NOW THERE WERE SIX

"Pearlie, you ready?"

"I guess I have to be, seein' as I've already voted on it," Pearlie replied.

Smoke pointed to the left. "Looks like there are several rocks, trees, and logs over there," he said. "You work your way up on that side. I'll go up the right."

"Give me the word," Pearlie said. Gone was the joking, he was all business now.

Smoke and Pearlie started up the trail toward Tatum. They were violating every dictum in the book of military strategy—a book that says that those on the attack need many more men than those in defense in order to balance the scales. And if the attack is made against higher ground, then the number needs to be even greater.

Smoke and Pearlie were only two men, and they were attacking seven men—seven men who had good positions of cover on higher ground. As they worked their way up the hill, they heard Tom's rifle bark from behind them, and at almost the same time, they saw one of Tatum's men pitch forward into the snow.

Now there were only six.

BOOK YOUR PLACE ON OUR WEBSITE AND MAKE THE READING CONNECTION!

We've created a customized website just for our very special readers, where you can get the inside scoop on everything that's going on with Zebra, Pinnacle and Kensington books.

When you come online, you'll have the exciting opportunity to:

- View covers of upcoming books
- Read sample chapters
- Learn about our future publishing schedule (listed by publication month *and author*)
- Find out when your favorite authors will be visiting a city near you
- Search for and order backlist books from our online catalog
- Check out author bios and background information
- Send e-mail to your favorite authors
- Meet the Kensington staff online
- Join us in weekly chats with authors, readers and other guests
- Get writing guidelines
- AND MUCH MORE!

**Visit our website at
http://www.kensingtonbooks.com**

WARPATH OF THE MOUNTAIN MAN

William W. Johnstone

PINNACLE BOOKS
Kensington Publishing Corp.
http://www.kensingtonbooks.com

PINNACLE BOOKS are published by

Kensington Publishing Corp.
850 Third Avenue
New York, NY 10022

All Kensington Titles, Imprints, and Distributed Lines are available at special quantity discounts for bulk purchases for sales promotions, premiums, fund-raising, and educational or institutional use. Special book excerpts or customized printings can also be created to fit specific needs. For details, write or phone the office of the Kensington special sales manager: Kensington Publishing Corp., 850 Third Avenue, New York, NY 10022, attn: Special Sales Department, Phone: 1-800-221-2647.

Pinnacle and the P logo Reg. U.S. Pat. & TM Off.

First Printing: July 2002
10 9 8 7 6 5 4 3 2 1

Printed in the United States of America

One

Smoke Jensen was in front of the hardware store, looping the reins of his horse around the hitching rail, when he heard the gunshot. Sometimes, in drunken play, shots were fired into the floor or in the air. Most of the citizens of Big Rock had learned to tell the difference between the sound of a shot fired in play and one fired in anger.

This shot, fired at ten-fifteen A.M. on a Tuesday morning in October, was fired in anger.

Suddenly, a man burst from the front door of the bank, which was located about two blocks west of the hardware store. It was Rich Flowers, one of the bank tellers.

"They're robbing the bank! They're robbing the bank!" Flowers shouted. "Help, somebody, they're . . ."

That was as far he got before a masked man appeared in the doorway of the bank, clutching a bag in one hand and a pistol in the other. The masked man raised his pistol and fired at Flowers, hitting him in the back. Flowers fell face-down in the dirt.

Up and down the street there were screams and shouts of fear and alarm. Citizens of the town scrambled to get out of the way: running into nearby doorways, ducking behind watering troughs or around the corners of buildings. Three more masked men appeared in the bank door, firing their weapons indiscriminately. There was a scream from inside Mrs. Pynchon's dress shop. The crash of glass followed as a woman tumbled through the window and fell onto the boardwalk, bleeding from her wound.

"Clear the street, clear the street!" one of the bank robbers shouted, waving his pistol. "Everybody get off the street!" He punctuated his demand with more pistol shots.

Although most of the citizens obeyed the bank robbers' orders, Smoke Jensen did not. Instead he strolled, almost casually, to his horse, and pulled his rifle from its saddle holster. Then, jacking a shell into the chamber, he stepped out into the middle of the street, raised the rifle to his shoulder, and fired at one of the bank robbers. The bank robber went down.

"What the hell!" one of the other robbers shouted. "Where did that come from?"

"Down there!" another said, pointing to Smoke.

The robber aimed at Smoke and fired, but he was using a pistol, and he missed. Smoke returned fire, and didn't miss.

Now there were only two of the robbers left.

"Get the money and let's get out of here!" one of the two shouted. The other robber tried to retrieve the money bag from the hands of one of the two robbers Smoke had killed, but Smoke put a bullet in his leg and he went down.

The last robber, now seeing that he was alone and outgunned by the man with the rifle, threw his pistol down and put his hands up.

"Don't shoot! Don't shoot!" he shouted. "I quit!"

Keeping the robber covered, Smoke walked toward him. By now, most of the townspeople realized that Smoke had everything under control. They started coming back into the street, heading toward the bank and the two robbers who were left alive: one standing with his hands up, the other, groaning and bleeding, lying in the dirt.

"Who are you, mister?" the one who was still standing asked.

"Why do you need to know?" Smoke replied. "It's not like we're going to be friends, or anything."

Some of the citizens of the town, now close enough to hear the exchange, laughed.

"Mister, you just been brought down by Smoke Jensen," someone said. "And if it's any consolation to you, he's beaten many a man better than you."

By now, Sheriff Monte Carson was also on the scene, and he took the two robbers into custody.

"What about my leg?" the wounded robber asked. "I got me a bullet in my leg. I need a doctor. I'm your prisoner, and the law says you got to get me a doctor."

"We've only got one doctor in this town, mister," Monte replied. "And right now he's seeing to Mrs. Pynchon and Mr. Flowers. You better hope neither one of them dies, 'cause if either of them does, you'll both be hung for murder. Let's go." Monte made a motion toward the jail.

"I can't walk on this leg, I tell you."

" 'Couple you men . . . help him," Monte said.

With assistance from two onlookers, the wounded man and his uninjured partner crossed the street and entered the jail.

"We've got two nice rooms just waiting for you," Monte said, opening the doors to adjacent jail cells.

"When's the doctor going to look at my leg?"

"When he gets around to it," Monte replied. "In the meantime, if I were you, I'd just lie on the bunk there and take it easy."

"It hurts," the wounded prisoner insisted.

"Yeah, I reckon it does. What are your names?" Monte asked.

"I'm Jack Tatum," the uninjured man said. He nodded toward the other robber, who had taken Monte's advice and was now lying on the bunk. "His name is Billy Petrie."

"Tatum?" Monte said. "I've seen that name." He opened the drawer of his desk and took out a pile of wanted posters. After looking through several of them, he pulled one out. "Ah, here it is. This is you, isn't it?"

Monte turned the poster so Tatum could see it.

WANTED
JACK TATUM
For Murder and Robbery
$5,000
Reward to be paid
DEAD OR ALIVE

"Only five thousand? They're a bunch of skin-flints," Tatum snorted. "Hell, I'm worth more than that."

"Proud of it, are you?" Monte asked. He pulled out a tablet and began writing. "I reckon I'd better get a telegram off. No doubt some folks are going to be happy to hear that you are out of business."

"Sheriff, what are you going to do about that fella that murdered my two friends?" Tatum asked.

Monte looked up from his desk. "I beg your pardon? Did you say murdered?"

"Yeah, I said murdered, 'cause that's what he done. We wasn't shootin' anybody, we was just shootin' in the air to clear the street. Next thing I know, that bank teller was down, then that woman come crashin' through the window, then Fuller and Howard, then

Billy was shot. The fella doing the shooting—Jensen, I think someone said—was a crazy man, sending bullets flying everywhere. You ask me, he's the one who should be locked up in here."

"Are you trying to tell me that you didn't have anything to do with shooting Mr. Flowers or Mrs. Pynchon?"

"That's what I'm telling you," Tatum said.

"I'll give you this, Tatum. You've got gall, telling a lie like that when the whole town saw what you did."

"Well, now, some folks may have seen it one way and some the other," Tatum replied. "We are going to get a trial, aren't we? Or do you plan to just hang us?"

"You'll get a fair trial," Monte replied. He paused for a moment, then chuckled. "Then we'll hang you."

Dr. Spaulding came into Monte's office then, and set his bag on the corner of Monte's desk.

"How's Mrs. Pynchon?" Monte asked.

"She'll be all right. The bullet went all the way through her upper arm, but it didn't hit any bones."

"Rich Flowers?"

Doc Spaulding shook his head. "Dead. He was dead before I even got to him."

"That's a shame. Flowers was a nice man."

"Yes, he was. And the really sad thing is, Edna, his wife, is going to have a baby."

"Damn, that's a shame. What about the two bank robbers? Both dead?"

"Yes."

"Listen, Doc, I want you to do me a favor. Take the bullets out of the bodies. No doubt the court will need them for evidence."

"All right. I understand one of your prisoners is wounded?"

"Yeah, he's on his cot back there. He took a bullet in his leg."

"I'll take a look at it," Spaulding said, picking up his bag and heading toward the cell.

"Sheriff," Tatum called.

Sighing, Monte looked up at him. "What is it now, Tatum?"

"I want to see a lawyer. That's my right, ain't it? To see a lawyer?"

"You have that right," Monte agreed.

"And if I don't have one, you have to appoint him?"

"That's right."

"Then appoint a lawyer for me and get him over here," Tatum demanded.

In the cell next to Tatum, Billy Petrie started screaming.

"Hold still, young man," Doc Spaulding said. "If I don't get this bullet out, you're likely to lose that leg. Here, here's some laudanum."

The laudanum took effect, and the prisoner's screams turned to a few moans and groans. Doc Spaulding, ever the caregiver, spoke in quiet, reassuring tones as he worked on Petrie.

Monte was just finishing the telegram he was going to send when Dewey Wallace, a recently hired deputy, came in.

"Whoowee, the town is really buzzing over all the excitement this morning," Wallace said, walking over to the little stove to pour himself a cup of coffee.

"Is Welch seeing to the bodies yet?" Monte asked.

"You bet. He had his measuring tape out before they were cold. Want a cup of coffee?"

"No, thanks," Monte said. He tore the sheet of paper off his pad. "As soon as you finish your coffee, take this down to the telegraph office."

"All right," Wallace said. Sipping the coffee, he

looked at the sheriff's message, then whistled. "You think they'll pay Smoke Jensen that reward?"

"I don't know why they shouldn't," Monte said.

Wallace walked over to the jail cells and stood just outside the bars, looking at the two prisoners as he drank his coffee. "So, what were you fellas thinkin'?" Wallace asked. "Did you think we're such a small town you could just come in here and rob our bank, then leave without so much as a fare-thee-well?"

Tatum glared at the deputy, but said nothing.

"Quiet, huh?" Wallace said, chuckling. "Well, I reckon you won't be so quiet when we string you up." Holding his hand beside his neck to represent a rope, he made a jerking motion, then gave his impression of a death rattle. He followed that with a laugh. "Yeah, you won't be so quiet then," he said.

"Wallace, get the hell away from the cells and quit bothering the prisoners," Monte said. "Take that telegram down to Western Union like I told you."

"All right, Sheriff. Whatever you say," Wallace said, draining the rest of his coffee.

As Wallace was leaving, Doc Spaulding came back from Petrie's cell.

"I don't know what I was thinking when I hired that boy," Monte said.

"Ahh, he'll come around," Spaulding said. He dropped a small piece of lead on the corner of Monte's desk. "Here's the bullet I took from his leg."

"What is it? A .44-40?"

"Is that what Jensen was shooting?"

"Yes."

"Then that's what it is. Of course, it's pretty hard to tell the difference between a .44 and .44-40, seeing as they are so close to the same size and weight."

"That's true," Monte agreed. He had opened a small notebook and was looking through it. Then, when he found what he was looking for, he groaned. "Jensen's not going to like this."

"Who's not going to like what?" Doc Spaulding asked as he closed his bag.

"Sam Covington is next in line to be the public defender."

Doc Spaulding chuckled. "You're right," he said. "He's not going to like it."

"I'll tell you who else won't like it. Norton, the prosecuting attorney. If anyone can make a case out of this, it will be Sam Covington."

"Covington's good, all right."

"Good has nothing to do with it. As far as I know, every lawyer in the county is good. But Covington is more than good, he is ruthless. He'll do anything it takes to win a case, any case. It doesn't matter to Covington whether something is right or wrong or whether someone is guilty or innocent. All that matters to him is who wins and who loses."

When Smoke Jensen returned home to Sugarloaf, he dismounted and untied a sack from the pommel. He had gone into town to get a few things at the hardware store, and despite the excitement of the morning, he had not lost sight of his objective.

The aroma of fried chicken assailed his nostrils as he entered the house, and going into the kitchen, he saw Sally standing over the stove. He stepped up behind and put his arms around her, then pulled her to him, nuzzling his cheek against hers. She leaned back into him.

"Uhmm-uhm, that smells good," he said.

"What smells good?" Sally replied. "The fried chicken, or the five-dollar-an-ounce perfume I'm wearing?"

"Uh . . . the, uh . . . perfume of course," Smoke stammered. "Well, the chicken too, but definitely the perfume."

Sally laughed. "You are the biggest liar I know. Not only am I not wearing any perfume, you know full well that I would never be foolish enough to spend five dollars for one ounce. Especially when I could put essence of fried chicken behind my ears and accomplish the same thing, as far as you are concerned.

"Well, as far as I'm concerned, you don't need perfume or fried chicken," Smoke said. "To me, you always smell good."

"Uh-huh, don't you try and butter me up now, Mr. Smoke Jensen. Especially after what happened in town today. You go into town to make a simple purchase at the hardware store and you wind up in a gunfight."

Smoke picked up a drumstick from the platter of chicken that was already done and began eating. "How'd you hear about it so fast?"

"Well, I'm glad to see that you aren't going to deny it. Mrs. Fremont was in town and she saw the whole thing. You better believe she couldn't wait to stop by and tell me about it."

"She always was a busybody."

"You can't blame her. She figures that is her purpose in life."

"Then you also heard about Rich Flowers?"

Sally nodded. "Yes, I heard. And poor Edna is pregnant. Pregnant and a widow. It's terrible. But you had no business putting yourself on the line like that. One man against four? Did you want to make me a widow too? What were you thinking?"

"I don't know. It just seemed like the thing to do at the time," Smoke said.

Smoke knew that Sally's bark was worse than her

bite, because he knew that had she been there, she quite likely would have joined him. Sally was as good with a gun as just about any man Smoke had ever met. She was lightning fast and deadly accurate with a pistol. A trick she liked to do was to put a pie pan on the ground at her feet and a steel washer on the back of her hand, then hold her arm out straight and go for her pistol. Of course the moment she turned her hand, the washer would start to fall and, as it was falling, Sally would begin her draw. She could pull the pistol, fire, and hit her target, before the washer hit the pie pan. And with a rifle she was even deadlier, for she could drill a dime from a fifty yards.

"You aren't mad, are you?" he asked.

Sally chuckled. "Do I get mad at a raindrop for getting my hair wet? Some things are just acts of nature. And when you see someone in trouble, you have just naturally got to come to their rescue. It's who you are."

"You're a good woman, Sally. I don't know how I was ever lucky enough to find you, or why you were foolish enough to marry me. All I know is, you are the best thing that ever happened to me."

"Better be careful, cowboy," Sally said with a seductive smile. "Talk like that will get you . . ."

"Whooeee, am I starved!" a voice suddenly shouted from the front of the house. "And does that ever smell good."

"Damn, Pearlie, if you don't have the worst timing in the world," Smoke said.

"The timing seems pretty good to me," Pearlie said. "I mean, the food's about ready, isn't it?"

Smoke and Sally laughed.

"Yes, it's ready," Sally said. "Wash up, I'll have it on the table shortly.

Pearlie, a young man just past twenty, was the acting

foreman of Sugarloaf, having come to work for Smoke after a stint as a hired gun. But the concept of being a hired gun had soured when some of the men Pearlie was working with had raped and killed a young girl. Pearlie had quit that job and thrown in with Smoke, whose ranch had been the target of the man Pearlie was working for at the time. Since then, Pearlie had proven to be one of the most loyal—and hungry—people Smoke had ever known.

Cal came into the house right behind Pearlie. Cal was a couple of years younger than Pearlie, and while his appetite wasn't quite as large, his loyalty to Smoke and Sally was just as intense.

Smoke and Sally had no children of their own, but if they had, they would have wanted them to be exactly like the two young men.

"Wish I'd been with you for the little fracas in town," Cal said as they all sat down to eat.

"Why?" Pearlie asked as he spooned a pile of mashed potatoes onto his plate. "What could you have done that Smoke didn't do?"

"Watch," Cal said simply.

The others laughed.

Two

While Big Rock did not have a courthouse, it did have a city administration building, with an area that was set aside specifically to be used as a courthouse when the occasion demanded. However, there was no permanently sitting judge. Because of that, there was a two-day delay while they waited for Harry Tutwyler, circuit judge of the third judicial district, to come to town to conduct the trial. The judge was met by Sheriff Monte Carson; Abner Norton, the prosecuting attorney; and Emil Bartholmew, the president of the bank. In addition, there were several other townspeople on hand because the upcoming trial was a big event for the small town of Big Rock.

The judge, a man of considerable girth, was wheezing from exertion as he stepped down from the train. "Have you made arrangements for my accommodations?" he asked.

"Yes, Your Honor," Monte replied. "We've put you up at the Homestead Hotel."

"Is there a restaurant nearby?"

"Yes, sir, the City Pig is right next door. It's a very fine restaurant, and I have arranged for the town to pick up your tab."

"Thank you," Tutwyler said. "I take it that everything is ready for the trial?"

"Oh, yes, we're all ready for it," Monte said.

"Do the accused men have a lawyer? I'm not going to conduct the trial if they don't have a qualified attorney representing them."

Monte and Norton looked at each other for a moment. Seeing their hesitation, Judge Tutwyler stopped. "Don't tell me they aren't represented?"

"Oh, they're represented, all right," said Norton. "Sam Covington is their lawyer."

Tutwyler looked at Norton with an expression of surprise on his face. "Sam Covington? Isn't he the governor's man?"

"Hand in glove."

"How did he wind up representing a couple of bank robbers and murderers?"

"It was his turn, Your Honor. As you know, every lawyer in the county is on a roster and must take his turn representing the indigent. Covington's name came up."

"From what I know of Covington, Mr. Norton, you can be sure that he will be a powerful adversary. He doesn't like to lose at anything."

"No, sir."

"Well, if you gentlemen will show me to the hotel, I'll freshen up, have some dinner, then retire for the night. Court will convene sharply at nine tomorrow morning. Please make certain that all interested parties are so informed."

"Yes, sir," Monte said.

The next morning, Smoke, Sallie, Cal, and Pearlie came to town to watch the trial of Jack Tatum and Billy Petrie. It wasn't mere curiosity that brought them to town, because Smoke had been subpoenaed as a witness for the prosecution.

The four of them arrived in a trap that was driven by Cal. Pearlie sat beside him on the front seat, Smoke and Sallie on the backseat.

"What time does the trial start?" Pearlie asked.

"Nine o'clock," Smoke answered.

"It's just now a little after eight. Maybe we could get something to eat while we're waiting."

"Heavens, Pearlie, after that huge breakfast you had, you are still hungry?" Sally asked. Then, almost immediately, she laughed. "What am I saying? Of course you are still hungry. I don't think there is ever a time when you aren't hungry."

"I could use a cup of coffee myself," Smoke said.

The four went into the City Pig and found a table.

"Good morning, Mr. Jensen, Mrs. Jensen," Kathy said, coming over to the table. "Are you folks in town for the trial?"

"Yes," Smoke said without elaboration.

"It seems that everyone is. We've never been so busy. Oh, and everyone is talking about what a hero you were."

"Yes, well, people talk too much," Smoke said, self-conscious at being the recipient of such accolades.

"Well, what can I get for you?" Kathy asked, realizing that she was embarrassing him. "Our pancakes are awfully good this morning."

"Thanks, but we've had breakfast," Sally said. "We're just waiting around until the trial starts. All I want is coffee."

"That'll do for me," Smoke said.

Cal also ordered only coffee, but when Kathy got to Pearlie, he was still studying the menu.

"Pearlie?" she asked.

"Uh, I had breakfast too," Pearlie said, "but it was fairly light."

Sally gasped, then looked at Smoke and Cal. All three laughed.

"Well, I mean, it wasn't all that heavy," Pearlie said. "So I might have just a little something to tide me over until lunch. Maybe a stack of pancakes, three eggs, 'bout half a pound of sausage, some biscuits and gravy ought to do it."

"I'll get a work crew started on it right away," Kathy said, laughing as she started toward the kitchen.

Forty-five minutes later, Smoke, Sally, Pearlie, and Cal were in the courthouse, sitting in the second row of seats. They were there when Monte and Deputy Wallace brought in the prisoners, Jack Tatum and Billy Petrie.

Jack Tatum looked out over the gallery. The courtroom was packed for the show, and he intended to give them one. No stranger to court appearances, Tatum was a man who had spent at least half of his forty-two years in various jails and prisons.

He had a misshapen eye, the result of a knife fight that left him permanently scarred, and his adversary permanently dead. There were few laws he hadn't broken, and none he wouldn't. He had started his life of crime when, at the age of fourteen, he sneaked into his mother's bedroom, killed the man she was sleeping with, took his money, and ran away into the night. He had neither seen nor contacted his mother since then, and neither knew nor cared whether she was dead or alive.

Billy Petrie was considerably younger than Tatum. Petrie's mother, a soiled dove, died when he was twelve. He never knew who his father was, so when he was orphaned, he became a ward of the state. They put Petrie in a reform school because there was no room for him in the orphanage. He broke out of reform school when he was sixteen, and had lived a life of crime ever since.

Although the bullet had been removed from Petrie's leg, the wound was still bothering him. He was limping noticeably as the prisoners were brought into court to await the arrival of the judge. It also didn't help matters that he and Tatum were chained together.

Sitting at the defendants' table, and greeting them when they arrived, was Samuel B. Covington, appointed by the court as counsel for the defense.

Covington was a dapper, distinguished-looking man, exceptionally well dressed, complete with vest and gold watch chain. His hair was dark, except at the temples, where it was gray. He had a small, well trimmed mustache.

Sam Covington was a well-known lawyer who was very active in politics. In the most recent election, he had directed the successful campaign of the sitting governor. As a result, he was now one of the most powerful men in the state, with the governor's ear any time he wanted it.

Mrs. Edna Flowers was in court, the grief over the recent loss evident in her face. The widow's weeds she was wearing did little to hide the fact that she was pregnant. Margaret Pynchon was in court as well, sitting next to Mrs. Flowers. Mrs. Pynchon's arm was in a sling, and both she and Mrs. Flowers glared at the defendants as they were brought in.

Before the judge entered the court, Smoke and Sally went back to speak to the two ladies who had suffered most from the aborted bank robbery.

"Edna, I was so sorry to hear about Rich," Sally said. "The entire town will feel his loss deeply. If there is anything I can do for you, please let me know."

"Thank you, Mrs. Jensen," Edna said, dabbing at her eyes. "Everyone has been so kind."

"And that goes for you as well, Margaret. I know with your arm hurt like that, you can't work. So if you need anything, please let me know, would you?"

"Thank you," Margaret said. "Dr. Spaulding said he was sure I could get back to work in a couple of days, so I'm sure everything will be all right.

At that moment the bailiff came into the courtroom.

"All rise!"

The court fell silent as everyone stood.

"Oyez, oyez, oyez, this court is now in session, the Honorable Harry Tutwyler presiding. All who have business with this honorable court draw near and listen. God bless this honorable court, and God bless the United States of America. Order in the court!"

Judge Tutwyler, wearing black robes, came in and stood behind the bench for a moment, then sat. Not until then did everyone else sit.

"Who comes now before this court?" said Tutwyler.

"Your Honor, before this honorable court comes the case of the state against Jack Tatum and William, also known as Billy, Petrie. They are charged with murder in the first degree, aggravated assault with the intent to commit murder, bank robbery, and conspiracy to commit bank robbery."

"Will the defendants please stand?"

At Covington's urging, both Tatum and Petrie stood.

"You have heard the charges against you," Judge Tutwyler said. "How do you plead? Guilty, or not guilty?"

"We didn't do all them things that was just said," Tatum said. "I mean, to listen to all that, you'd think . . ." That was as far Tatum got before Covington was able to put his hand out toward his client to quiet him.

"The defendants plead not guilty, Your Honor," Covington said.

"The plead of not guilty is entered," the judge said.

After they spent nearly an hour selecting the jury, the judge finally turned to Norton and said, "Mr. Prosecutor, make your case, sir."

Norton gave his opening remarks, called upon witnesses from the bank, then called his star witness, Smoke Jensen.

Reaching over to pat Sally's hand, Smoke walked up to the front of the courtroom, where he was sworn in.

"Mr. Jensen, would you please, in your own words, tell the court what happened on the morning of the fourteenth of last month?"

Without elaboration, Smoke told the story of being in front of the hardware store when he heard the shooting. He told of watching Mr. Flowers shot down in the street before he himself joined the action. His statement was concise but complete, with no self-aggrandizement.

"Your witness, Counselor," Norton said as he walked back to his table.

Covington approached Jensen, looked at him for a long moment without saying a word, then moved over to stand in front of the jury.

"Mr. Jensen, how many men have you killed?"

"Objection, Your Honor!" Norton shouted, leaping up from his own chair. "That question is inflammatory and irrelevant!"

"Your Honor, by definition, anytime someone is killed, it is inflammatory," Covington replied. "But if you will allow me to pursue this course, I will be able to establish the relevance."

"I will allow the question, Counselor, but be cautioned, I will be keeping an eye on you. And if I see you misusing my generosity, I'll withdraw permission in a heartbeat."

"Thank you, Your Honor," Covington said. He turned back to Smoke. "How many men have you killed?"

"I'm not sure," Smoke replied.

"You're not sure? You mean the act of killing another human being is so insignificant to you that you can't even remember how many you have sent to their Maker?"

"I've never killed anyone who wasn't trying to kill me."

"Would you say you have killed more than ten men?"

"Yes."

"More than twenty?"

"Your Honor, I object. The witness has answered the question. He has killed more than ten men. I see no reason for carrying this any further," Norton protested.

"Objection sustained. Continue the cross-examination."

"I am curious, Mr. Jensen. When you killed Mr. Fuller and Mr. Howard, did you pause to reflect upon it?"

"I'm not sure what you mean."

"Before you pulled the trigger that sent Mr. Fuller and Mr. Howard hurling into eternity . . . did you hesitate, even for a moment?"

"No."

"Did you not even ask yourself if you were doing the right thing?"

"Mr. Covington, much is said about the speed of a gunfighter's draw. But in reality it isn't the speed of drawing the gun as much as it is the speed of making the right decision. Once I realized what was going on, I made the decision to intervene. I knew it was right and I didn't have to reconsider."

"I see. Mr. Jensen, what caliber bullets were you shooting on the day in question?"

"The rifle I fired used .44-40-caliber ammunition."

"Are you aware that the shots that killed Fuller and Howard were made from a distance of one hundred seventy-five yards?"

"I didn't measure the distance," Smoke said.

"I did. Given the distance of the shot, don't you think some hesitation might have been prudent? Especially since Richmond Flowers and Mrs. Pynchon were both struck by bullets that are consistent with the caliber of the bullets you were shooting?"

"Objection! Is defense trying to suggest that Smoke Jensen shot Mr. Flowers and Mrs. Pynchon?" Norton asked.

"Your Honor, I am making no such claim," Covington said quickly. "I am merely making the observation that Mr. Flowers was killed and Mrs. Pynchon was wounded by bullets that are consistent with the caliber of the bullets Mr. Jensen was shooting. It goes to establishing doubt."

"Objection overruled."

"Thank you, Your Honor." Turning back to Smoke, Covington continued with his cross-examination. "Mr. Jensen, you do admit to killing Howard and Fuller, do you not? I mean, that issue is not in doubt?"

"I killed them," Smoke said.

"Would it be fair to say then that, on that day, you were their judge, jury, and executioner?"

"Objection, Your Honor. Inflammatory," Norton protested.

"Sustained."

"Withdraw the question. Mr. Jensen, are you an officer of the law?"

"No."

"Would you consider yourself a vigilante?"

"No."

"Then, by what right did you kill Fuller and Howard?"

"Objection, Your Honor, the witness is not on trial here. Jack Tatum and Billy Petrie are on trial. It is clear to anyone with reason that, by his actions, Mr. Jensen saved more innocent lives. I'll not have him browbeaten like this."

"Your Honor, this goes to witness credibility," Covington said. "As far as I know, there has been no hearing to determine whether or not Mr. Jensen's homicide was justifiable. And unless or until that happens, any testimony Mr. Jensen may give this court could be said to be self-serving."

"Objection sustained," Judge Tutwyler said. "Unless you can prove that the witness has perjured himself, his testimony will be given relevant weight. Now, please continue."

"I have no more questions for this . . ." Covington turned his back on Smoke as if disgusted, then added in a derisive tone, "Witness."

"Redirect?" the judge asked Norton.

"No redirect, sir. And, as Mr. Jensen was my last witness, prosecution rests."

Three

"Prosecution having rested, you may now present your case, Mr. Covington."

"Thank you. Your Honor, defense wishes to call Sheriff Monte Carson to the stand."

There was a buzz of curiosity throughout the courtroom as Monte was called. He had been one of the prime witnesses for the prosecution, and everyone wondered what use Covington could make of him for the defense.

"Sheriff, I remind you that you are still under oath," the bailiff said as Monte took the stand.

"I understand," Monte replied.

"In the course of your investigation of the events on the fourteenth of October, were you presented with the bullet that killed Mr. Flowers?"

"I was."

"And I believe you testified that it was a .44-caliber bullet?"

"It was."

"And the bullet that wounded Mrs. Pynchon? Also a .44-caliber?"

"It was."

"And, under questioning from prosecution, you stated that the pistols you took from the defendants, Jack Tatum and Billy Petrie, were also .44-caliber?"

"They were."

"Now, Sheriff, I would like to ask you a question that prosecution did not ask you. Did you also take the pistols from the two men that Smoke Jensen killed?"

"Yes."

"What caliber were they?"

"The pistols were Colt .44's."

"And the bullet that Dr. Spaulding took from Mrs. Pynchon's shoulder, as well as the bullet he took from Mr. Flowers' body, what caliber were they?"

"The bullets were .44-caliber."

"What about the bullets taken from the bodies of Mr. Howard and Mr. Fuller?"

"They were .44-40."

Covington walked over to his table and picked up two envelopes. Returning to the witness stand, he held the envelopes in front of him. "Your Honor, I have defense exhibits marked A and B. I beg permission to perform an experiment."

"You may proceed."

"Sheriff Carson, would you hold your left hand out, please?"

Monte did as directed.

"I am removing an object from the envelope marked A and placing it in your hand. Would you identify it for the court, please?"

He placed a small piece of lead in Monte's hand.

"It is a spent bullet," Monte said.

"Caliber?"

Monte hefted it, and examined it closely. "I'd say it was a .44-caliber."

"And now this one?" Covington put another bullet in Monte's right hand.

"It's also a bullet."

"Caliber?"

"It's a .44-caliber."

"You are correct, Sheriff, this is a .44-caliber bullet."

Monte smiled and nodded at the jury.

"But the bullet you are holding in your left hand is a .44-40."

The gallery reacted with a buzz of wonder and surprise.

"Thank you, Sheriff Carson. No further questions," Covington said. "Defense calls Mr. Jack Tatum to the stand."

The bailiff held the Bible out toward Tatum, who looked it for a second, then placed his hand on it.

"Do you swear to tell the truth, the whole truth, and nothing but the truth, so help you God?"

"Yeah, yeah, sure," Tatum snorted.

"Be seated, please."

Tatum took his seat.

"Mr. Tatum, on the fourteenth of October, at approximately ten-fifteen in the morning, did you, Mr. Petrie, Mr. Howard, and Mr. Fuller attempt to rob the bank of Big Rock?"

"Yeah, we tried," Tatum said.

"Your Honor, if he is confessing to this, why are we continuing with the trial?" Norton called from the prosecutor's table."

"Your Honor, if the court will indulge," Covington said quickly. "There is a greater purpose to this."

"Continue the questioning," the judge said.

"Tell the court, in your own words, what happened that morning," Covington said.

"Yeah, well, like I said, me, Petrie, Howard, and Fuller was robbin' the bank. And everything was goin' along just fine. I mean, nobody was getting hurt or anything like that, and nobody was going to get hurt. Then, when we come out of the bank, someone started shooting at us. First thing I know after that, the bank teller went down. I yelled out to Fuller and Howard, 'What'd you shoot him for?' But instead of answerin' me, I seen that they was shootin' at Jensen. That's when I first found out that Jensen was the one shootin' at us."

"Did either you or Petrie return fire?"

"We shot at Jensen in self-defense, but only at Jensen. And we didn't even do that until he started shooting first. Then I seen that he was out of range, so I yelled at Petrie to just forget the money so we could get out of there! But that's when he got shot in the leg. I figured then that we'd better surrender before anyone else got hurt, or maybe kilt. This Jensen fella was goin' wild, you know what I mean? He was just shootin' up the whole town. I admit I come to town to steal money, but I never had it in mind to hurt anyone. When I seen what Jensen was doin', I figured the only way to keep anyone else from getting shot was if I surrendered."

Billy Petrie's testimony was almost an exact duplicate of Jack Tatum's. According to Petrie, Smoke Jensen started the shooting. The bank teller was killed, not intentionally, but by a wild shot. Mrs. Pynchon was also hit with a wild shot. Neither of them was shot, Petrie insisted, until after the shooting was started by Smoke Jensen. He added one more thing to his testimony. Looking directly at Mrs. Flower and Mrs. Pynchon, he said, "Ladies, didn't none of us want anyone hurt. I'm sorry you lost your husband, Mrs. Flowers, and I'm sorry you got shot, Mrs. Pynchon, but wasn't neither one of us that done it."

When Petrie stepped down, Covington presented his closing argument.

"Some may regard Smoke Jensen as a hero for what he did. I don't share that opinion of Mr. Jensen,"

Covington began. "By opening fire in an otherwise peaceful street, he placed the lives of everyone in town in mortal danger. Did my clients kill Mr. Flowers?" Covington paused for a moment, then nodded. "They may have. It is entirely possible. They were shooting, and so were Mr. Howard and Mr. Fuller. Bullets from one or more of their guns may well have killed Richmond Flowers and wounded Mr. Pynchon.

"However, it is also possible that Smoke Jensen killed Richmond Flowers." From his pocket, Covington held up two unfired bullets.

"Here you see an unfired .44-40 rifle bullet, and an unfired .44-caliber pistol bullet. When they are like this, it is easy to tell the difference. Ahh, but the spent bullets"—returning to his table, Covington picked up the two chunks of lead he had shown to Sheriff Carson—"are a different story. Not even Sheriff Carson, who everyone will concede is an expert in these matters, was able to tell, for certain, which bullet was which. And though I am not saying with certainty that Smoke Jensen killed Mr. Flowers, I am proving to you that it is possible that he did.

"Now, why would a man like Smoke Jensen open fire when doing so would place ordinary people in danger? That's a good question, and I think it deserves an answer. Smoke Jensen is a successful rancher to whom money is everything. To such a man, money means more than the life of an ordinary person.

"What, exactly, is an ordinary person? Rich Flowers was a simple teller, so he was an ordinary person. Mrs. Pynchon is a simple tailor, so she is an ordinary person."

Covington walked away from the jury, and fixed his gaze upon Mrs. Flowers and Mrs. Pynchon.

"Our government was founded upon the principle of the sovereignty of the ordinary person. People like these two noble ladies." He took them in with a wave of his hand, milking the moment. Then he walked away from them to stand just across the railing from Smoke Jensen. He glared at Smoke. "In Jensen's world, such people as Rich Flowers and Margaret Pynchon are unimportant." He turned to the jury. "In Smoke Jensen's world, you, the gentlemen of this jury, are all ordinary people. Thus, you are unimportant."

After a pause to let his point sink in, Covington continued. "But those of us who are unimportant know something that people like Smoke Jensen will never understand. We know that, while money can be replaced, human life cannot.

"It wasn't lives Jensen thought to save that terrible Tuesday morning. It was money. After all, Jensen's own money is kept in that bank, so he did have a vested interest in stopping the robbery. Incensed by the idea that his money might be stolen, Smoke Jensen began shooting, and now we all know the sad and tragic consequences of that action. Gentlemen of the jury, I do not have to prove that Jack Tatum and Billy Petrie are innocent beyond a shadow of a doubt." He paused for a moment, and held up his finger. "But the prosecution must prove they are *guilty* beyond a shadow of a doubt. So, think about that. You heard Sheriff Monte Carson testify that Fuller and Howard were carrying .44-caliber pistols. In order to find Jack Tatum and Billy Petrie guilty beyond the shadow of a doubt, you must be absolutely certain that it was one of their bullets that killed Mr. Flowers—not a bullet fired by Fuller, nor a bullet fired by Howard, nor even a bullet fired by Smoke Jensen. Because it is entirely possible that Mr. Flowers was killed by one of those three. And if that is the case, then you have no choice but to find these defendants *not guilty*. Defense rests, Your Honor."

Abner Norton stood at his table, then looked toward the jury.

"Mr. Covington has just made a brilliant closing argument for his case, and I applaud him for his attempt to spin straw into gold. My closing won't take long. We have seven witnesses who testified about what they saw that day. Their stories varied somewhat, but no more than could be expected in relating accounts of such horrifying events. But all of them agreed on one thing. Smoke Jensen only fired three times, and all three of those bullets are accounted for. One killed Howard, one killed Fuller, and the third was taken from Billy Petrie's leg.

"Finally, it does not matter whether the bullet that killed Rich Flowers was fired by Howard or Fuller. Legally, the act by any one of the four men who attempted to rob that bank is shared equally by all four parties. And if anyone is killed resulting from *mala in se,* which is a legal term meaning an act of malice, then that killing—whether by intent or accident—is murder.

"There is only one finding you can return, and that is the finding of guilty. Prosecution rests, Your Honor."

When the jury retired for deliberation, Smoke, Sally, Cal, and Pearlie went back to the same restaurant where they had had their morning coffee.

"Do you think Mr. Covington really believes everything he said?" Sally asked.

"If he does believe it, then he is an even bigger fool than he looks," Pearlie said, shoveling a large piece of pie into his mouth.

"He is a lawyer. His job is to get his clients off by whatever means possible," Smoke said, trying to pla-

cate Sally, who had been bristling with anger ever
since Covington had started attacking her husband.

"Well, he doesn't have to lie about it, does he?"

Smoke chuckled. "Well, I don't think we have
much to worry about. Abner did a pretty good job of
taking Covington's argument apart. And let's not forget that Tom Burke is foreman of the jury. I can tell
you for a fact that he won't be buying any of Covington's bluster."

Just down the street from the restaurant, in the defendants' room of the courthouse, Tatum and Petrie
sat across a table from Covington.

"So, what do you think?" Tatum asked. "Will the
jury let us go free?"

"Let you go free?" Covington replied. "Are you in-
sane? You were caught red-handed robbing the bank.
You even admitted as much from the stand. The best
you can possibly hope for is that you don't hang.
Either way you're going to prison."

"Prison?" Tatum said. "I thought you were supposed to be such a good lawyer."

"There's not a lawyer alive who could get you declared not guilty," Covington said. "As it is, I've alien-
ated everyone in town by the way I've attacked Smoke
Jensen. He is held in very high regard by folks in
these parts."

"Yeah? Well, he's not held in high regard by me,"
Tatum said. "If it hadn't been for him we'd be in New
Mexico now, spending our money."

There was a quick knock on the door; then the
bailiff stuck his head in.

"Jury's in," he said.

* * *

After taking his seat at the bench, Judge Harry Tutwyler adjusted the glasses on the end of his nose, then cleared his throat.

"Would the bailiff please bring the prisoners before the bench?"

The bailiff, who was leaning against the railing with his arms folded across his chest, spat a quid of tobacco into the brass spittoon and looked over toward Tatum and Petrie.

"Get up, you two," he growled. "Present yourselves before the judge."

Tatum and Petrie were handcuffed together, and they had shackles on their ankles. They shuffled up to stand in front of the judge.

"Mr. Foreman of the Jury, have you reached a verdict?" the judge asked.

"We have, Your Honor," Tom Burke replied.

"What is the verdict?"

"Your Honor, we have found these guilty sons of bitches guilty," Tom Burke said.

"You damn well better have!" someone shouted from the court.

The judge banged his gavel on the table.

"Order!" he called. "I will have order in my court." He looked over at the foreman. "So say you all?" he asked.

"So say we all," Tom replied.

The judge took off his glasses and began polishing them as he studied the two prisoners before him.

"Jack Tatum and Billy Petrie, you have been tried by a jury of your peers and you have been found guilty of the crimes of robbery and murder. Before this court passes sentence, have you anything to say?"

"What? You mean like beg for mercy or something like that?" Tatum asked. He laughed, an evil cackle without mirth. "Go on, you fat-assed son of a bitch. Sentence us and get it over with."

There were several shocked gasps from the gallery, followed by an outbreak of shouts and curses. Judge Tutwyler had to use the gavel to restore order. Finally, everyone was quiet for the sentencing.

"Jack Tatum and Billy Petrie, it is the sentence of this court that you be taken from this place and put in jail just long enough to witness one more night pass from this mortal coil. At a time to be fixed by the sheriff, though no later than noon on the morrow, you are to be removed from jail and transported to a place where you will be hanged by the neck until you are dead."

"Your Honor, we can't hang 'em in the mornin'. We don't have a gallows yet," Monte said.

Judge Tutwyler held up his hand to silence Monte, indicating that he had already taken that into consideration. "This court authorizes the use of a tree, a lamppost, a hay-loading stanchion, or any other device, fixture, apparatus, contrivance, agent, or means as may be sufficient to suspend the prisoners' carcasses above the ground bringing about the effect of breaking their necks, collapsing their windpipes, and in any and all ways, squeezing the last breath of life from their worthless, vile, and miserable bodies."

Four

Deputy Wallace had been napping at his desk in Monte's office when something—a noise, or perhaps a dream—awakened him.

"What?" he asked, startled awake. "What is it?" He opened his eyes and looked around the inside of Monte's office. The room was dimly lit by a low-burning kerosene lantern. A plethora of wanted posters fluttered from the bulletin board. A pot of aromatic coffee sat on a small wood-burning stove. The Regulator clock on the wall swept its pendulum back and forth in a measured tick-tock, the hands on the face pointing to ten minutes after two in the morning. Wallace rubbed his eyes, then stood up and stretched. He went to the stove to pour himself a cup of coffee, then stepped over to the jail cell to look inside. Expecting to see the prisoners asleep, he was startled to see that both Tatum and Petrie were wide awake, sitting on the edges of their bunks.

"What's the matter?" Wallace asked. He took a slurping drink of his coffee. "Can't you fellas sleep any?"

"No," Tatum growled.

"Well, I wouldn't worry about it," Wallace said. He took another drink of coffee. "In just about four more hours or so, you won't have no trouble at all goin' to sleep. You'll be sleepin' forever!" He laughed at his joke, then took another swallow of his coffee.

"Ahh," he said. "Coffee is one of the sweetest pleasures of life, don't you think? But then, life itself is sweet, ain't it?" He laughed again, then turned away from the cell.

Wallace gasped in surprise at seeing a Mexican standing between him and his desk. He had not heard the Mexican come in. The Mexican was wearing an oversized sombrero, and had a dark mustache, which curved down along each side of his mouth.

"What the hell are you doin' in here, Mex?" Wallace asked gruffly. "You aren't supposed to be in here."

"I have come to work, *señor,*" the Mexican said. He made a motion as if he were sweeping the floor. "Sweep floor."

"Sweep the floor at two o'clock in the morning? Are you crazy? Get the hell out of here!"

"Deputy?" Tatum called.

"Now what do you want?" Wallace asked, turning back toward the jail cell. He was surprised to see both Tatum and Petrie smiling broadly.

"I want you to be nice to our friend Senor Sanchez," Tatum said.

"Your friend?" Wallace asked, confused by the strange remark. Suddenly, he realized what he had done! He had just turned his back on the Mexican.

Too late, Wallace felt the Mexican's hand come around to clasp over his mouth. Wallace dropped his cup of coffee and started reaching for his gun. That was a mistake, for even as his fingers wrapped around the grip of his pistol, he felt something sharp at his throat. The Mexican's hand flashed quickly across his neck. There was a stinging sensation, then a wetness at his collar. The Mexican let go of him and stepped back. Wallace felt his legs turn to rubber, and he fell to the floor. He put his hand up to his neck, then pulled it away and looked in horror at the blood on his fingers. He tried to call out, but could not because his windpipe had been cut. He could make no sound at all, save the silent scream in his head.

As he was losing consciousness, he saw the Mexican opening the cell doors. Tatum and Petrie hurried out. Tatum came over to look down at him.

"Deputy, when you get to hell, tell ole Fuller an' Howard hello for us, will you?" he asked.

"Horses in ally behind calaboose," Sanchez said. "Come."

"Not yet. We got us a little job to take care of," Tatum said.

"What's that?" Petrie asked.

"The judge is stayin' over in the hotel till after the hangin'. We need to give him our regrets, tell 'im we're sorry but we can't make it."

Petrie laughed.

The three men left the jail, then slipped through the shadows down the street to the hotel. Moving in through the front door, they walked quietly over to the counter. As the desk clerk snored loudly, they checked the registration book.

"He's in two-oh-three," Tatum whispered.

Taking the spare key to the room, the three men left the desk clerk undisturbed, then moved quickly and quietly up to the second floor. They walked down the carpeted hallway until they found the door. Slowly, Tatum unlocked the door and pushed it open.

The judge was snoring loudly.

"The son of bitch ain't losin' no sleep over sentencin' us to hang, is he?" Tatum whispered. He pulled his gun.

"No, señor," Sanchez said, shaking his head. He put

his finger over his mouth to indicate the need for silence.

"Sanchez is right," Petrie whispered. "You use the gun it's goin' to make too much noise."

"I kill him for you," Sanchez offered. Pulling his knife, Sanchez stepped over to the judge's bed.

"Wait!" Tatum said. "I want the son of a bitch to wake up long enough to know what happened to him."

Sanchez nodded.

Tatum put his hand on the judge's shoulder.

"Judge. Judge, wake up," he said.

The judge snorted, then opened his eyes.

"What is it? Who is there?"

"It's a couple of friends of yours, Judge. Jack Tatum and Billy Petrie. We just killed the deputy and broke jail. We've come to tell you good-bye."

"What?" the judge gasped. He started to sit up, but before he was halfway in the upright position, Sanchez's knife flashed quickly across his neck. The judge's eyes opened wide in shock and fear, and he put his hands up to his throat, then fell back down onto the pillow.

"Let's get out of here," Petrie said.

Tatum started looking around the room.

"Come on!" Petrie said. "What the hell are you lookin' for? You know this old fart doesn't have any money. Let's go, before someone hears us!"

"This is what I was lookin' for," Tatum said a moment later, holding something up that gleamed softly in the dim light.

"What is that?"

"The judge's gavel," Tatum said triumphantly. "I want something to remember him by."

The three men went downstairs, walking quietly so as not to awaken any of the guests. When they passed through the lobby the clerk was still sleeping behind the desk. Slipping down through the alley, they mounted their horses and rode off into the night.

When Monte walked down to the jailhouse at just after seven o'clock the next morning, he passed the carpenters who were working on the gallows. Because of the time constraints, and the fact that the judge had authorized the hanging to be from any such contrivance as they might be able to find, Monte and a few others had come up with an ingenious solution. The stoutest of any of the pillars in town holding a porch roof were the pillars of the hardware store. Thus it was there that they decided to attach a crosspiece that would protrude out into the street.

At the street end of the protruding crosspiece, a second post was placed to support it, resulting in an upside-down U. Underneath the U, there was a plank for Tatum and Petrie to stand on. When the support post for the plank was suddenly removed, the drop would be sufficient to break the necks of the condemned men.

Several people were already gathered around the makeshift gallows, watching and talking.

"What time is the hangin' to be, Sheriff?" someone asked.

"Eight-thirty," Monte said. He took out his watch, opened it, and glanced at the time. "About another hour and a half. Has anyone seen the judge this morning?"

"No, and we don't think we will. A highfalutin fella like the judge don't get out of bed *this* time o' day. He said any time before noon. My thinkin' is, he was hopin' that's about when you would do it so he wouldn't lose any sleep."

The others laughed at the observation.

"Well, if any of you see him, tell him I'm down at

WARPATH OF THE MOUNTAIN MAN   41

the jail," Monte said. "I'm going down to relieve Wallace so he can get some breakfast."

"We'll tell him, Monte," someone said. Then, as Monte walked away, he heard the same voice saying, "You better put another brace right there if you don't want this whole thing to come crashing down on you."

"Now, who's building this contraption, Paul, you or me?" the carpenter replied.

"Well, you are, I reckon. You just ain't doin' that good a job with it, that's all."

"It's just temporary. How good does it have to be?"

"Good enough to get these fellas hung, and the way you're doin' it, might not get the job done."

"Would you like to test it out, Paul?"

Monte grinned as he heard the others laugh at the carpenter's retort. He reached the jailhouse door and tried to open it, but was surprised to find it locked. He tapped on it.

"Dewey? Dewey, you in there?" He tapped on the door again. "Why have you got the door locked?"

When he got no answer, he fished in his pocket until he pulled out his own key. Then, opening the door, he stepped into the jail. "Dewey, I'm here," he called. "If you want any breakfast you'd better . . ." That was as far as he got. Even from the door he could see blood on the floor, and when he stepped around the desk for a better look, he saw his deputy lying in a pool of blood, his throat cut and his eyes open, opaque now, but still reflecting the horror of his last moment on earth.

"Jesus, Dewey," Monte said quietly. He didn't know if it was prayer or a curse.

Monte hurried back down the walk toward the hotel. He passed the carpenters and their audience on his way.

"You forget something, Monte?" one of the men asked.

Monte stopped. They might as well know it now as later. He drew a deep breath, then sighed. "Deputy Wallace is dead," he said. "The prisoners are gone."

"The hell you say. How did it happen?"

Monte shook his head. "He's lying on the floor with his throat cut," he said. He shook his head. "The judge isn't going to like this."

Monte hurried down to the City Pig, figuring to catch the judge at breakfast. When he came in, Kathy walked over to him. "You mean Mary's going to let you have breakfast with us this morning?" Kathy teased. Kathy and the sheriff's wife, Mary, were good friends.

Monte shook his head. "No, I'm looking for the judge. Has he come in for breakfast yet?"

"I haven't seen him."

"Hmm, I would've thought he would have been here by now. All right, I'll check the hotel. If I miss him and you see him, would you tell him I'm looking for him?"

Sure thing, Monte," Kathy promised.

When Monte crossed through the lobby of the hotel, he saw the clerk sweeping the lobby floor.

"Has the judge come down yet?"

"Not yet."

"What's his room number?"

"Two-oh-three."

Monte went upstairs. When he reached the second floor, he stepped over to Room 203 and knocked on the door.

"Judge? Judge Tutwyler, you awake? Judge?" Monte knocked again, more loudly this time. "Judge, wake up!"

When the judge still didn't answer, Monte went

back downstairs. "Do you have an extra key to the judge's room?" he asked.

"Yes," the clerk said, starting back toward the registration desk. He reached up toward a large board covered with nails from which keys were hanging. His hand started toward 203, then stopped. That nail was empty. "That's funny."

"What's funny? What is it? What's wrong?"

"The extra key is gone."

"You sure? You sure you didn't give two keys to the judge?"

"I'm positive. The extra key was hanging right here," the clerk said. "I know it was here last night because I saw it. I don't have the slightest idea what happened to it."

"Damn," Monte said. "I'm afraid I do." Turning, Monte went back up the stairs, this time taking them two at a time, although he knew in his gut that any need for hurrying was long over.

Puzzled by the sheriff's strange behavior, the hotel clerk hurried up behind him.

This time Monte made no effort to knock on the door, or even try the doorknob. Instead he backed away from it, then raised his foot and kicked hard right beside the knob.

"Here, what are you doing!" the clerk asked in alarm.

The door popped open, along with part of the door frame. Monte took one step into the room, then stopped.

"Holy shit," he said.

The bed on which the judge was lying was soaked in blood. Like Deputy Wallace, the judge's eyes were open and opaque. And like Wallace's eyes, these too reflected the horror of his death.

* * *

Jack Tatum had met Raul Sanchez six months earlier when the Mexican came to him with information about a shipment of rifles to the Mexican Army. Tatum, Sanchez, and a half-dozen others had hit the freight wagon, killed the Mexican Army guards, and taken the shipment of repeating rifles. Their initial plan had been to sell it to one of the several revolutionary groups operating in northern Sonora, but none of the groups had enough money to make the deal worthwhile. So Tatum came up with a new plan, a particularly ambitious one, which would require several more men. After breaking Tatum and Petrie out of jail, Raul Sanchez went his own way, intending to round up the men they would need to carry out Tatum's plan. Sanchez and Tatum had agreed to meet in Risco, a tiny town in northern New Mexico Territory.

Tatum was pulled out of his reverie by a call from Billie Petrie, who was riding behind him.

"Jack," Petrie called. "Jack." His voice was strained and filled with pain.

Twisting in his saddle, Tatum saw that Petrie had fallen from his horse. With a disgusted sigh, Tatum rode back to look down at him.

"We ain't makin' no time with you fallin' off your horse ever' mile or so," he said.

"I can't help it, Jack," Petrie said in a pained voice. "This here leg is killin' me. The wound has festered."

Tatum dismounted, then pulled a knife, knelt down by Petrie and ripped his pants leg open. The leg was swollen and blue. He put his hand on the leg near the bullet entry wound and felt its heat.

"You're in bad shape," Tatum said matter-of-factly.

"I'll be all right soon's I get to where I can rest a little," Petrie insisted.

"No, you ain't going to get all right."

"Maybe a doctor could . . ."

"There ain't no doctor in Risco," Tatum said. "And even if there was, 'bout the only thing he could do for you is take the leg off."

"No," Petrie said, shaking his head. "I ain't goin' let no doctor do that."

Tatum turned away from Petrie and started back toward his horse. "Think you can get mounted?" he asked.

"Yeah," Petrie said. Painfully, he got up, then reached for the saddle horn. He tried to pull himself up into the saddle, but he couldn't do it. Then, with a mighty effort, he heaved himself up, only to fall from the other side.

"Sorry, Billy, but I ain't got time to take care of you," Tatum said.

"Don't you worry about me," Petrie said.

"Oh, I ain't worried," Tatum said. There was something about the tone of Tatum's voice that caused Petrie to look up at him. When he did, he saw that Petrie was holding a gun on him.

"Jack, no!" Petrie said. "What are you going to do?"

"It's best this way, Billy. You wouldn't want to go through the rest of your life without a leg now, would you?"

"Listen, Jack, no, don't—" That was as far he got before Tatum pulled the trigger. The bullet hit Petrie in his heart, stopping it instantly.

Tatum started to leave him there, then looking down, saw the snakeskin boots Petrie was so proud of.

"No sense in lettin' these go to waste," he said. "I'll just take 'em with me—as a keepsake, so to speak." Kneeling at Petrie's feet, he pulled the snakeskin boots off, one at a time. Then, taking the reins of Petrie's horse, he rode off, even as the vultures were circling

Five

Tom Burke, the man who had acted as foreman for the jury that convicted Tatum and Petrie, gave a barbecue on his ranch, Timber Notch. It was a gala event, with half a steer turning on a spit over an open fire, tended to by a couple of Tom's hired hands. He had invited everyone who served with him on the jury, as well as the sheriff, the bailiff, and all his neighboring ranchers. Sugarloaf was adjacent to Timber Notch, which meant that Smoke, Sally, Pearlie, and Cal were included in the invitation.

The barbecue was given as a way of getting everyone together and settled back down again after the events of the recent past: the attempted bank robbery, the killing of Richmond Flowers, and more recently, the killings of Deputy Wallace and Judge Tutwyler.

The party was supposed to help people put everything behind them, but throughout the large house there were little groups of guests all talking about the same thing: the events of the recent past. Not until one of the hands came in, carrying a large joint of beef, did the subject change.

"Here's the first carving, folks!" Tom said. "If you'll get in line at the table there, when you get to the meat, I'll serve you."

Although the steer had been cooked over an outdoor pit, it was a little cold outside, so the serving was inside. A long table, laden with vegetables and salads, provided the side dishes. There were at least forty people in attendance, and they were going down each side of the table, loading their plates with the salads and vegetables. Then they took their plates to another table where Tom was carving the meat. As Tom carved the meat, his wife, Jo Ellen, served.

Jo Ellen was wearing a gold chain, from which hung a sparkling diamond. It was an anniversary gift from Tom, and she had been showing it off proudly.

"Have you seen my new diamond?" she asked as Smoke held his plate out to be served.

"It's pretty, all right," Smoke agreed. "But I'd just as soon you not be showing it off to Sally. Next thing you know, she'll be wantin' one."

"Hah! As if you wouldn't get it for her, Smoke Jensen," Jo Ellen said. "I know you. You'd do anything Sally asked you to do. And why wouldn't you? She's a wonderful woman."

"Well, I reckon I'll confess to that," Smoke agreed with a little laugh.

Pearlie was right behind Smoke, and he held his plate out to Jo Ellen while she put a generous portion of beef on it. When Pearlie looked a little disappointed, she smiled at him.

"Would you like a little more?"

Grinning broadly, Pearlie held his plate out again. "Yes, ma'am, if you don't mind," he said.

"Say when." Jo Ellen put another large slice of beef on his plate, and when he didn't pull it back, she put another.

"Damn, Smoke, you didn't tell me I was going to have to butcher half my herd just to feed Pearlie," Tom said, laughing.

"The boy does have an appetite," Smoke agreed.

"Appetite? He doesn't have an appetite, he has a bottomless pit."

After Tom had carved enough meat, he got his own plate, then found Smoke and joined him. Tom had recently announced that he would soon be going to Texas to buy blooded bulls, and some of the other ranchers were already making arrangements to buy stud service from him.

"When are you leaving, and how long do you think you'll be gone?" Smoke asked.

"I'll be leaving sometime in the next two weeks," Tom replied. "It'll take me two days to get there by train, maybe a week to find the bulls, and two days back. So, make it about two weeks that I'll be gone."

Tom's young son brought his own plate over and sat down beside them.

"What are you doing here, Buddy? I thought all the kids were outside, playing down at the pond," Tom said.

"They're running around putting frogs down the girls' dresses," Buddy said disgustedly. "I don't have time for that kid stuff."

Tom laughed. "You're twelve years old. If you don't have time for it now, when will you have time for it?"

"Never," Buddy said. "Anyway, you're talkin' about goin' to Texas to get the bulls, aren't you?"

"Yes."

"That's more interesting than playing with frogs."

"Buddy, would you please come take this plate over to Mrs. Pynchon?" Jo Ellen Burke called.

"Yes, ma'am," Buddy replied, putting his own plate down and going over to do his mother's bidding.

Pearlie pointed to him as he walked away. "That kid acts older'n you do, Cal," he teased.

"Jo Ellen and I are convinced that Buddy's not really

a kid," Tom said, laughing. "We think he's a full-grown man, passing himself off as a kid."

"Well, look at it this way. If he keeps up his interest in the ranch, you'll have a home-grown foreman in no time at all," Smoke suggested.

"Did you read that letter in the paper from Judge Tutwyler's wife, thankin' the town for the flowers it sent to his funeral?" Tom asked.

"Yes. It was a nice letter," Smoke said.

"It's a shame, what happened to him and the deputy."

"You should've killed both those sons of bitches while you had the chance," Pearlie said.

"It would've been better if I had," Smoke agreed.

"Where do you think they are now?" Cal asked.

"If I were them, I'd be in California," Tom said. "Or Washington State maybe. Anywhere, as long as it's somewhere far away from here."

It was after midnight when Tatum rode into the tiny town of Risco, in northern New Mexico Territory. It had been six days since he escaped, and four days since he left Billy Petrie dead on the desert floor. Using some of the money he had stolen from the deputy and the judge, he bought a bottle of tequila at the cantina, then picked up a Mexican whore, taking her as much for her bed as for any of the special services she could provide for him.

Risco was a scattering of flyblown, crumbling adobe buildings laid out around a dusty plaza. What made it attractive to people like Tatum was the fact that it had neither constable nor sheriff, and visitations by law officers from elsewhere in the territory were strongly discouraged. In fact, there was a place in the town cemetery prominently marked as "Lawman's

Plot." There, two deputy sheriffs, one deputy U.S. marshal, and an Arizona Ranger—all uninvited visitors to the town—lay buried.

Tatum woke up the next morning with a ravenous hunger and a raging need to urinate. The *puta* was still asleep beside him. The covers were askew, exposing one enormous, pillow-sized, blue-veined breast and a fat leg that dangled over the edge of the bed. She was snoring loudly, and a bit of spittle drooled from her vibrating lips. She didn't wake up when Tatum crawled over her to get out of bed and get dressed.

There was an outhouse twenty feet behind the little adobe crib, but Tatum chose not to go inside, peeing against the outside wall instead.

Finished, Tatum went back in to get dressed. He looked at the snakeskin boots, then smiled as he pulled them on. They were every bit as comfortable as Petrie had said they were. "Hell, if I'd known the boots felt this good, I'd'a shot you a long time ago," Tatum said quietly, laughing at his little joke. Dressed now, he walked over to the table where he had seen the woman put the money last night. He took his money back, then let himself out and went downstairs.

Tatum was sitting at a table in the back of the cantina, having a breakfast of beans, tortillas, and beer, when Pigiron McCord came in. Pigiron wasn't very tall, but he was a powerfully built man, bald, with a prominent brow ridge, thick lips, and heavily muscled arms that seemed too long for his body. Seeing Tatum, Pigiron came back to join him.

"Sanchez told me you would be here," he said.

"Did he tell you what I've got in mind?"

"He said you were going to sell guns to the Indians."

"That's right."

Pigiron shook his head. "You ain't going to make no money that way. The Indians have gone straight. They've got their own money; they can buy guns anytime they want. Hell, they can even order them from a catalogue."

Tatum shook his head. "The treaty allows them to buy guns for hunting purposes only, and there is a limit to how many they can buy."

"Why would they want any more than they can buy?"

"Because they are going to be in a war," Tatum said. "And you can't fight a war if you don't have enough guns."

"Hell, Tatum, you been in jail too long," Pigiron said with a snort. "Except for a few Sioux and their Ghost Dancers, there ain't no Indians nowhere that's on the warpath."

"That's the way it is now," Tatum said. "But it don't have to stay that way."

"What do you mean?"

"Soon's we get through causing trouble, there will be Indians on the warpath. I guarantee it." Tatum concluded his comment by shoving half a bean-loaded tortilla into his mouth. When bean juice ran down his chin, he wiped it off with his shirt cuff, then licked the juice from the accumulation of filth that was on his sleeve.

"What are we going to do?" Pigiron asked.

"You let me worry about that. In the meantime we're going to need some men. Think you can round a few up?"

"Sure, if they don't all have to be white Anglos."

"They don't. In fact, I already got me a couple of half-breed Injuns goin' to throw in with us. We need them to make the plan work."

"How soon you want me to get 'em?"

"Soon as you can. Is there any paper out on you up in Colorado?"

"No, not that I know of."

"Good. Soon as you get a few men rounded up, I want you to take one of them with you and go on up to Big Rock to have a look around. Wait for me up there. I'll join you soon as everything's ready."

"All right." Pigiron was silent for a moment. "You said take a look around. What am I lookin' for?" he asked.

"The man who was the foreman on the jury that convicted me is named Tom Burke. I understand he has a ranch somewhere near to Big Rock. I want you to find out where it is and how many men he's got workin' for him. 'Cause the first thing I aim to do after I get back up there is pay that son of a bitch a little visit."

When Pigiron McCord and Jason Harding rode into Big Rock some days later, they rode right past Tom Burke, though, never having seen him, they didn't realize it. Pigiron and Harding headed straight for Longmont's Saloon, while the buckboard they had just passed, containing Tom Burke and his family, continued on toward the railroad station. Tom had driven in from Timber Notch so he could catch the afternoon train.

Tom's ten-year-old daughter, Sue Ann, had been bribed by the promise of a sarsaparilla, but Buddy had needed no inducement. He'd come willingly. When they reached the depot, Tom stopped the team and set the brakes on the buckboard. He left for a few minutes to check his suitcase and buy his ticket, then came back to sit on the buckboard and wait for the train with his family.

Because trains were the town's contact with the rest of the world, nearly every arrival and departure were major events. Therefore, the depot platform was crowded with men, women, and children. There was nearly always someone there to take advantage of the crowd: a musician, an artist, or even a public speaker looking for an audience. Today a juggler was entertaining the crowd by keeping brightly colored balls in the air, in exchange for whatever coins might be tossed in his hat. Getting permission, Sue Ann got down from the buckboard and went over for a closer look. She'd asked Buddy to come with her, but he'd declined, concentrating instead on the purpose of his father's visit to Texas.

"Pop, I know bulls near 'bout as good as you do. You sure you don't want me to come along?"

"Not this time, Buddy," Tom said. "Maybe next year."

"All right, next year," Buddy said, pleased by the concession. "You think I won't remember that, but I will."

Tom chuckled. "Oh, I've no doubt but that you will remember."

In the distance they heard a whistle and looking north, saw smoke in the sky.

"Well, here it comes," someone called, though as everyone had heard the whistle and seen the smoke in the sky, no such announcement was necessary.

Tom stepped down from the buckboard, stretched, then reached for a small valise. He saw his suitcase, along with a dozen other bags, on the little steel-wheeled cart that was being rolled out to the track, where it would be loaded onto the baggage car.

Tom stood alongside the buckboard as the train

arrived. When it drew even with him, he could feel the pounding of the big driver wheels rolling against the track as wisps of spent steam spewed out of the actuating cylinder. The train slowed, then stopped, with the cars alongside the platform while the engine, venting steam and popping and snapping as the metal cooled, sat on the far side of the depot.

"Well, this is it," Tom said. He kissed Jo Ellen and Sue Ann good-bye. Then he put his hand on Buddy's shoulder. "Take care of them while I'm gone," he said.

"I will, Pop," Buddy said.

Tom started toward the train, but Jo Ellen called out to him. "Tom?"

He turned.

"Kiss me good-bye again?"

Tom chuckled, then came back and kissed her. During the embrace she held him very hard.

"Easy, darlin'," Tom said gently. "I'm only going to be gone a couple of weeks."

"I know," Jo Ellen said.

Tom kissed her once more, then walked out to the train. Jo Ellen and her two children watched as Tom climbed onto the train and disappeared inside. The conductor called all aboard, and the train began to pull away from the station. Jo Ellen could no longer see him, but just in case he could see them, she wanted them to all be there when he took his last look back. For that reason they stayed right where they were until all that could be seen of the departing train was its smoke, hanging in the distant sky.

"Mom? Mom, aren't we going to get my sarsaparilla?" Sue Ann asked.

"What?"

"You promised me a sarsaparilla, remember?"

"Oh, yes," Jo Ellen said. "Of course."

Suddenly, and unexpectedly, Jo Ellen's body quaked as she shivered. Sue Ann laughed. "Why did you do that?" she asked.

"Oh, no reason," Jo Ellen replied.

"Ben says when you shiver like that, it means some-one just stepped on your grave," Buddy said.

"Don't be saying such things," Jo Ellen said more harshly than she intended.

"It's just a joke, Mom."

"Well, it's not a very funny one," Jo Ellen said. For some reason she had a strange feeling of foreboding that she couldn't shake.

Six

By coincidence, Smoke Jensen was in town the same afternoon that Tom Burke left for Texas. And though he had come to run a few errands, he allowed himself enough time to stop by Longmont's to have a drink.

The owner of the saloon, Louis Longmont, was a lean, hawk-faced man, with strong, slender, always clean hands and long fingers with nails that were carefully manicured. Louis had been Smoke's friend for many years, and though he was sitting at his special table in the back, he got up and came over to the bar specifically to serve Smoke, pouring his drink from a special bottle he kept just for his friend.

Louis was dressed in a black suit with white shirt and dark ascot. He wore low-heeled boots and a pistol hung in a tied-down holster on his right side. The saloon owner was an enigma to many people. On first glance, he was just another dandy. But in fact, he was worth a great deal of money, and in addition to the saloon, owned a large ranch up in Wyoming, several businesses in San Francisco, and a rather significant share of a railroad.

"Did you hear about Billy Petrie?" Louis asked as he poured the drink.

"No, what about him?"

"They found his body about fifty miles south of here."

"His body?"

"Yes, he'd been shot. Sheriff took the noon train down to see about it. Looks like Tatum may have shot him to keep him from slowin' him down. So much for friendship."

"I'm not all that surprised," Smoke said. "Tatum struck me as the type of person who might do something like that."

"You crazy bitch!" someone shouted. The shout was followed by the sound of a slap, and when Smoke looked around, he saw that a big man had just hit one of the bar girls.

"You come back here!" the big man bellowed when the girl ran from him.

"Who is that?" Smoke asked.

"He gave his name as Pigiron McCord," Longmont answered. "He's a stranger in town, must've just come in today." Louis started to pull his pistol, but Smoke put out his hand to stop him.

"Wait, no need for that yet."

When the big man started toward the girl a second time, Smoke called out to him.

"Leave the girl alone, McCord."

The big man looked toward Smoke in surprise. "How'd you know my name?"

Smoke didn't answer.

The man chuckled. "So, you've heard of ole Pigiron McCord, have you? What have you heard? That I'm not someone you mess with?"

"What makes you think I would have heard of a worthless pile of shit like you?"

The smile left Pigiron's face. "Well, you will have heard of me by the time I get through with you. Then I'm goin' to settle accounts with that whore."

Pigiron started toward Smoke, but he was stopped when Smoke snapped a quick, slashing left into Pigiron's face. It was a good, well-placed blow, but Pigiron just flinched once, then laughed, a low, evil laugh.

"Fight!" someone shouted across the batwing doors of the saloon. "Smoke Jensen and some big bastard are havin' a fight in the saloon!"

Within a few seconds, there were twice as many people in the saloon as there had been when Smoke came in, and though Smoke was concentrating on the task at hand, in the back of his mind he couldn't help but wonder where all the people had come from. It wasn't as if they were out on the street, and yet here everyone was, gathered in a large circle to watch Smoke Jensen and the stranger going against each other.

"Ole Smoke may of bit off more'n he can chew this time," someone said.

"I know. Did you see a moment ago when Smoke hit him? Hell, it would'a laid just about anyone in here out, but that big bastard hardly blinked."

Pigiron rushed Smoke, and Smoke stepped to one side, causing Pigiron to slam into the bar. With a roar like an angry bull, Pigiron ran his arm down the bar, clearing it of a half-dozen glasses or more. Then he turned to face Smoke a second time.

"Why don't you stay in one place, you yellow-bellied bastard?" Pigiron asked, his words a low growl.

"I haven't gone anywhere," Smoke said. He held his left hand out, palm up, curling his fingers in invitation. "Come on, if you want me, come get me. I'm right here."

Again Pigiron lunged, and again he missed. Finally, he gave that up as a fruitless tactic and, panting heavily now, raised his fists in front of his face. For the next few minutes, the two men circled each other, holding their fists doubled in front of them, each trying to test the mettle of the other.

Pigiron swung, a clublike swing that Smoke leaned away from. Smoke counterpunched, and scored, but again, Pigiron laughed it off. As the fight went on Smoke continued to score, and though Pigiron had laughed off his early blows, he was beginning to show some effect from the punches. His eyes began to puff up, and there was a nasty cut on his lip. Then Smoke landed a punch that broke Pigiorn's nose, causing blood to flow.

So far Pigiron hadn't landed a single blow, and Smoke was glad. He had a feeling that if just one of Pigiron's blows landed, it would be like getting kicked by a mule.

Then Smoke saw an opening, and took it. He timed it just right, and landed a solid right on Pigiron's already smashed nose. He hit it perfectly, and had the satisfaction of hearing a bellow of pain from Pigiron for the first time.

Then, when Pigiron put both hands over his nose, Smoke drove his fist hard into Pigiron's solar plexus. As Pigiron bent over, stunned by the blow, Smoke finished it with a roundhouse right to the jaw. Pigiron went down and out.

Pearlie was standing in the crowd with the others, watching the fight as he ate boiled eggs he had scooped from the jar on the bar. When Smoke scored his telling blow, Pearlie started to cheer along with the others. His cheer was interrupted when he saw a man in front of him slip his pistol from his holster, aiming it at Smoke.

Dropping his eggs, Pearlie pulled his own pistol, then brought it down hard on the man's head. The would-be shooter fell forward across Pigiron's prostrate form, the pistol in his hand clattering to the floor.

"Damn!" Pearlie said. "The son of a bitch made me drop my boiled eggs."

Smoke and the others laughed. "Come on home," Smoke said to his friend. "I'll have Sally boil you up a dozen. I reckon you've earned them."

"Smoke," Louis called. "What do you think we should do about these two? Monte's gone."

"Ah, throw a bucket of water over 'em and let 'em go," Smoke said. "I don't think they'll bother anyone else. I seem to be the one that pissed them off."

"What about me?" the bar girl asked.

"Yeah," Smoke said. "Well, maybe you'd better stay out of sight until they're both gone."

When Smoke and Pearlie stepped out in front of the saloon, Smoke saw that Pearlie had picked up three of the dropped boiled eggs. He was blowing on them, brushing them against his shirt.

"I thought you dropped those."

"Yeah, I did, but the floor wasn't that dirty."

Smoke laughed. "Tobacco quids, ground-out cigarette and cigar butts, spilt beer, whiskey, and other things I don't even want to know about, and you say it isn't that dirty?"

Pearlie was about to take a bite of one of the refurbished eggs, but he got a funny expression on his face, and pulled the egg away from his mouth.

"Yeah," he said. "Yeah, you're right. They're probably pretty dirty, aren't they?"

"I'd say they were."

Seeing a stray dog under the porch, Pearlie tossed the eggs to the animal. "You'll have Sally cook me a dozen eggs, you say?"

"An even dozen," Smoke promised as he mounted his horse.

"Those will probably be better anyway."

Smoke laughed. "I'm sure she will be flattered that you think so."

Smoke and Pearlie rode out of town as an unsteady Pigiron McCord and his equally groggy partner were tossed out of the saloon.

It was dark by the time Pigiron and Jason reached the mesa where Tatum had told them he would meet them.

"You sure this is the place?" Jason asked, looking around. "I don't see no one here."

"You think they're going to put up a sign or something?" Pigiron replied. He put his hand on his jaw and worked it back and forth a couple of times. "That son of a bitch nearly broke my jaw."

Jason rubbed the top of his head. "Yeah, and whoever hit me nearly broke my head," he said. "What the hell did you start that fight for in the first place?"

"I didn't start it. That fella Jensen did. All I was doing was having a little fun with one of the whores. Next thing I know he was comin' after me, like I'd stepped on his boots, or somethin'."

Their conversation was interrupted by the quiet hooting of an owl.

"Did you hear that?" Pigiron asked.

"What, that owl?"

"That ain't no owl," Pigiron said. "Like as not, it's one of Tatum's half-breeds."

The owl sounded again.

"That's an owl," Jason insisted.

Looking back at him, Pigiron smiled, then raised his hands to his lips. He made an owl call that almost perfectly duplicated the one they had just heard. A moment later, a man appeared out of the darkness.

He was obviously an Indian, and his appearance startled Jason, who jumped—but Pigiron held his hand out to stop him.

"This is Russell Swift Bear," Pigiron said. Then Pigiron asked the Indian, "Where's Tatum?"

"Come," was all Swift Bear said in reply.

Pigiron and Tatum followed Swift Bear for a short distance until they came to a little draw. There, several shadowy figures sat around a flickering campfire. Tatum came over to greet the two men.

"Did you find out what I wanted to know?" he asked Pigiron.

"About Tom Burke? Yeah, I found his ranch. It's about seven miles northwest of Big Rock. Burke ain't there, though."

"Burke ain't there? What do you mean, he ain't there? Where is he?"

"He went down into Texas."

"Damn! He's moved?"

"No, he ain't moved. He just went to Texas to get some bulls, they was sayin'. His family is still there at the ranch. It's a placed called Timber Notch."

"His family? Who's he got in his family?"

"Don't know, didn't get all that. Just heard that his wife and kids were staying back at the ranch."

"How many hands working at the ranch?"

"Didn't find that out," Pigiron said.

"How do you expect me to plan anything if you don't get all the information I need to . . ." Tatum stopped and looked more closely at Pigiron's face. "What the hell happened to you?"

"What do you mean?" Pigiron asked, self-consciously putting his hand to his nose.

"I mean, you've always been an ugly son of a bitch, but damn if you ain't uglier now than you was last time I saw you." Tatum put his hand out and touched the puffed up bruise on Pigiron's jaw. "You been beat up."

"He got into a fight with Smoke Jensen," Jason said.

Tatum laughed. "You let him whip you like that?"

"He got in a lucky punch," Pigiron said.

"Yeah, well now we both got a case against Smoke Jensen," Tatum said. "He's the one killed Fuller and Howard. He killed Billy too."

"You ask me, he's the one we should go after, instead of Tom Burke."

"Not yet. I'll get around to taking care of him when the time comes, but that time ain't here yet. Did you boys eat any supper?"

"No."

"They's prob'ly some beans left in the pot."

Getting their kits from their saddlebags, Pigiron and Jason went over to the little black pot that was suspended over the fire and helped themselves.

Tatum climbed up on a rock and looked toward the distant horizon, approximately where he thought Burke's ranch might be.

Tomorrow, he would put his plan into operation. It was a good plan, and the beauty of it was, it didn't matter whether Burke was there or not. In fact, this might even be better.

Seven

The morning sun, a bright red orb just beginning to gather warmth and brilliance, rose in the east. A dark gray haze was still hanging in the notches, though it was already beginning to dissipate, like drifting smoke. Timbered foothills, covered with blue pine and golden aspen, marched down from the higher elevations. One of the mountains, scarred by some ancient cataclysmic event of geology, shone blue-green in the early morning light.

On Timber Notch, a cock crowed. In the barn of the neatly laid-out ranch, a horse whickered. A cow, anxious to be milked, moved nervously in her stall. The morning air was perfumed by the smell of coffee, frying bacon, and baking biscuits.

"Buddy, don't forget, you need to get that cow milked," a woman's voice called.

"I'm going to do it, Mom, soon as I'm dressed," Buddy answered.

"And put on a coat. It's cold this morning."

From a bunkhouse adjacent to the big house, a cowhand came outside carrying a handful of paper with him, his breath creating puffs of vapor in the brisk morning air. The door to the outhouse creaked as he opened it. He stepped inside, then slammed the door shut behind him.

In the corral a windmill answered a slight freshening and turned into the breeze, its fan blades spinning. The actuating piston rattled as water spewed from the pump's wide mouth and splashed into a big, wooden trough.

Unnoticed by any of the residents of the ranch, ten riders sloped down the side of a nearby hill, their appearance making an ugly scar on this idyllic scene. The leader of the group was Jack Tatum.

Raul Sanchez was riding directly behind Tatum. Although he wasn't technically second in command, because Tatum knew that some of his men wouldn't accept a Mexican as second in command, he was probably the one Tatum depended on more than any other.

Behind Sanchez rode Pigiron McCord. Pigiron's face still showed signs of the beating he had taken the day before. One eye was swollen shut, his nose was flattened, his lips were puffy and deformed, and there were scars on his chin and jaw.

The next three in the line of riders who were coming single file down the side of the mountain were Jason Harding, Orville Clinton, and Dirk Wheeler. They were petty outlaws who had been in and out of jail several times over the years, but even though all three were wanted men, the government didn't consider any of them important enough to go to the expense of having reward posters printed for them.

Like Pigiron, Jason had been in town the day before, and also, like Pigiron, he was showing the effects. He had a large knot on top of his head, the result of a pistol being brought down hard on his cranium.

In addition to Raul Sanchez, there was another Mexican in the group, Paco Arino. Perry Blue Horses and Russell Swift Bear rode just behind Raul Sanchez. Blue Horses and Swift Bear were half-breed Indians who were equally unwelcome in both Indian and white society. The last rider in the group was a man known simply as Jim. Jim was completely alone, not only within this group, but in most of the territory he roamed, for he was black. Jim was a big, muscular man who seldom spoke, but whose eyes and demeanor did little to hide the hatred that smoldered within him.

When they reached a rock outcropping that was no more than one hundred yards from the house and outbuildings, Tatum gave silent hand signals to put his men in place.

"All right, boys, get ready," he said once they were in position.

All but Blue Horses and Swift Bear raised rifles to their shoulders, waiting for an order from Tatum. Blue Horses and Swift Bear also had rifles, though for this particular operation they were using bows and arrows.

The door to the outhouse opened, and the man who had entered it a few moments earlier now exited, hooking his suspenders over his shoulders as he did so.

"Now," Tatum shouted, and everyone opened fire.

Blue Horses aimed for the man at the outhouse, and had the satisfaction of following his arrow in its swift flight, all the way across the open space between them, until it buried itself in the man's chest. Swift Bear's arrow plunked into the wall beside the door of the outhouse.

"Indians!" someone shouted. "Get your guns, boys, and get to shootin'!"

Now Blue Horses and Swift Bear were shooting fire arrows into the compound. The bunkhouse and barn were quickly enveloped in flames. Within a few minutes the hired hands ran from the bunkhouse, coughing and gasping for breath. That was exactly what Tatum wanted, and he and the others directed their firing at the men who were so devastated by smoke inhalation that they were unable to put up any kind of effective response. Within moments, all were down.

"Hold it! Hold it!" Tatum shouted to his men. "Stop firing. I think we've got 'em all."

"What about from the house?" McCord asked.

"Anyone hear any shootin' come from the house?" Tatum asked.

"I didn't hear nothin'," Clinton said.

"You boys here anything?" Tatum asked the Indians. Both responded in the negative.

"Could be they're already dead. Or maybe, nobody was there in the first place."

"How do we find out?" McCord asked.

"We'll surround the house," Tatum replied. "Pigiron, you, Jason, and Wheeler go round front and bust in through the front door. Sanchez, Arino, you two go in through windows there on the left side of the house. Jim, you, Blue Horses, and Swift Bear go in through windows on the right. Me'n Clinton will bust in through the back door."

Tatum led his men down to the main house. There were four bodies on the ground: the hand who was killed as he left the outhouse and the three who had run out from the bunkhouse. The outlaws approached the main house cautiously, not sure of who was still inside, or even if whoever was inside was still alive.

Tatum gave the signal, and his men moved into the positions he had assigned them.

"All right, boys! Let's go!" he shouted. He started toward the back door, then stepped to one side, indicating that Clinton should go in first. Clinton hesitated for just a moment, then he burst in through the door. As he did so, he caught a charge of double-ought buckshot from a ten-gauge Greener shotgun. The blast knocked him back outside, and he fell on the porch with his guts ripped open and his head hanging halfway down the steps. Looking cautiously around the door frame, Tatum saw a boy of about twelve trying desperately to reload the shotgun he had just fired.

"Hold it right there, boy!" Tatum shouted, jumping in through the door and pointing his gun at Buddy. "You're pretty damn handy with that scattergun."

"Not handy enough," Buddy said. "If I was, you'd be dead too."

"You've got a big mouth. Where are the others?"

"What others? There ain't no one here but me."

"You expect me to believe you are all alone here?"

"That's what I said."

"Where's your pa?"

"He's down in Texas, buying bulls."

"What about your ma?"

"I told you, nobody else is here."

Looking over toward the sideboard, Tatum saw a plate of biscuits and bacon. "You plannin' on eatin' all this yourself, were you?" Tatum said. He broke apart a biscuit, laid several pieces of bacon on it, then making a sandwich of it, began eating.

"Let me go!" a woman's voice said from the front of the house. "Who are you people? What are you doing here?"

An attractive woman and a young girl were dragged into the kitchen.

"Look what we found," McCord said.

"Are you Mrs. Burke?" Tatum asked, his words muffled by the fact that his mouth was full of biscuit and bacon.

"It's none of your business who I am," Jo Ellen answered defiantly.

Almost distractedly, Tatum backhanded Sue Ann, knocking the little girl against the wall. She slid down to the floor, her nose and mouth bleeding. Immediately, she began crying.

"What are you doing?" Jo Ellen screamed in rage.

"If you don't want the little girl hit anymore, answer the question, woman. Are you the wife of the jury foreman who sentenced me to hang?"

"Yes," Jo Ellen said. "I'm only sorry that the state didn't get the job done."

"Good. That's all I wanted to know," Tatum said. He took another bite of his biscuit sandwich.

"What do we do with them?" McCord asked.

"Kill 'em," Tatum said, his words muffled by the fact that his mouth was full of biscuit and bacon.

"You sure? Seems to me like if we keep the woman alive, we could have a little fun with her," McCord said. But almost before he could finish his statement, Tatum drew his own pistol and shot the woman.

"Mama!" Sue Ann screamed. Tatum's next shot stopped the little girl in mid-cry.

"You son of a bitch!" Buddy shouted.

Tatum pointed his gun at the boy. "I saved you till last so you could watch your mama and sister die," he said evilly.

Buddy glared at him.

"I guess you think your mama and sister are in heaven, huh?"

"I know they are."

"Then look at it this way. You won't be apart very long, because I'm about to send you to heaven to be with them."

Buddy shook his head. "Uh-uh. I'll get around to going heaven," he said. "But first I'm going to wait for you in hell so I can soak your ass in kerosene and watch you burn, you sorry son of a bitch."

"Ha, ha! Gutsy little shit, ain't he?" Pigiron said, laughing.

"Like I said, kid, you've got a big mouth." Tatum shot Buddy in the heart. Then, holstering his pistol, he made himself another bacon and biscuit sandwich. Some of the others started to eat as well, but Tatum waved them away.

"We ain't got time to eat," he said. "Get busy. Remember, this has to look like the work of Indians."

Tatum looked back toward Jo Ellen's body. That was when he saw, for the first time, the gold chain with diamond pendant that was around her neck.

"I reckon I'll just take that as a little souvenir," he said. He grabbed the chain, then hung it around his own neck. "All right, let's go, get busy. We can't hang around here all day," he shouted to the others.

There was a little grumbling about not getting to enjoy the grub, but the men went to work as ordered, scalping and mutilating the bodies. Perry Blue Horses and Russell Swift Bear left a few more arrows around.

"Hey, Jack, ole Clinton here is still alive," Wheeler called from the back porch.

"He can't still be alive. Hell, that Greener purt' nigh took out all his innards."

"Yeah, it did that, all right. But he's still groanin'. What'll we do with him?"

"Leave him, he'll die soon enough," McCord said.

"No, we can't leave him here. This is supposed to be the work of Indians, remember?" Tatum said. "Drag 'im back to the horses, then throw him belly down across his. We'll take him somewhere else to get rid of him."

After a few more minutes of leaving Indian sign, Tatum ordered his men away and, dragging the nearly lifeless body of Clinton with them, they mounted and rode off. Three quarters of an hour later they were ten miles south.

It was Cal who discovered the carnage at Timber Notch Ranch. He had been riding the fence line when he saw the smoke. Realizing that so much smoke had to mean a burning building, he rode hard to get there. From the looks of the smoke the fire had a pretty good start, so he wasn't sure he would be able to do anything to help once he arrived, but he intended to be there to help nevertheless.

His first suspicion that something was wrong was when he reached the place and saw that, while the fire outside was still raging, no one was attempting to fight it. The barn was burning and the stock was still in the corral, gathered in a frightened bunch at the far end. The horses were wild-eyed and restless; the milk cows were milling about as if dazed. Although the barn, bunkhouse, and granary were on fire, the main house and the outhouse were not. It was then that he saw someone lying on the ground near the outhouse. Urging his horse to a gallop, he crossed the remaining distance very quickly, then dismounted.

"Oh, shit!" he said aloud. The man on the ground was the foreman of Timber Notch, Ben Goodpasture. Ben had an arrow sticking from his body, and he had been scalped. In various positions around the burning bunkhouse lay the bodies of Tom Burke's remaining ranch hands.

"Mrs. Burke!" Cal shouted, running toward the house. "Mrs. Burke, are you here?"

Cal darted up the steps and into the kitchen. There, just inside the kitchen door, he saw young Buddy's body. Like the hands outside, Buddy had been scalped. Mrs. Burke had been scalped as well as mutilated. Both breasts had been cut off. Only the little girl was neither scalped nor mutilated, though there was blood on her face, as if she had been beaten before she was shot.

Cal felt sick, and he turned and went back outside, then walked over to the edge of the porch, where he grabbed hold of one of the supporting posts. He stood there for a long moment, breathing deeply and trying hard to force the image of what he had just seen out of his mind. Then, when he was no longer afraid he was about to throw up, he walked back out to his horse, mounted, and started the long ride back to Sugarloaf.

It was nearly noon by the time he got back. Smoke, Sally, and Pearlie were just sitting down to eat when Cal came in.

"Cal, good, you're just in time," Sally started. "Wash up and . . ." Sally stopped in mid-sentence as she stared at Cal. "Good heavens, Cal, what is it? You look as if you have seen a ghost."

"It's Mrs. Burke," Cal said.

"Jo Ellen? She's here?"

Cal shook his head. "Not just Mrs. Burke. It's her, the boy, the little girl, Ben, and all the hands. All of them. Every one of them." Cal stopped for a moment, then took a deep breath. "They're dead."

"What?" Sally asked with a gasp.

"They're dead. Every one of them," Cal said. "I just got back from their place. Looks like they were attacked by Indians."

"Indians? That's impossible. There aren't any warring Indians around here," Smoke said.

"They burned the barn, the bunkhouse, the granary. There's arrows all over the place and every one of them have been scalped."

"Oh, God in heaven, Smoke, what will we do?" Sally asked.

"If it's already done, there's nothing we can do," Smoke replied. "Except see to it that Tom gets the word."

"Oh, that poor man," Sally said.

The lunch Sally had just put on the table went uneaten. Even Pearlie had no appetite for this meal.

Eight

It had been three days since the massacre at Timber Notch. Smoke Jensen, wearing a black suit and black bolo tie, was leaning against the wall in the kitchen of his house with his arms folded across his chest. Sally, who was wearing a black hat, was fussing with the veil, part of the funeral ensemble she was wearing. Pearlie was sitting at the table eating a piece of pie left over from supper the night before. Pearlie didn't own a black suit, but he was wearing a brown suit and a white shirt. The door opened and Cal came in. Cal didn't have a suit of any kind, but he was wearing clean jeans and a clean and pressed white shirt, complete with closed collar and a bolo tie he had borrowed from Smoke.

"The surrey is all hitched up, Smoke," Cal said.

"Thanks, Cal. If we can pull Pearlie away from the pie, we're ready."

"Uhmm, if you're waiting on me, you're backing up," Pearlie said, making a point to jump up quickly. He took one step away from the table, then reached back, picked up the last piece of pie, and shoved it in his mouth as they started toward the door.

"Has anyone heard from Tom Burke yet?" Pearlie asked as they climbed into the surrey. Pearlie rode in the front seat alongside Cal, who was driving. Smoke helped Sally into the backseat, then got in beside her.

"Tom wired back that he would be on the five o'clock train this morning," Smoke said. "So I suspect he's already here."

"How awful this must be for him," Sally said. "There he was down in Texas, buying cattle, when he gets the telegram that his family and all his hired hands were killed by Indians."

"If it was Indians," Smoke said.

Cal snapped the reins and the team pulled the surrey away smartly. As it rolled up the road, its wheels singing on the hard-packed dirt, Smoke turned to look back. The house and buildings of his own ranch gleamed brightly in the morning sun. It was a neatly kept, well-laid-out ranch that spoke well of Smoke's success, and even more of Sally's industry and creativity, for it was she who had made Sugarloaf the showplace that it was.

Seeing his ranch made Smoke feel an even greater sense of sympathy for his friend Tom Burke, for Tom had been every bit as proud of Timber Notch as Smoke was of Sugarloaf. Now, with his family dead, what was the purpose?

There were scores of buggies, surreys, buckboards, wagons, carriages, and horses around the cemetery in Big Rock, for Tom Burke was a well-liked and highly respected man in the area. Ben Goodpasture and one of the hired hands who had been killed at Tom's ranch had been buried the day before. Even before Tom returned, he'd made arrangements, by telegram, to pay for their funerals. The other two hired hands had been sent, by train, back to their families, one in St. Louis, the other in Memphis, also at Tom's expense. The funeral today was for Jo Ellen, Tom Jr.— who was called Buddy by everyone—and Sue Ann.

Cal parked the surrey behind one of the several long lines of conveyances that were arrayed around the cemetery; then the four climbed down and walked up the path toward the three open graves. There were more than five hundred people gathered for the funeral. That number included nearly everyone from Big Rock as well as people from all over the Las Animas County. When Smole and his companions reached the top of the hill where the three were to be buried, Smoke saw Tom Burke sitting in a chair next to the open graves. Tom's uncovered head was bowed, his silver hair shining. Smoke knew that the loss of his family was a particularly cruel blow for Tom, because family life had come late to him.

"Oh, Smoke," Sally said, putting her hand on his arm. "Look at the poor man. Have you ever seen anything so sad? We must speak to him."

"All right," Smoke agreed.

The four moved through the crowd until they reached Tom. From this position they could see the three coffins waiting to be lowered into the openings, one full-sized and two smaller ones. The air was redolent with the many floral arrangements that were scattered around, including a full bouquet of roses on top of the larger coffin, and a single rose on top of each of the two smaller coffins, red for Sue Ann, yellow for Buddy.

"Oh, Tom, I am so sorry about this," Sally said as she leaned down to embrace their friend and neighbor.

"Thank you," Tom mumbled.

"Tom," Smoke said, taking his friend's hand. It was all he could think to say.

"Smoke, I don't aim to just let this go," Tom said.

Smoke shook his head. "No, I didn't expect you would."

"Can I count on you?"

Smoke felt, rather than saw, Sally's quick glance toward him.

"Yes, of course you can," he said.

Pearlie and Cal paid their respects as well; then the four of them moved away from the bereaved rancher, finding a nearby place to stand that would keep them away from the crowd, yet afford them a good view.

"What was that all about?" Sally asked.

"What?" Smoke replied innocently, though he knew exactly what she meant.

"He said he wasn't going to let it go. Then he asked if he could count on you. You said, and I quote, 'Yes, of course you can.' "

"I'm sure he intends to go after whoever did this," Smoke said.

"Why? Going after the murderers isn't going to bring Tom's family back."

"I know it won't, but that's not the point," Smoke said. He put his arm around Sally and pulled her closer to him. "I don't quite know how to explain it, Sally, but leaving Sugarloaf this morning, I looked back at it and thought about it, and you and . . . well, I reckon it just gave me a deeper feeling about what Tom's going through right now. I know we can't bring his family back, but getting the ones who did it and making them pay? That can go a long way toward bringing him some peace of mind. And if there's any way I can help him do that, I aim to do it. I hope you understand."

"Whether I understand or not, you're going to help him find the renegade Indians who did this, aren't you?"

"I reckon I am," Smoke said. "But it would set a lot easier with me if you understood and approved."

Sally sighed. "Of course I understand," she said.

"You have a tremendous generosity of spirit, Smoke Jensen. I think that is one of the reasons I fell in love with you."

The preacher stood up then and the buzz of conversation halted. The tall, gaunt man looked out over the assembled mourners, giving them a moment to interrupt their conversations and focus on the task at hand, that of burying some of their own.

Once he had their attention, the preacher delivered a homily invoking God's wrath upon the evil savages who would perpetrate such a thing. After that, he reminded everyone of the promise of a joyous reunion in the hereafter. Finally, after the coffins were lowered into the grave, the preacher invited Tom to drop a handful of earth onto each of them. As Tom did so, the preacher intoned his final prayer.

"For as much as it hath pleased Almighty God in his wise providence to take out of this world the souls of Jo Ellen, Sue Ann, and Thomas Jr., we therefore commit their bodies to the ground; earth to earth, ashes to ashes, dust to dust; looking for the general Resurrection in the last day, and the life of the world to come through Our Lord Jesus Christ; at whose second coming in glorious majesty to judge the world, the earth and the sea shall give up their dead; and the corruptible bodies of those who sleep in him shall be changed, and made like unto his own glorious body; according to the mighty working whereby he is able to subdue all things unto himself. Amen."

When the funeral was over, the mourners began leaving the cemetery, walking quietly through the nearly one hundred tombstones that marked the last resting places of the late citizens of Big Rock. Like the living citizens of a town, the deceased ran the gamut from innocent children to murderers who were there because they had paid the ultimate penalty to the state. Four of the graves were so recent that the pile of dirt was still fresh over them. Those were the graves for the two would-be bank robbers, and for Richmond Flowers and Deputy Wallace.

One by one the mourners went their own way, some on foot, others on horseback, and still others by buggy, surrey, carriage, buckboard, or wagon. The quiet cemetery echoed with the sounds of subdued conversation, the scratch of horse hooves on the ground, and the creaking roll of wheels.

"He is still there, isn't he?" Sally asked as she climbed into the surrey. "He's all alone."

Settling into his own seat, Smoke looked back toward the three graves. Only one person remained, and that was Tom Burke, still sitting in the chair that had been put there for him by Nunley Welch, the undertaker.

"Looks like it," Smoke said.

"Oh, Smoke, I feel so sorry for him. I wish there was something we could do for him."

"There's nothing we can do to bring back his family," Smoke said.

"Do you think it was Indians?"

"I don't know," Smoke said. "I do know this. If it was Indians, it had to be a band of renegades. I'm sure it wasn't any of the regular tribes. We haven't had any Indian trouble in years. Soon as I can get around to it, I plan to have a good, long look around over there."

"Then you're going after whoever did it?"

"I am as soon as Tom feels up to going. I don't think he's quite finished saying good-bye yet."

"I'm glad you are going with him, Smoke. I only wish I could go."

Smoke reached over and patted her hand. "Don't think I don't believe for one minute that you couldn't handle it," he said. "But I think I would rather you and Cal stay back to watch the ranch."

"Wait a minute!" Cal said sharply. "You mean you aren't going to let me go with you?"

"Cal," was all Smoke said.

Cal looked down for a moment, then nodded contritely. "Sure, I'll stay here," he said.

"I knew I could count on you."

As the last mourner left the cemetery, Angus Pugh, the grave digger, stuck a wad of tobacco in his mouth, then glanced over at Nunley Welch.

"He's still there, Mr. Welch. Still just sittin' in that chair over there. Do you think maybe I ought to go start closing the grave anyway?"

Welch shook his head. "We don't let our people see the dirt thrown in on their loved ones," he said. "It's just too painful. Give him a little more time."

"How much time should I give him?"

"As much time as he needs," Welch answered. "He isn't like one of our normal bereaved. He has lost his entire family."

"Yes, sir, I know that."

"Then we will give him as much time as it takes."

"Yes, sir."

Sam Covington went straight from the funeral to the telegraph office. The Indian attack on Tom Burke's ranch was a tragedy of tremendous proportions. In fact, Covington could not recall any other incident in the brief history of the little town, or the even longer history of the county, that could quite compare with it. Covington was sorry it happened, but it had happened, so it just didn't make sense not to take advantage of the situation.

Covington was a man with political ambition, and he made no effort to hide that ambition. He wasn't that great an admirer of Governor Cooper. In fact, when Cooper was running for election, Covington chose to support him only because Cooper was obviously losing, and if Covington could turn it around, it would put Cooper deeply in his debt. Covington did turn it around, running a brilliant campaign for Cooper which ultimately snatched victory from the jaws of defeat. And now he was still calling the shots for Cooper.

Cooper was going to be a one-term governor, Covington would see to that. Then, after Cooper stepped down, Covington intended to run for governor. And in Covington's grand scheme of things, he too would be a one-term governor, but would persuade the legislature to send him to the U.S. Senate. From the Senate there was only one more step up the ladder, to the office of President of the United States. And who was to say that Covington couldn't take that step?

Fred Dunn, the Western Union clerk, looked up as Covington went into his office. "Is the funeral over?" Fred asked.

"Yes."

"I thought it must be, when I saw all the traffic out on the road. I wish I could've gone to pay my respects, but the wire has to be manned twenty-four hours a day."

"And it's a fine job you're doing too," Covington said. "Has there been any reply to the wire I sent this morning?"

"Oh, yes, here it is," Fred said, picking up an envelope from a small pile that was on the desk.

Covington received the envelope, then tore it open quickly and began to read:

> YOU ARE HEREBY APPOINTED TO RANK OF FULL COLONEL IN STATE MILITIA STOP INCUMBENT WITH RANK IS AUTHORITY TO RAISE AND EQUIP ONE CAVALRY REGIMENT STOP ONCE REGIMENT IS RAISED AND READY YOU ARE TO EMBARK ON CAMPAIGN AGAINST INDIANS WHO ATTACKED TOM BURKE RANCH STOP YOU ARE FURTHER AUTHORIZED TO USE ALL FORCE REQUIRED END

The telegram had been sent by Gerald Cooper, the governor.

Smiling, Covington put the telegram back in its envelope, then put the envelope in his pocket.

"So, am I to call you Colonel now?" Fred asked, reserving any comment on the contents of the telegram until after Covington read it.

"Yes . . . for now," Covington replied. Although he didn't say it aloud, he thought that if things went well—and so far they had gone very well—Fred and everyone else would be calling him Governor.

Nine

After taking Sally back home, Smoke got out of his suit, put on his jeans and a shirt, then changed from the surrey to the buckboard for a drive back to town. Before he could leave on an extended campaign with Tom Burke, he would need some things from the store. Going into the hardware store, he gave his list to the clerk.

"Whew," the clerk whistled. "You've got quite a list here, Smoke. Three boxes of .44-caliber bullets, three boxes of .44-40, ten sticks of dynamite, two boxes of lucifers, a gallon of kerosene, rope . . ." There were many more items listed, but he stopped reading aloud. "What are you going to do with all this stuff?"

"Pay for it," Smoke joked. "That is, if you've got it and will get it packed for me."

The clerk laughed. "That's what I get for being too nosy, I guess. Yes, sir, I've got it. It'll take me a good half hour or so to get it all gathered and packed, though."

"I can wait. I'll be over at Longmont's," Smoke said.

Leaving the store, Smoke saw someone posting a circular, and curious, he went over to read it.

* * *

Attention!
INDIAN FIGHTERS
Having been authorized by GOVERNOR
COOPER OF COLORADO to raise a MILI-
TIA COMPANY OF CAVALRY for immediate
service against hostile Indians, I call upon all
who wish to engage in such service to contact
me soonest for the purpose of enrolling your
names and joining your friends and neigh-
bors for this great adventure. Weapons and
uniforms will be furnished by the State. Pay
and rations will be the same as U.S. Army.
Those who volunteer shall be entitled to all
horses and other plunder as may be confis-
cated from the Indians.

COLONEL SAMUEL B. COVINGTON
COVINGTON'S MILITIA
COMMANDING

Longmont's saloon was more crowded than normal
for this time of day. That was understandable, though,
since nearly every ranch hand within fifty miles of
town had been given the day off in order to attend
the funeral. And, as might be expected, the conversation was about the funeral and what had happened
out at Timber Notch.

"What I don't understand is why them fellas there
at the ranch didn't put up any more of a fight than
they done," one of the men was saying. "Hell, if I'd
been there, there would'a be dead Injuns lying all
over the place."

"We don't know that there weren't any Indians

killed," one of the other patrons said. "Indians tend to carry away their dead."

"Yeah? Well, if I had been there, I would'a killed so damn many of them redskin bastards, they couldn't of carried them away."

"Dingo, you're full of shit," someone said, and all laughed.

"You think I haven't killed my share of Indians? I fought against the Apaches."

"Well, if you still have it in you to kill Indians, you can always join the militia cavalry," still another suggested. "Covington is sittin' back there at a table, signing up folks right now."

"By God, maybe I'll just do that," Dingo said.

Seeing Smoke standing at the bar, Louis came over to see him.

"It was a very impressive funeral, didn't you think?" Louis asked.

"Yes, it was," Smoke replied.

"Tom took it real hard," Louis said. "Of course, under the circumstances, I can see why. Smoke, is he going to be all right? Do you think there's anything I can do for him?"

"He'll be all right," Smoke said. "He's just got to get through this." Smoke nodded toward a table in the back corner where half a dozen men were standing in line. Sam Covington, normally a lawyer, was sitting at the table wearing the uniform and insignia of an Army colonel. "I see Mr. Covington is busy."

"Oh, hell, it's Colonel Covington now, and don't think he isn't quick to let you know that," Louis replied with a little laugh. "Yesterday he was a lawyer, foreclosing on widows and orphans, and today he is their savior."

"How did he ever talk the governor into giving him

a commission in the first place? What does he know about the military?"

"About the military? Not a blasted thing," Louis replied. "But he doesn't need to know anything. Don't forget, he was the governor's right-hand man during the last election."

"If I had known the governor's character judgment was so weak, I never would have voted for him," Smoke said. Then he chuckled. "Hell, now that I think of it, I *didn't* vote for him."

Louis laughed with him. "I can't find anybody who did vote for him, or at least, who will own up to it now. But there he is, sitting up in Denver as our governor, and here is Sam Covington, colonel of militia."

"Well, I don't guess it can hurt anything for them to dress up like soldiers, then ride around in the countryside for a while," Smoke said.

"If that's all that happens, I agree with you," Louis said. "But knowing Covington, there's no telling what that dumb bastard might stir up."

Although he was too far away to know he was being talked about, Covington looked up from his table and saw Smoke and Louis standing together at the bar.

"Excuse me, boys," Covington said, getting up.

"Wait a minute, where you a-goin'?" Dingo asked. "I aim to sign up here."

"I'll be right back," Covington replied with a wave of his hand. "There's plenty of time and room for all of you to sign up. Don't worry."

Stepping up to the bar, Covington slapped a coin down. "Mr. Longmont, another for Mr. Jensen, if you don't mind."

Nodding, Louis poured another drink for Smoke.

"Thanks," Smoke said, holding his glass up.

"Mr. Jensen, I hope you have no hard feelings

about the things I said during the trial," Covington said. "I was just trying to win the case."

"You lost," Smoke said simply.

"Yes, I did," Covington admitted. "And though I hate to lose anything, I must confess that I'm glad Tatum isn't free because of me. Who would've thought he would do something like kill Deputy Wallace and the judge? That was a terrible thing, absolutely terrible."

"Yeah," Smoke said, indicating by the tone of his voice that he wasn't buying what Covington was trying to sell.

"Well, enough about Mr. Tatum. He'll wind up in custody again somewhere. His kind always does. And I won't be defending him next time."

"No, I don't suppose so," Smoke replied.

"Anyway, right now, we have an even bigger problem on our hands."

"What problem would that be?" Smoke asked.

Covington looked at Smoke with a surprised expression on his face. "What do you mean, what problem? Why, Indians of course," he replied. "My God, man, you know what happened out at Timber Notch."

"No, I don't know," Smoke replied.

"What do you mean you don't know?" Covington replied, the expression on his face growing even more confused. "You were at the funeral. I saw you there."

"Yes, I was. Tom Burke is a close, personal friend of mine."

"Then I don't understand. Why do you say you don't know what happened out there?"

"Because I don't know. At this point, I don't think anyone knows."

"Of course we know. Everyone knows. The ranch was attacked by Indians."

"Is that a fact?"

"Of course it is. Everyone knows that it was Indians who murdered Tom Burke's family and hands."

"Covington, do you have any idea how long it has been since we've had any Indian trouble in these parts?"

"Quite a while, I'm sure. Do you know anything about volcanoes, Mr. Jensen? Sometimes they remain dormant for hundreds of years before they erupt."

Smoke chuckled. "And you are suggesting that the Indians are what? Like a volcano?"

"The comparison isn't strained," Covington said. "We all know what the Indians are capable of. And don't think for one minute that they aren't living out there in their reservation villages envious of the life we lead and seething inside with hate and resentment. I've always known they could break out of the reservation someday. Well, they have. And now it's our duty to punish them severely enough that they will think long and hard before they ever try anything like that again. So, what do you say, Mr. Jensen?"

"What do I say about what?"

"I'm asking you to join my militia as a scout. The rank of major comes with it. That would put you second in command."

"And allow me a share of the booty?"

"Yes, indeed," Covington said, smiling broadly in the belief that he was winning Smoke over.

Smoke finished his drink and looked at Covington. He stared at him for such a long time that Covington's smile faded. He got nervous and began to fidget under Smoke's gaze. Finally, Smoke wiped the back of his hand across his mouth.

"No, thanks," he said.

"What?" Covington asked in surprise. "Jensen, do you realize that by your action, you are showing that you don't care about what happened to poor Tom Burke?"

Smoke sighed in disgust. "You do have a way with words, don't you, Covington? You don't let truth bother you. I suppose that's what makes you a good lawyer."

"It's just that I am surprised that you don't want to help your friend."

"I am going to help him," Smoke said. "But I'm going to do it in my own way."

"What does that mean? In your own way?" Covington asked.

"It means I have no intention of running around with a bunch of fools in pretend-Army uniforms who'll probably get lost before they get more than ten miles out of town."

"You need have no fear about that," Covington said, sputtering. "I'll be leading them."

Smoke laughed. "My point exactly. Using both hands and a compass, you couldn't find your own ass."

Covington's face became purple, and the vein in his temple began to pulsate. "We'll just see about that," he said. "After we make a couple of successful scouts and kill us a few Indians, we'll bring this uprising to a halt."

"Uprising? There is no uprising," Smoke said.

"No? How do you explain what happened out at Tom Burke's ranch?"

"If it was Indians, it was a party of renegades at best," Smoke said. "I hardly think we have an Indian war on our hands."

"An Indian is an Indian. And you might remember that a famous general once said, 'The only good Indian is a dead Indian,' " Covington said. He paused for a moment, then smiled and held his hand out, offering to shake with Smoke. "Anyway, we shouldn't be arguing about this, you and I," he said in a conciliatory voice. "After all, we are the natural leaders of this community. We should be allies in this noble endeavor. So, what do you say, man? Will you join us?"

Instead of taking Covington's proffered hand, Smoke reached for his glass and took another drink, staring over the rim at Covington. "I thank you for the drink," he said, and there was such a finality to his voice that it stopped all further conversation between the two men.

Covington stared at Smoke for a moment longer, then turned and walked back to his table.

"You think he finally got the message?" Louis asked.

"Maybe. But it takes a while for anything to get through a head as thick as his is."

All right, men!" Covington called out to the others in the saloon. "I'm still signing up volunteers for the cavalry. Who's next?"

"I am," Dingo said.

"Your full name?" Covington asked.

"Marcus W. Dingo."

"Do you have any military experience, Mr. Dingo?"

"Yes, sir. I was a sergeant with General Miles when we fought the Apache."

Covington looked up from the paper he was writing on. "You were a sergeant, you say?"

"Yes, sir."

"Why did you leave the Army?"

"After we whupped the Apache, there wasn't nothin' else to do 'cept drill and the like. So when it come time, I took my discharge and moved on."

"But you are willing to come back in now? To serve

in whatever capacity I assign you, and to recognize the authority of the officers appointed over you?"

"Yes, sir," Dingo said. "I know what armyin' is all about."

"Why do you want to serve now?"

"Well, sir, I don't know 'bout the rest of these boys, but after what them heathens did to Mrs. Burke and those children, I'm by God ready to start killin' me some Injuns."

"Hold up your right hand," Covington said.

Dingo did as instructed.

"You swear to follow the orders of those in authority over you, and to defend your state and your fellow citizens against all enemies, foreign and domestic?"

"Yeah, that is, yes, sir, I do," Dingo said.

Coving stuck his hand out to shake with Dingo. "Welcome to Covington's militia, First Sergeant Dingo."

Dingo grinned broadly. "First Sergeant?"

"Yes, First Sergeant. I feel that is the best way to utilize your experience."

At the far end of the bar, a small man with weasel eyes finished the rest of his beer, then wiped his mouth with his sleeve.

"Another one?" the bartender asked.

"No," the small man replied. "I've got to go." Turning, he left the bar, then pushed through the batwing doors and walked out into the street. As he headed toward the livery, he took out a plug of chewing tobacco and stuck it in his mouth. As a result, he had worked up a good spit by the time he got there.

Standing just inside a Dutch door, looking through the open top, was Pigiron McCord.

"Did you see him, Wheeler?" Pigiron asked.

"Yeah, I seen him. Jensen's in there, all right."

Pigiron smiled broadly. "Good. Good. Now it's time to pay him back for what he did."

"Pigiron, you sure you want to do this? I mean, Tatum told us to just hang around to see what was goin' on, then get back to him. He didn't say nothin' 'bout killin' anyone."

"If you got no stomach for it you can go on back, far as I'm concerned," Pigiron said. "But I aim to kill that bastard Smoke Jensen." Pigiron opened the door so Wheeler could come into the livery.

The three men in the livery stable were Pigiron McCloud, Jason Harding, and Dirk Wheeler. Because Pigiron didn't want to be recognized, he'd sent Wheeler into the saloon to see if Jensen was there. Harding, who had had his own run-in in the saloon, had also stayed away. He was stretched out on the barn floor, his head on a sack of grain and his hat pulled down over his eyes.

"Seems to me like killin' a man is a long way to go just to get back at him for whuppin' you," Wheeler said.

"Well, now, that's just 'cause you didn't see how bad ole Pigiron here got his ass whupped," Harding said from under his hat.

"I told you, he got in a lucky punch," Pigiron said, turning away from the open window and glaring at Harding. "Besides which, you ain't got a lot of room to talk. Seems to me like you got your head bashed in as well. Hell, I'd think you would be with me on this."

"I am with you," Harding said. "I'm here with you, ain't I? I just want to make sure nothin' goes wrong. I asked some of the boys back at Risco about Smoke Jensen. And from what they tell me, he ain't a man you want to mess with. And I don't aim to get myself kilt before we get some of that money Tatum's been talkin' about."

"There ain't none of us goin' to get kilt if we all stick together," Pigiron said.

"What's goin' on over there in that saloon anyhow?" Pigiron asked. "They's an awful lot of people just goin' in and out."

"They're raisin' an army," Wheeler said. "They's a man there in a Army suit signin' folks up to go fight the Injuns."

Pigiron laughed. "Is that a fact? Well, you got to hand it to ole Tatum. He was right about that. After these fellas get all dressed up in their Army suits and march around an' salute for a while, they're goin' to get tired of playin' army. When that happens, they're goin' to attack some Injuns some'ers. And soon as they do that, well, we got us some customers for our rifles."

"Yeah, well, I wish Jensen would get back out here so we can get this over with. I'm hungry," Harding said.

"You're always hungry, or sleepy, or thirsty, or gotta piss or somethin'," Pigiron said. "I swear, you'd bitch if they hung you with a new rope."

Harding stood up and dusted himself off. "I seen Muley Thomas hung with a new rope," he said. "Ole Muley didn't bitch about it. He didn't do nothin', 'cept maybe twitch a little."

Wheeler shuddered. "Don't talk like that," he said. "I don't like to hear that kind'a talk."

Harding held his fist alongside his neck, then tilted his head and ran his tongue out in a mockery of someone being hanged, while making the sound of a death rattle. He laughed at his own impression.

"I said, I don't like that kind'a talk!" Wheeler said.

"Shhh!" Pigiron hissed. "Quiet! Here he comes."

"We goin' to shoot him, Pigiron? Or are we goin' to brace him?" Wheeler asked.

Harding raised his pistol and aimed it at Smoke. "I say let's just shoot the son of a bitch and be done with it," he said.

"No," Pigiron said. "I want him to know who it was shot him. I want my ugly face to be the last thing that son of a bitch sees before he dies."

"Pigiron, I don't know," Harding said. "I told you, I've heard a lot about him since we run into him. They say he's faster'n greased lightning."

"I ain't no virgin in this business," Pigiron said. "I think I can beat him."

"You thought you could whup him too," Harding said. "But look what happened."

"I told you, he got in a lucky punch. Anyway, there are three of us. I don't care how fast the son of a bitch is." He can't take all three of us. I say we brace him."

"You brace him," Wheeler said. "I ain't goin' to."

"What?"

"You want to kill the son of a bitch from here, I'm with you," Wheeler said. "But if you're countin' on me walkin' out there in the street and callin' him out, you goin' to have to do it without me."

"And without me," Harding added.

"You two yellow bellied bastards!" Pigiron swore.

"We kill him from here, or you go it alone," Harding said.

In frustration, Pigiron pinched the bridge of his nose. "All right," he finally said. "If that's the way it is to be, then that's the way it'll be. I don't care how we kill the son of a bitch, as long as we kill him."

The three men, in agreement now as to their tactics, walked back to the Dutch door and looked through the top window. Jensen was nowhere to be seen.

"What the hell? What happened to him?" Pigiron asked.

"There he is over there, going into the hardware store," Wheeler said.

By the time Pigiron saw him, Jensen was just going into the store, with the door closing behind him.

"All right, we'll get him when he comes out," Pigiron said.

Ten

"I've got everything you asked for, Smoke," the hardware clerk said. "Beans, bacon, coffee, sugar, salt, flour, three boxes of .44's, three boxes of .44-40's, and two boxes of lucifers. That comes to three dollars and twenty-five cents." The clerk put everything into two boxes. "Will you need help carrying that out to your buckboard?"

"No, thank you, I can get it," Smoke said. He paid for his purchases, then picked up the two boxes and headed for the door. The clerk beat him to the door and held it open for him.

"Here he comes!" Pigiron said to the others, and they pulled the hammers back on their pistols as they took aim. "Wait until he gets into the buckboard. It'll be a closer shot."

They watched as Smoke put his boxes in back, then untied the reins and climbed into the driver's seat.

Suddenly, the stagecoach rolled into town, the six-team hitch sweating and breathing hard as they trotted the final hundred yards. The stage was filled with passengers and piled high on top with luggage and cargo. Its route to the stage depot went between the livery and the hardware store.

"Damn it!" Pigiron swore, lowering his pistol until the stage passed. They waited for a moment. Then when the stage was gone, they raised their pistols again, but Smoke wasn't there.

"What the hell? Where is he? What happened to him?" Pigiron asked.

"There he is, down there," Wheeler said.

Smoke had driven away, matching the speed of the stagecoach all the way down to the depot. As a result, he had been shielded by the coach until he was now too far down the street for any kind of a shot.

"Now what?" Wheeler asked.

Sighing in disgust, Pigiron put the pistol back in his holster. "Let's get on over to the saloon and see what we can find out about this army they're raisin'," he said.

"Thought you didn't want to go to the saloon," Wheeler said.

"I said I didn't want to be seen by Jensen. Now that he's gone, it don't matter whether I'm seen or not."

"The saloon sounds good to me," Harding said. He rubbed his mouth with the back of his hand. "Yeah, I like that idea. In fact, it's your best idea yet."

When Louis Longmont saw Pigiron and Harding come into his saloon, he got up from his table and walked over to confront them.

"I'll take your money, McCord," he said, "but I won't take anything from *you*. Stay away from my girls, and don't start anything."

"All me 'n my pards want is a couple of drinks," Pigiron said. "We ain't lookin' for no trouble."

Louis looked toward the bartender, then nodded. "You can serve them," he said.

As the three stood at the bar drinking, they listened

to several of the conversations, hoping to hear something they could take back to Tatum. Much of the conversation was about the militia company being formed, but Pigiron heard something that caught his attention right away.

"I would'a thought Smoke Jensen would'a joined up with the militia," someone said. "Him an' ole Tom Burke been friends for a long time."

"You heard him say he was goin' to help in his own way, didn't you?"

"Yeah, but I don't know what that means."

"I figure it means he'll be goin' out on his own to find whoever done this."

"On his own? What can he do by his ownself?"

"What can he do? He can track, hunt, shoot, and live out in the mountains better'n anyone I ever heard of. If I was the one that done this, I'd rather have two companies of milita after me than to have Smoke Jensen doggin' my trail."

"When you think he'll leave?"

"He's probably left by now. I was over to the hardware store while ago, and Mr. Clark told me that Smoke bought a lot of provisions to take with him."

"What about Mrs. Jensen? You think she'll stay out at the ranch by herself? Or will she come stay in town till he gets back."

"Sally? Oh, she'll stay out there and run the ranch." The speaker chuckled. "And probably do as good a job with it as any man would."

"Probably. I'll say this for her. She's a good-lookin' woman."

The first speaker chuckled. "I agree, but if you ever say that around Smoke, you better make damn certain he don't misunderstand it."

The second speaker chuckled as well. "You didn't have to tell me that. You think I'm some kind of fool?"

"Well, now," Pigiron said very quietly, "That's good information to know."

"Beg pardon?" Wheeler asked.

"Never mind," Pigiron said. "We'll talk about it later."

As Smoke and Pearlie were saddling their horses, Cal was leaning against the fence, his arms folded across his chest, looking on with an expression of disappointment.

"Cal, did anyone ever tell you that if you make a bad face, it could freeze like that?" Pearlie asked with a laugh. "Cheer up."

"Easy for you to say. You're going," Cal said. "I have to stay here."

Smoke tightened his cinch, then sighing, looked over at Cal. "I've explained it to you, Cal," he said. "Whoever did this, whether it's renegade Indians or just a gang of outlaws, might still be around. If they double back while we're tracking them, we could miss them. That would leave Sugarloaf vulnerable. I'd feel a lot better if you were here with Sally."

"I know," Cal said. "And I'm honored that you trust me with it. But if nothing happens here, and you find them, then I'm going to miss out on it."

"I'll tell you all about it," Pearlie promised.

"I'd rather hear it from Smoke. If you tell it, no doubt it will be a pack of lies."

"Well, yeah, it probably will be," Pearlie said. "But it'll be a lot better story than you can get from a dime novel."

All three laughed.

"What is this?" Sally asked, coming out to join them. "Here I expected to see long faces, sad because you're going away. Instead, you are laughing. Are you that happy to get away from me?"

"You know better than that," Smoke said, putting his arm around her. They kissed, then Sally held up a little bag.

"I thought you might like a sack full of sinkers for your trip."

"You made doughnuts?" Pearlie asked, reaching for the sack.

"I did. If I told you to go easy on them, to try and make them last a couple of days, would I just be wasting my breath?"

"Ma'am?" Pearlie replied, the work muffled by a mouthful of doughnut. Even as he answered, he was reaching for a second one.

Sally laughed. "Never mind. Smoke, if you plan on getting any of those, you'd better carry the sack yourself."

"Looks that way, doesn't it?" Smoke said, taking the sack from Pearlie and sticking it down into his own saddlebag.

"Don't worry, Cal, I held some back for us," she said.

Cal grinned broadly. "Well, for once I won't have to fight Pearlie for them."

Smoke and Sally kissed again. Then Smoke swung into the saddle. He looked down at his wife.

"I don't have any idea when I'll be back," he said. "Just look for me when you see me. And take care."

"I will," Sally replied. "Smoke?"

Smoke had just started to turn his horse and he stopped to look back at her.

"Be careful?"

"Careful? Damn, now there's an idea. I hadn't even thought about that," he said, teasing her.

"Oh!" Sally said in an exasperated tone of voice. "Go on, the sooner you leave the better."

Laughing, Smoke urged his horse ahead and it broke quickly and easily into a trot.

Smoke and Pearlie were over at Timber Notch, preparing to leave on their hunt for whoever had raided the ranch. Pearlie was sitting on the edge of the porch of the Burke house, already into the little bag of doughnuts Sally had made for them. Tom Burke was cinching up the saddle on his horse, while Smoke was kneeling by the steps of the porch, studying the dirt.

Reaching down, he picked something up, then examined it closely. "Well, now. It looks like they didn't get away clean," Smoke said.

"What have you found?" Tom asked.

"Do you have a shotgun in the house?"

"Yes, a double-barreled Greener ten-gauge. At first I thought maybe they stole it, but I found it out by what's left of the barn."

"Did you keep it loaded with double-aught buck?"

"As a matter of fact I did. Why?"

"Because this shot is double-aught buck," Smoke said, holding out his hand. There were three large shotgun pellets in his palm. "And if you look close enough, you can see that they are bloodstained."

"So one of them is wounded?" Pearlie asked.

Smoke shook his head. "I doubt that. Whoever caught a bellyful of these pellets is more'n likely dead."

"I hope so."

"There's something else about these pellets," Smoke said. He held something up. "This thread was sticking to one of them. It's red and black."

"Red and black thread. Came from a shirt maybe?" Tom asked.

"That would be my guess. But the question is, what would an Indian on a raiding party be doing wearing a white man's shirt?"

"That doesn't seem all that unusual to me, Smoke," Pearlie said. "Since they've all started getting paid for allowing grazing on their land, most of the Indians have more money than most of the cowboys I know. They buy all sorts of white men's things."

"That's true," Smoke agreed. "But let's think about it for a moment. These Indians were out on a war party, right? Now, it's been a long time since any of our Indians around here were hostile. They've got no reason to be. It's like you say, most of them are making more money than most of the cowboys as it is. So the only reason I can think of that Indians might be on the warpath would be for some holy reason known only to them. If they're goin' to war for some holy reason, then they would want it to be in the old way. That means they would paint their face, wear feathers and traditional warrior getup. And to tell the truth, I have a hard time picturing a warrior in a red and black plaid shirt."

"Maybe they aren't out to make medicine," Tom said. "Maybe they're just out to steal what they can."

"Are you missing anything, Tom? Anything that the Indians might want?"

Tom shook his head. "The only thing that was taken was that gold chain and diamond I had given to Jo Ellen. You remember it, don't you?"

"Yes, of course I do."

"That was gone, but nothing else was missing. Not any of the horses. Not even the shotgun. Come to think of it, none of the guns were taken from my hired hands either."

"Have you thought about that?" Smoke asked. He walked over to mount his horse. Tom and Pearlie mounted as well.

"Sort of curious, isn't it," Tom replied.

"Very curious," Smoke agreed. "I mean, here we find arrows all over the place, which means they were armed with bows. Wouldn't you think they would want to replace those bows with guns?"

"So, what do you think all this means?"

"I believe it means someone wants us to think it was Indians."

"Think we'll be able to follow the trial, Smoke?" Cal asked.

"I don't see why not. They didn't make any effort to cover it up," Smoke said. "Let's see where it leads us."

Eleven

The sun was high overhead at Sugarloaf, a brilliant white orb fixed in the bright blue sky. Pigiron McCord, Jason Harding, and Dirk Wheeler looked down on the ranch from atop a nearby hill. As they watched, a woman came out onto the back porch. There, in broad daylight, she took off her shirt, and would have been naked from the waist up had it not been for the fact that she was wearing a camisole.

"Goddamn!" Pigiron said, nearly choking on the word. "Look at that!"

The woman poured water into a basin, then began washing her hair.

"Is that Jensen's woman?" Wheeler asked.

"Who else would it be?" Pigiron replied.

"You think she's alone?"

" 'Course she is. If they was some hired hands here, you think she'd be out on the back porch damn near nekkid?" Pigiron chuckled.

"What is it?" Wheeler asked. "What are you laughing about?"

"I'm laughing about Jensen," Pigiron said. "He's out looking for us, and we're here with his woman." Pigiron rubbed himself. "You know what? I think I'm going to enjoy this more than I would have enjoyed killing Jensen back in town."

"We goin' to take turns with her, aren't we?" Harding asked.

"Yeah," Wheeler said. "We are going to take turns, aren't we? I mean, I ain't plannin' on just standin' by and watchin' you have all the fun. I figure to get in on it too."

"Don't worry, you will. We'll take turns," Pigiron said. "Long as you boys both know that I'm first."

Sally looked at the pile of towels she had brought out onto the back porch with her. Under the top towel was a loaded pistol. She looked at it to reassure herself by its presence, then, without being too obvious, checked the progress of the three riders who were coming toward the house.

What Pigiron and the others didn't realize was that Sally and Cal knew they were there. A few minutes earlier Cal had gone up into the loft of the barn to push down a couple of bales of hay. While he was up there, he just happened to walk over and stand in the attic opening to have a look back toward the distant tree line. He didn't know what made him walk over there, or what made him look, but whatever it was was fortuitous, because that was when he saw the three riders coming.

The way they were approaching—avoiding the road, staying back in the trees, and never crossing a hill in silhouette—told Cal that whoever they were, they were up to no good. He hurried to the house to tell Sally.

"Cal, do you think you could manage to get around behind them without being seen?" Sally asked.

Cal nodded. "Yeah, I think I can. I can get across to the ridgeline before they are close enough to see me cross in the open. The ridge will give me cover until I reach Bushy Draw. By then, they'll be beyond Bushy Draw, which will put me behind them."

"All right, you do that. And while you're sneaking around behind them, I'll do something to keep their attention here."

Cal hurried back to the barn, saddled his horse quickly, then rode hard to get across a field that would let him go along the back side of the ridge. He figured to come back down behind them about the time they hit the edge of south pasture.

Sally decided to get their attention by washing her hair. And to make certain that she kept their attention, she upped the ante a little by taking off her shirt. It would also give her the opportunity to carry a pistol outside without anyone knowing she had it, by slipping the revolver in between the towels.

In the meantime, Cal reached Bushy Draw, a pass through the ridgeline. Bushy Draw was so well protected by vegetation that unless someone knew it was there, they would never see it. In fact, even knowing it was there, one had to be right on it to see it. Because of that, Cal was able to get within twenty yards of the riders, close enough to hear them talking.

"They said she was a good-lookin' woman," one of the men said. "I reckon I just didn't know how good-lookin' she was until I seen her."

One of the others laughed. "Hell, Wheeler, what difference does it make to you whether or not she's a good-lookin' woman? I've seen you with women that was so ugly they'd gag a maggot on the gut wagon."

"Yeah, but just once, I'd like to have me a good-lookin' woman," the one called Wheeler replied.

"Well, you boys better enjoy her while you can," the third man said. " 'Cause I don't aim to leave her alive."

"You goin' to kill a good-lookin' woman like that? Why? Seems to me like we could take her with us.

That way, anytime we wanted to, why, we could just take our pleasure with her."

"Nah, she'd just be getting in the way all the time. And I don't aim to leave her here where she can talk."

"Yeah, I reckon you're right."

Cal pulled his pistol. "You fellas just hold it right there," he called.

"What the hell? Where'd you come from?" Harding hissed, startled by Cal's sudden appearance.

"Who are you?" Cal asked.

"What's it to you?" Harding asked.

Cal fired at Harding. His bullet clipped Harding's earlobe, sending out a misty spray of blood and leaving a bloody wound.

"Ahhh!" Harding yelled in pain, slapping his hand to his ear. "Are you crazy, mister?"

"If somebody doesn't answer me really quick, I'm going to take off another earlobe," Cal said. He smiled. "Only, I'm going to let you three guess which earlobe it will be. Am I going to take your other one?" He pointed his pistol at Harding. "Or one of yours?" He pointed to the other two. "Now, I'm askin' again. Who are you?"

Suddenly there was an angry buzz, then the *thocking* sound of a heavy bullet tearing into flesh. A fountain of blood squirted up from the neck of Cal's horse and the animal went down on its front knees, then collapsed onto its right side. It was a good half second after the strike of the bullet before the heavy boom of a distant rifle reached Cal's ears.

The fall pinned Cal's leg under his horse. He also dropped his pistol on the way down, and now it lay just out of reach of his grasping fingers.

"What the hell? Who's that shooting?" Wheeler shouted, pulling hard on the reins of his horse, which, though not hit, was spooked by seeing another horse go down.

"Who the hell cares?" Harding shouted back. "Look at him! He's pinned down!" Harding drew his gun and fired at Cal.

Though Cal's right leg was still pinned, he was able to flip his left leg over the saddle and lay down behind his horse, thus providing himself with some cover. Harding's bullet dug into his saddle and sent up a little puff of dust, but did no further damage.

"Shit!" Harding said. "I can't get to him from this angle."

"Come on, let's get the woman and get out of here!" Pigiron shouted.

"Not till I put a bullet in that son of a bitch!" Harding insisted. "The son of a bitch shot off my ear!" Harding slapped his legs against the side of his horse and moved around to get a better shot at Cal.

Cal made one more desperate grab for his pistol, but it was still out of reach. His rifle, however, was in the saddle sheath on the side of the horse that was on the ground, and Cal could see about six inches of the stock sticking out. He grabbed it, gratified when it pulled free. He jerked it from the sheath and jacked a shell into the chamber, just as Harding came around to get into position to shoot him.

"Good-bye, asshole!" Harding said, raising his pistol and taking careful aim. The smile left his face as he saw the business end of Cal's rifle come up and spit a finger of flame. The bullet from Cal's rifle hit Harding just under the chin, then exited the back of his head, taking with it a pink spray of blood and bone as Harding tumbled off his horse.

"He got Jason!" Wheeler shouted.

"Let's get out of here!" Pigiron shouted.

Pigiron and Wheeler started riding away hard now,

forgetting all about their original intention of going after Jensen's wife. They didn't even bother to look back to see what happened to Harding. In the meantime, another bullet whistled by from the distant rifle. When Cal located the source of the shooting, he saw a mounted man with one leg thrown casually across his saddle. Using that leg to provide a stable firing platform, the shooter raised his rifle to fire again. There was a flash of light, the man rolled back from the recoil, then the bullet whizzed by so close to Cal's head that it made his ears pop. All this before the report of the rifle actually reached him. With a gasp of disbelief, Cal realized that the man was shooting at him from over five hundred yards away.

Suddenly Cal heard hoofbeats and, looking around, he saw Sally riding hard toward him.

"No! Sally, get back!" he shouted.

The distant rifleman also saw Sally approaching, and his next shot went toward her. Cal watched with alarm as dust puffed up from her hat, and he was sure she had been hit. He was greatly relieved when she reached his fallen horse, leaped down with a rifle in her hand, and slapped her own animal on the rump to get him out of the way. She dropped to the ground behind Cal's horse.

"Thank God you weren't hit!" Cal said. "When I saw that bullet hit your hat, I thought you were a goner."

"The bullet hit my hat?" Sally asked. Reaching up to pull it off, she saw the hole in the felt. "Oh, my, that was very close, wasn't it?"

Another bullet whizzed by, this one so close that both of them could hear the air pop as it passed.

"We've got to get you out from under that horse and over on this side," Sally said.

Cal tried to pull his leg free, but couldn't. Then he

got an idea. He stuck the stock of the rifle just under the horse's side and grabbed the barrel. Using the rifle as a lever, he pushed up and wedged just enough space between the horse's flesh and the ground to allow him to slip his leg free.

"Is your leg broken?" Sally asked.

Cal felt it. "No, I don't think so. But the blood circulation was cut off and now it's numb."

"Let's try and make it over to the dry streambed," Sally suggested, pointing to a depression that snaked its way across the ground. Only in the freshet season was the channel a stream. Then it caught the runoff waters from the snow of the higher elevations. Now it was just a low spot in the ground, but if they could reach it, it would give them more protection from the distant shooter.

Crawling on their bellies, Sally and Cal slithered and twisted their way down to the dry streambed. They reached the bank and rolled over behind the berm just as another bullet ploughed into the dirt beside them. Then they twisted around behind the bank and looked back up toward the place where the shots were coming from.

"Well, with this cover and the rifles, we aren't easy targets," Sally said. "And if he tries to come any closer, he'll be playing with our deck of cards."

The shooter, whoever he was, had come to the same realization, because he put his rifle back in the saddle sheath, then turned and rode away as casually as if he were riding down Main Street. And why not? There was no way Cal and Sally could reach him from where they were.

As Pigiron and Wheeler got close to the rifleman who had rescued them, they recognized him. He was easy to recognize. His skin shone black in the sun.

"Jim!" Pigiron said. "What are you doing here?"

"Tatum sent me after you."

"What does he want?"

"He didn't say," Jim said.

"Well, I'm glad you come when you did," Wheeler said. "I reckon we owe you."

Jim, always a man of few words, didn't answer.

Twelve

Pigiron and the others rejoined Tatum just before dark that night. Tatum was sitting on a fallen log near a fire, eating beans. He looked up as they arrived.

"Find out anything?"

"Yeah," Pigiron said. "They've raised 'em an army. A fella by the name of Covington is leading it."

"Covington?" Tatum asked. "A lawyer?"

"Yeah, a lawyer."

Tatum laughed out loud. "Well, what do you know. My lawyer leading the army. Why, this couldn't have worked out better if I'd planned it."

Tatum looked around, as if just noticing that someone was missing. "Where is Harding?" he asked.

Pigiron and Wheeler glanced at each other, hesitant to answer.

"I said, where's Harding?" Tatum repeated.

"We, uh, run into some trouble," Pigiron finally said.

"What kind of trouble? I told you to lay low when you were in town. Last time you were there you got yourself whipped by Smoke Jensen, as I recall. So what happened, did you run across him again?"

"Not exactly," Pigiron replied.

"Not exactly. What the hell is that supposed to mean?"

"Well, Jim was there, weren't you, Jim?" Wheeler said.

Jim just stared at Wheeler with an absolutely emotionless expression. Then, without saying a word, he got his kit from his saddlebag, went over to the pot, and spooned out a serving of beans.

"Hah!" Tatum said. "I can just see the kind of fracas Jim might get into, him being black and so talkative and all. Now I'm going to ask you one last time to tell me what the hell happened to Harding."

"We went out to Smoke Jensen's ranch," Pigiron said.

"Did I tell you to go to his ranch? No. What I said was, hang around town and see what was going on."

"I know you didn't tell us to, but I figured maybe we could find out something out there too."

"Bullshit, Pigiron. You figured you would get even with him for beating you up," Tatum said. "Hell, I don't blame you none for that. Truth is, I'd like to see the son of a bitch dead myself, and when all this is over, I may just arrange that. So, did you kill him?"

"He wasn't there," Pigiron replied. "There wasn't no one there except his wife and some hired hand, a kid."

"Well, did you kill them?"

"No," Pigiron admitted.

"Wait a minute," Tatum said, stroking his chin. "Let me get this straight. There was no one there except Jensen's wife and a kid, but Harding is the one who wound up gettin' hisself kilt?"

"Yeah," Pigiron said. "That's about the size of it."

"What did Jim have to do with it?"

"Well, the kid . . . uh . . . he got the drop on Harding. . . ."

"He got the drop on Harding?"

"Yeah, he got the drop on Harding, and when he

did, well, he sort of had us over a barrel too. He was going to kill Harding unless we give up to him."

"So you let him kill Harding," Tatum said. "Yeah, I can see that. Two for one, that's a pretty good exchange."

This wasn't at all where Pigiron was going with the story, but when Tatum accepted it this way, Pigiron looked over at Wheeler in a silent suggestion that they let him believe it this way.

"Yeah," Wheeler said, catching on quickly. "That's exactly the way it happened. Then, ole Jim here come along with his rifle and he kilt the kid's horse. That gave us a chance to get away."

"Get away? You didn't kill the kid?"

"No. Jensen's wife was comin' by then. She had a long gun, we only had pistols. We didn't have no choice but to leave."

Some miles away, Smoke, Pearlie, and Tom Burke were also sitting around the fire. They had eaten well tonight, for Smoke had killed a turkey, and the aroma of its cooking still hung in the air. Tom was cleaning his .52-caliber Spencer rifle.

"I'll be damned," Smoke said, nodding toward the rifle. "You've still got that rifle."

"Yep," Tom answered.

"What rifle?" Pearlie asked.

"The rifle he made the shot with," Smoke answered.

"The shot?"

"You mean you've never heard about the shot? The shot that won the battle of Adobe Springs?" Smoke asked. "How far was it, Tom?"

"They measured it later, said it was twelve hundred yards."

"Wait a minute," Pearlie said. "Are you trying to tell us he made a shot from twelve hundred yards?"

"At least that far," Smoke said. "To tell the truth, it looked even farther to me."

"To you? Wait a minute, you mean you were there too?"

"Oh, yes," Smoke replied. He looked at Pearlie. "I can't believe I've never told you the story."

"No, but I have a feeling I'm going to hear about it now," Pearlie said, smiling.

"Tom was a buffer then, and from time to time I would do a little of it myself."

"A buffer?" Pearlie asked.

"That's what they called buffalo hunters," Smoke explained. "Anyway, about fifteen of us just happened to wind up in a stage depot called Adobe Springs."

As Smoke told the story, he did so with such vivid imagery that Pearlie could almost see himself in the little adobe trading post where the fifteen buffalo hunters had come together.

It was early in the morning and Smoke had just awakened. Spread out all over the floor of the little stage way station were the bedrolls of other buffers who had gathered there. Some of them had whiskey and one of them had a guitar. In addition, there were two women passengers from the stagecoach, headed for Denver. They were saloon girls, known to nearly all the buffalo hunters, so most had stayed awake, drinking and singing far into the night. As a result, nearly everyone else was still asleep this morning.

Smoke went outside to relieve himself, and was just finishing when he saw a large group of mounted Indians advancing slowly toward them.

"Indians!" he shouted, running back inside.

Barricading the door, Smoke ran to the window and looked outside. The Indians weren't approaching as they normally did, either by stealth or by riding back and forth. Instead, they were heading straight for the building in a massive charge, their horses leaping over obstacles, feathered bonnets flying in the breeze.

By now everyone else in the building had responded to Smoke's warning and rushed to the windows. There was the sound of glass breaking as the defenders cleared the way for them to shoot.

Nobody gave the order to fire, because no one was in charge. Instead, the defenders fired at targets of opportunity, and the opening salvo was devastating. Half-a-dozen Indians went down. Stunned by the unexpected volley, the Indians withdrew about two hundred yards, then formed for a second attack.

"Anyone get hit?" Smoke called.

"Yeah, Johnny got hit, but I don't think it's bad," Tom said.

"I'll look after him," Jo Ellen offered. Jo Ellen was the more attractive of the two prostitutes who had come in on the stage.

The Indians came again, three abreast this time, galloping through the dust, shouting and whooping their war cries. They charged all the way up to the building, firing from horseback, shooting arrows and bullets at the cracks between the logs. They hurled lances toward the open windows. Two of them jumped down from their horses and tried to force the door open by hitting against it with the butts of their rifles.

Once again, the buffalo hunters took very careful aim, making every shot count. Several Indians went down, and their riderless horses whirled and retreated, leaving their riders dead or dying on the ground behind them. The rest of the Indians waited a few minutes, then launched a third attack.

"Here they come again," someone shouted and, once more, the defenders fired at targets of opportunity.

This time, however, the Indians made a much more traditional approach. Using a stone wall and a barn as cover, they were almost on top of the defenders before anyone could get a shot at them. The Indians fired through the windows, and bullets buzzed about like angry hornets.

Three more of the defenders were hit, including Lily, the other woman.

"Lily!" Jo Ellen shouted, running to her friend. She sat on the floor and held her friend's head in her lap.

"Never figured I'd go out this way," Lily said, smiling up at Jo Ellen. "I always thought some drunken cowboy would shoot me in a jealous rage."

"Hang on, Lily, you'll be . . ." Jo Ellen said, but Lily's head fell to one side and her open eyes began to glass over.

Suddenly, fire arrows came streaking in through the window, starting several small fires.

"Get 'em out, quick!" Smoke shouted.

Grabbing blankets and rugs, the defenders managed to beat out all the arrows but one, which continued to burn out of control.

"We're going to need water!" someone yelled, and another grabbed the water bucket and with it, finally got the upper hand over the last fire arrow.

"Was that our drinking water?" someone asked.

"Yeah," Tom said.

"We're going to get awful thirsty."

"Where's the well?" Smoke asked.

"Out there," the depot manager said, pointing to

the well out in the front yard. Anyone who went after water would be completely exposed to the Indians.

"I'll go," someone said, grabbing the bucket.

"Speaker, no!" Smoke shouted, but Speaker was out before anyone could stop him, and he dashed across the open space toward the well.

Watching through the window, Smoke saw a puff of dust fly up, then a gush of blood spurt from Speaker's shirt. He went down and the bucket rolled, clanging, across the yard.

"I wish he hadn't done that," Smoke said.

"Yeah, he should've thought more about it. He never had a chance," Tom said.

"That's not the only thing," Smoke replied. "Now the Indians know we are out of water. All they have to do is wait us out."

That's exactly what the Indians did. They did not launch another attack. Instead, they waited just out of range. The afternoon grew long and very thirsty, aggravatingly so when the Indians, who had plenty of water, would appear, just out of range, and pour gourds of water over their heads.

The Indians didn't leave during the night. From every window, the defenders could see campfires. They could also hear the drums and singing.

"We've got to have water," someone said. "I'm going out to get the bucket."

"You won't make it," Smoke said.

"I might. It's dark, they might not see me."

"Do you think they don't know we need water?" Smoke replied. "You saw how they were pouring water over themselves today, tantalizing us. They're waiting at the well for anyone who is crazy enough to try."

"We've got to do something. We can't make it another day without water."

"How long can we last?" Jo Ellen asked, and Tom was surprised to see that she had come up to stand right beside him.

"Maybe another day," Tom replied.

Tom looked out across the open ground toward the ridge where the Indians were. Though the fires had mostly burned down, he could still see faint glowings here and there. There was also enough of a moon that he didn't think the Indians could sneak up on them, even if they wanted too.

"You're going to think I'm crazy," Jo Ellen said. "But I'm glad this happened. That is, if I live through it, I'm glad it happened."

Tom chuckled. "Well, I don't know as I think you're crazy. But that is a curious outlook."

"I reckon it is. But I aim to change my life after this. I don't plan on being a whore anymore."

"Good for you," Tom said.

"What about you? You plan to go on being a buffalo hunter?"

"Doesn't make much difference whether I plan to or not," Tom replied. "There aren't many buffalo left. The truth is, I'm going to have to get into some other line of work pretty soon."

"You ever thought about ranching?"

"Thought about it. I wouldn't mind owning a ranch, but I don't think I'd care to cowboy for someone else."

"I own a ranch," Jo Ellen said.

"What?"

"That is, I own some land. It's out in Colorado. A . . . uh . . . friend left it to me."

"He must've been a good friend."

"He was," Jo Ellen said without elaborating.

"Have you ever seen it?"

"No, but I know it's there. The county clerk sent

me a letter describing it to me. And I've kept the taxes up. You aren't married, are you, Mr. Burke?"

"No, I'm not."

"You think you could marry someone who was once a whore?"

Tom stared at Jo Ellen for a long moment. "Jo Ellen, are you asking me to marry you?" he asked in surprise.

"I reckon I am," Jo Ellen replied. "That is, if we get out of here. The way I look at it, we're both going to be making some big changes in our life. Seems to me like it might be easier if we made those changes together."

Tom laughed out loud.

"I'm sorry," Jo Ellen said, her face burning in embarrassment. "I had no right to . . ."

"No," Tom said, reaching out to her. "You don't understand. I'm not laughing at you. I'm laughing because I never thought anything like this would happen to me. Yes, I'll marry you."

Shortly after dawn, when everyone was awake, Tom told the others that during the night he and Jo Ellen had made plans to get married.

"When?" someone asked.

"Soon's we get out of here," Tom replied.

"Then you're both goin' to die single, 'cause there ain't no way we're ever goin' to get out of here. Them Indians out there are just goin' to wait us out till we either die of thirst or go crazy and start runnin' toward the well," someone said.

"Maybe not," Tom suggested.

"Maybe not? What do you mean, maybe not?"

"Well, I've been doin' some thinking." Tom walked back over to the window and looked out toward the Indians who were still there on the distant ridge. He studied them through a pair of binoculars, and took two large-caliber bullets from his bullet bag. Separating the bullets from the cartridges, he began pouring the powder from one of the cartridges into the other cartridge.

"What are you doing?" someone asked.

"I'm double-loading a shell," Tom said. He nodded toward the binoculars. "If you take a look through those glasses, you'll see some fancy-dressed son of a bitch up there givin' orders to the rest of the Indians. Seems to me like if someone was to kill him, the others might go home. So, that's what I plan to do."

"You mean next time he comes down here?"

"No, I mean now," Tom said.

"Hell, man, he's a thousand yards away if he's a foot. What are you talking about?"

"Light that candle for me, would you?"

Shaking his head, the man lit the candle, then handed it to Tom, who tapped the bullet back into the cartridge, then used the dripping wax to help seal it. After that, he loaded his rifle, then stepped back up to the window.

"You're wasting a bullet."

"Maybe not," Smoke said.

"Wait a minute, are you saying you think he can do it?"

"I've seen him shoot," Smoke said. "He's got a place to rest his rifle, and the target is right up on top of the ridgeline. Yeah, I think it's possible. At least it's worth a chance."

Tom picked up the rifle then and rested the barrel on the windowsill. He aimed, then lowered the rifle and adjusted his sights, lifted it up, aimed again, then lowered it for another adjustment.

No one said a word.

Tom aimed a third time. This time the rifle roared and bucked against his shoulder.

One of the others had been looking at Tom's target through the binoculars. "Missed," he called.

"I told you he couldn't—"

"Wait!" Smoke shouted. "You got him!"

Everyone rushed to the window then to watch as, far in the distance, the fancy-dressed Indian fell from his horse.

"They left after that," Smoke said. "All of the Indians turned and rode away."

"And the woman?" Pearlie asked. "Wait a minute, you said her name was Jo Ellen. You mean that's where you met Mrs. Burke?"

"Yes, Pearlie. Jo Ellen was a former whore," Tom said. "But I will tell you this. No man could have ever asked for a better woman." He had been quiet during the telling of the story, and now he used a burning brand from the fire to light his pipe. Walking away from the fire, he found a place to be alone for a while.

Thirteen

The Comanche village was near the Purgatory River and for this reason, the little settlement was called Purgatory by the white men, though not by the Comanche. The Indians had no specific name for their village. It was just where they lived, a part of them, and they would not think to name it, any more than they would give a name to the water they drank and the air they breathed. Here, an old chief sat in the center of a circle of men, women, and children.

"Listen," the old chief said, "and I will tell you the story of the Comanche."

Those who were around him, including the elders of the council and the young men, drew closer to hear his words. The one who held the attention of the others was Stone Eagle, the traditional chief of the Comanche. Stone Eagle was an old man who had fought many battles when he was younger. Because of that, he had the respect and admiration of everyone in the tribe.

The women and children grew quiet, not only because it was forbidden to make noise while stories were being told around the campfires, but because they knew it would be a good story, and it filled them with excitement to hear it.

"Once there was a young man," Stone Eagle said.

He held up his finger and wagged it slowly back and forth. "He was not Comanche, he was not Kiowa, he was not Crow, and he was not Lakota."

"What was he, Grandfather?" one of the children asked. It was a term of respect. Stone Eagle wasn't really his grandfather.

"He was before," Stone Eagle said. "He was in the time of the beginning, before the winter-counts, when men could speak with the animals and the spirits of the earth, fire, wind, and water. Now the young man did not know this was unusual, because he had always been able to do so and it seemed a natural thing for him to do. Then, one day as he stood watching an eagle fly, he thought that perhaps he would try and fly too, so he leaped into the air and he beat his arms like the wings of an eagle, but he could not fly and he fell to the ground . . . *ker-whump*."

Stone Eagle made the *ker-whump* sound in such a way as to amuse the children, and they all laughed.

" 'Foolish one, you cannot fly,' the eagle taunted, and he soared through the air and laughed at the young man.

"Then the young man saw a coyote running swiftly, so swiftly across the plains, and he ran after the coyote, thinking to catch him, but he couldn't. 'Foolish one, did you think you could run as swiftly as I?' the coyote mocked.

"Then the young man saw a bear. The bear smelled honey in a comb that was high in a tree, and the bear, with his great strength, pushed the tree over so he could have the honey. The young man was very impressed with the bear's great strength, so he too tried to push a tree over, but he could not. The bear, who was enjoying his honey, saw the young man, and he teased the young man and called him a weakling, and told him he had no business trying to push over a mighty tree in the first place."

Stone Eagle shook his head sadly, and clucked his tongue.

"What did the young man do next, Grandpa?"

"Oh, the young man felt very bad," Stone Eagle said. "He tore out his hair, and he gashed his face with rocks, and he cried out in anger and in despair. 'I cannot fly like the eagle,' the young man said. 'I cannot run as swiftly as the coyote, nor do I have the strength of the bear. Why am I on earth if I cannot do any of these things?'

"Suddenly, the young man heard a strange-sounding voice, carried on the wind. 'Go . . . to . . . the . . . mountain,' the voice said."

Stone Eagle made his voice wail in a terrible sound, and the smaller children were frightened. Some cried, and others clutched the hands of their mothers tightly. The older children were frightened too, but they welcomed the fright because it made them feel brave to listen to the story without betraying their own fear.

"The young man climbed the mountain," Stone Eagle went on. "And as he climbed, the voice in the wind continued to speak to him. 'You are a worm,' the voice in the wind said. 'You are a blade of grass. You are an ant, a mote of dust. You are nothing. You cannot fly, you cannot run swiftly, you have no strength. Climb to the top of the mountain.'

" 'Why should I climb to the top of the mountain?' the young man asked.

" 'You will know why when you get there,' the voice in the wind answered.

"The young man began to do as he was instructed, but he did so with a heavy heart. He believed that the voice had instructed him to climb the mountain so he could jump off and kill himself. He was frightened and sad, but he felt that he must do what the voice told him to do."

"And did he climb to the top of the mountain and jump off, Grandpa?"

Stone Eagle held up a finger, as if to caution the young questioner against impatience, then went on with his story. "As the young man climbed, a strange thing happened. He grew hungry and, looking for something to eat, he saw the buds of the peyote cactus. He ate the peyote buds and as he did, he began to see things he could not see before. He was no longer frightened, or confused, or ashamed. Only truth remained in his body, and with truth, he understood all.

"It was true, he thought, he could not fly like an eagle, but an eagle could not use his wings as hands. It was true he could not run as swiftly as a coyote, but a coyote could not walk upright. It was true he did not have the strength of the bear, but the bear could not make poems or music or dance to the rhythm of the drums. When the young man reached the top of the mountain, he thought of all this and he spread his arms wide and looked over the valley, far below.

" 'Why don't you jump?' a voice asked, and the young man looked around and there he saw a warrior, wearing many feathers and shining as bright as the sun."

"Who was the warrior, Grandpa?"

"Some say it was he who is called Shining Warrior, a messenger from the Great Spirit, and that is what I believe," Stone Eagle replied.

"And did the young man jump?"

Again, Stone Eagle held up a finger, calling for quiet.

" 'No,' the young man said. 'I will not jump. I am

not a worm, I am not a blade of grass, I am not an ant or a mote of dust. I am a man!'

" 'Now,' Shining Warrior said. 'Now your period of trial is over. Now you have the gift of the peyote and the sacred wisdom, and from this day forth you will be the master over all the animals and over all the things of nature. You shall have a name and your name shall be called Comanche, and your people shall be many, and they will be mighty hunters and warriors.'

" 'But wait,' the young man called. 'Wait, I have questions to ask. There are many things I do not know. How will I learn what is needed to know to be worthy of the fine name you have given me?'

" 'I have given you the gift of the peyote,' Shining Warrior said. 'Now I tell you, when you wish to attain wisdom, you need only to build a sweat lodge. Go into the sweat lodge and build a fire so that you may sweat as you chew the peyote.'

"And that is why, even today, wise men of our people use peyote to gain knowledge and to know the truth," Stone Eagle said.

"What happened next, Grandpa?"

"The young man left the mountain and returned to the valley below. When he returned, he discovered that all the animals had been struck dumb as their punishment for mocking Comanche. The animals could no longer speak to him. They couldn't even speak to each other, and every animal had to go for all time after that unable even to speak to their own kind."

"Is that why men can speak to each other, but animals cannot speak?"

"Yes," Stone Eagle said. "For it was intended for man to rule over the animals."

"And what happened to Comanche after that?" another child asked.

"Comanche took a wife and had many children, and the children took wives and had many children and those children took wives and had many children. I am the child of one of those children, just as you are the children of my children. And that is why we are known as Comanche."

After Stone Eagle finished his story, there were others who told stories as well. If the story was to be a story of bravery in battle, the one who spoke would walk over to the lodge pole and strike it with his coup stick. Then everyone would know that he was going to tell a story of an enemy killed in battle. Such stories were only told by the older men of the tribe, for it had been a long time since the Comanche had been in battle and none of the younger men could make such boasts. In such stories, the enemy warriors were always brave and skilled, because that made the warrior's own exploits all the greater.

Not all the stories were of enemies killed in battle. Some of the stories were of hunting exploits, and these stories could be told by the younger men. Some stories were even of things that had happened in the time of their father's father's father, which had been handed down through the generations to be preserved as a part of their history.

One of the men who had listened intently to all the stories was Quinntanna. Quinntanna was the nephew of Stone Eagle, though, as Quinntanna's father had died many years ago, Stone Eagle was more a father than an uncle.

Quinntanna, a handsome man with a broad chest, powerful arms, strong legs, had listened to all the stories because he hoped to find—in one of them—the answer to a troubling and recurring dream.

In the dream, Quinntanna had seen many people walking through a pall of smoke. The people were weeping, but they were not weeping because smoke was in their eyes. They were weeping from sadness. Quinntanna asked why they were sad, but he always awoke before anyone could answer him.

At first, Quinntanna was disappointed because he did not find the answer in any of the stories. Then, as he thought about it, he realized that perhaps he had. The story of Comanche was the story of the origin of the use of peyote buttons.

Only once before had Quinntanna used the peyote. Perhaps if he used it now, he would understand the meaning of this strange and disturbing dream. That night, before he went to sleep, Quinntanna mentioned his dream, and what he had decided to do about it, to his wife, Sasheena.

"Does that mean you will not go with the hunters then?" Sasheena asked as she nursed their baby.

"Ho!" Quinntanna laughed. "Do you think I would stay here, only to listen to the stories the others will tell when they return? Were I to do that, Teykano would have me believe that he took every animal with his bare hands. No, I will make the hunt, then when I return, I will seek the knowledge of the peyote."

"I will sleep cold until you return, my husband," Sasheena said.

Quinntanna, who was already lying in the bed of blankets and robes, turned back the top blanket for her. "That is true," he said, smiling at her. "But you will not sleep cold tonight."

Putting the baby in its own bed, Sasheena removed her dress, then slipped naked into the bed alongside her husband.

Fourteen

Smoke Jensen stopped at the edge of a grassy meadow where he saw hoofprints. Then, seeing some elk droppings, he squatted to get a closer look at them. The droppings were soft, which meant they had been made less than an hour ago. That meant that the elk was close by, more than likely in the clump of trees just ahead.

Smoke knew that the elk would think himself safe in the woods, but those same trees would also allow Smoke to get closer without being seen, provided he made no noise as he approached. For most men that would be difficult or impossible, but Smoke had learned from the old mountain man, Preacher, how to choose his steps so carefully that he could walk on a carpet of fallen leaves without being heard. He knew too to stay downwind of his prey.

A small bush, its limbs bare but for a few brown leaves, rattled dryly in the wind. The bush stood just on the edge of the open meadow, the last piece of vegetation between the woods and a small, swiftly running stream. Smoke was certain that when the elk left the woods for water, it would come this way. Smoke crouched behind a rock and waited.

He had been there for about thirty minutes when he saw a bull elk's head stick out from between a couple of trees. The animal stood perfectly still for a long time, its eyes sweeping over the open meadow, its nose twitching, its ears cocked. The elk was not about to commit itself until it had examined every possible danger.

Moving as slowly and quietly as he could, Smoke raised his rifle to his shoulder and took aim.

The elk started out into the open. It moved slowly and cautiously down to the edge of the stream, then stopped. The elk's head popped up, its rack held high. It stared for a long moment, remaining perfectly still as it did so. Smoke held his breath.

The creature's eyes twitched, and Smoke wondered what sound it had heard, for he had made no noise at all. The elk listened, then decided that whatever it had heard represented no danger. It stuck its head down into the stream and began to drink.

Smoke sighted down the barrel of his rifle, finding a target just above and behind the elk's left foreleg. He tightened the finger on the trigger.

At almost the precise moment he squeezed off his shot, he thought he saw something flying out of the trees toward the elk. But the white puff of smoke that billowed from the end of the rifle barrel so obscured his vision that he decided what he had seen was nothing more than a trick of light, or a moving shadow.

The boom of his shot echoed back from the trees just as the elk fell to its front knees. It got back up and tried to run, but could go no more than a few steps before it fell again.

Smoke got up and ran across the open field toward the still-twitching elk. When he reached the animal, he stopped cold and stared at it in surprise. It was lying on its left side with its legs stretched straight out in front. Sticking up from just behind the right foreleg was an arrow.

"It is my kill!" a voice shouted.

When Smoke looked toward the sound of the voice, he saw an Indian coming toward him from the edge of the woods. He was tall for an Indian, and he was wearing traditional Indian dress.

"My elk," the Indian said again, pointing to the fallen animal.

"No," Smoke said. "It was my shot that killed it."

"My arrow," the Indian insisted, pointing to the shaft sticking up from the flesh of the animal.

Smoke turned the animal over, then pointed to the bullet hole. "My bullet," he said. They were quiet for a moment. Then Smoke offered the Indian his hand. "I am Smoke Jensen."

"You are Smoke Jensen?"

"Yes."

"I have heard of you." The Indian stuck out his hand. "I am Quinntanna."

Smoke smiled. "I have heard of you, Quinntanna. By the way, there is a way to settle this, if you are interested."

"Yes, I am interested. What is the way you would settle this?"

"Well, I'm looking for meat, and I reckon you are too. And the way I look at it, half an elk is better than no elk at all. We could cut the animal in half."

"I want the front half," Quinntanna said. "And I want the heart."

Smoke chuckled. "All right, you can have the front half."

"I will cut the elk in two pieces," Quinntanna offered, dropping to one knee beside the slain animal. He took out his knife and began cutting

"Why are you hunting with a bow and arrow?"

"We wanted to make this hunt in the way of our fathers and their fathers," Quinntanna answered.

"If you went on the warpath now, would you go on the warpath in the way of your fathers?" Smoke asked.

Quinntanna looked up at Smoke and laughed. "Warpath? Why would we go on the warpath now? The days of war are over."

"For you perhaps, but not for everyone," Smoke said.

"Yes, I have heard of the Sioux and their Ghost Dancers and medicine shirts. They think they can bring back the buffalo, but I know they cannot."

"No, I'm not talking about the Sioux," Smoke said. "I am talking about the Comanche."

Quinntanna snorted. "It is not true. There are no Comanche on the warpath."

"Perhaps some who are renegades?" Smoke suggested. "Evil young men who have left your village?"

Quinntanna shook his head. "I know where every young man from my village is. Why do you ask this?"

"Because recently, some Indians attacked a ranch. They killed everyone on the ranch—the rancher's wife, his children, and those who worked for him. Then they burned the barn and the outbuildings."

"And people think we did it?" Quinntanna asked.

"The arrows did have Comanche markings."

"I do not understand this," Quinntanna said. "It is not good that a white man's ranch was attacked. And it is not good that people think Comanche attacked the ranch."

"So you are telling me that you know nothing about this?"

"I know nothing," Quinntanna repeated.

"I didn't think you did," Smoke said. "Truth to tell, I've thought all along it might be someone else, Comancheros perhaps, who wanted to make it look like Indians attacked."

"Yes, that would be smart," Quinntanna said.

"They could take what they wanted from the ranch, but people would think it was the Indians."

"No," Smoke said.

"No?"

"That is the strange part. The people who did this took nothing. They only killed and burned."

Quinntanna shook his head. "Such people I do not understand," he said. By now the elk was in two parts, and Quinntanna stuck the knife into the open cavity of the front half. He carved for a moment, then pulled out the elk's heart. "Make a fire," he said. "We will eat the heart together."

Smoke smiled. "Good idea," he said. "I was getting a little hungry anyway."

While Smoke made a fire, Quinntanna found two forked sticks. Then he peeled the bark of a third stick and used that as a skewer for the heart. With the flames dancing, Quinntanna placed the skewer across the forked sticks so that the heart was in the fire. Within a few moments the juices, dripping into the fire from the roasting heart, snapped and popped and perfumed the air with their aroma.

Smoke and Quinntanna talked of inconsequential things until finally, Quinntanna stood up and carved off a piece of the meat. It was too hot to hold in one hand, so he passed it back and forth between his hands as he gave it over to Smoke. Laughing, Smoke also passed it back and forth between his hands for a moment until he could hold it.

"Here, I have some salt," Smoke said, taking a little paper envelope from his pocket. He gave a pinch to Quinntanna, then salted his own meat before he took a bite. He smiled as the juices filled his mouth and ran down his chin.

"It is good," Quinntanna said.

"Yes," Smoke agreed.

"To eat the heart of the animal you kill is a good thing," Quintanna explained. He took a big bite and began chewing. "If it is a male animal, you will have his strength, and"—Quinntanna rubbed himself and smiled, then added—"that which makes him a male."

"Oh," Smoke said. "What if it is a female?"

Quinntanna laughed out loud. "Do not worry," he said. "From the female we get courage and cunning. And that which makes us male is not harmed."

"I'm glad of that," Smoke said with a laugh. "For I have eaten many female elk and deer."

The two men finished eating the heart. Afterward, they held their hands up to each other in the sign of peace; then each took his half of the elk and went his own way.

"Would you mind tellin' me how you managed to kill half an elk?" Tom asked with a chuckle when Smoke rode back into their camp carrying the elk's haunch. "And the back half at that?"

Smoke told Tom and Pearlie of his encounter with Quinntanna.

"You sound more than ever convinced that they didn't have anything to do with the raid on Tom's ranch," Pearlie said.

"Practically the whole tribe is out on some sort of ritual hunt," Smoke said. "They don't even have any weapons with them, except for bows and arrows. If they were the ones who had attacked the ranch, they sure wouldn't be wandering around without guns."

"I think Smoke's right," Tom said.

"I almost wish I wasn't right," Smoke declared.

"Why's that?"

"Because if we were after Indians, we would at least have some idea of what we are up against. Now, we don't know. The only thing we know about whoever did this is that they are pure evil."

Camp Covington, as Covington called it, was located just outside Big Rock. There, in a wide meadow, tents were pitched and a military camp was born. Covington had insisted that all those who signed up leave their homes, ranches, and hotel rooms in order to come together as a military unit.

Covington had absolutely no military experience, so he knew nothing about drilling. However, Marcus Dingo, who Covington had appointed as his first sergeant, did know drilling, and he spent a couple of days "whipping the troops into shape."

This was particularly rewarding for Dingo. Dingo was the kind of man who had a difficult time hanging onto a job. As a result, he was often unemployed, which meant that sometimes he had to accept the most self-demeaning of tasks just to keep body and soul together. When he was sweeping the barroom floor, or emptying the spittoons, it was easy for the others to make fun of him. Now the situation was changed. As first sergeant of Covington's Company, Dingo was someone who could, and did, demand and receive respect from the same men who used to tease him.

For three days Dingo drilled the men, taking special delight in making life difficult for those who, but a week earlier, had regarded him as their inferior. Throughout the three days, there was a great deal of talk and complaining from the men, who insisted they had not joined the company to drill, they had joined to fight. Covington kept them in line by quoting an old military adage: "Ten men wisely led are worth a hundred without a head."

"What that means," he explained, "is that without discipline and structure, we are nothing. But with discipline, structure, and tactics, combined with a willingness to follow orders, we will fight the Indians and we will beat them."

Finally, Covington called his troops together in order to give them word that on the next day, they would go after the Indians.

Breakfast the next morning was coffee, bacon, and biscuits. After breakfast, the order was given to strike tents, followed by Boots and Saddles. The latter called for them to saddle their mounts. Then, the order was given "To horse!" This put every soldier standing at the head of his horse. Finally, they were ordered to mount, then to move out.

The march continued on through the day. Because they were a newly activated unit, poorly led and with no economy of motion, the march was difficult and tiring. For twenty minutes of every hour the men dismounted and led their horses for ten minutes, then let them rest for ten minutes.

For miles upon miles, Covington's Cavalry moved toward the Purgatory River, on which was located the Indian village that Covington was convinced was responsible for the raid on the Burke ranch. Finally, just before nightfall, a stream of water was found and Covington gave the order that this would be their bivouac. A handful of hardtack crackers supplemented the coffee and served as their supper.

While the men were eating, Covington sent Dingo ahead on a little scouting expedition. Dingo returned less than an hour later with word that he had located the village.

"Good," Covington said with a broad smile. "We will attack it tomorrow."

"Tomorrow?" Dingo replied.

"Yes. We'll hit them just before dawn," Covington said. "I want to catch the heathen redskins before they get out of bed."

"Get up," Dingo said, shaking the shoulder of one of the men.

"Get up? What fer? Hell, it's two or three hours 'till dawn."

"We want an early start," Dingo said. "Wake up the others in your platoon."

One by one the orders passed through the command, rousting everyone from their bedrolls. Then, in the darkness, they saddled their horses and made them ready to go. They did it quietly, for from the point of their bivouac to the Indian village itself was no more than two miles, and any unnatural noise could give them away.

Finally, when the bivouac was struck and all the men were mounted, Covington ordered the men forward.

Fifteen

Even though all its young men were gone, leaving the village virtually defenseless, the people of the village were enjoying the peaceful sleep of the innocent. They were completely unaware that less than two hundred yards from the village's outer ring, in the lower reaches of a great pine forest, shadows were emerging from the darkness, and that these shadows represented danger to them.

The emerging shadows were the men of Covington's Militia, and they began to take up their positions around the village in accordance with Colonel Covington's instructions. Their horses moved silently, with only their movement and the vapor of their breathing giving any indication of life.

It was cold in the predawn darkness, and Colonel Covington and his staff officers moved to the crest of a small hill to stare down at the Comanche village. All the teepees appeared to be tightly shut against the cold, and no one was moving anywhere. Wisps of smoke curled up through the smoke vents in the top of all the tepees, and the smell of wood smoke mixed with the aroma of last night's cooking, clear indications of habitation.

"Are you sure the Indians who raided Tom Burke's ranch came from Purgatory, Colonel?" Captain

Roach asked. Normally, Roach was teamster for a wagon-freight line, but he had joined Covington's Company of Indian fighters.

"Of course they came from Purgatory," Covington said. "This is the closet Indian village, isn't it?"

"Yes, sir, but that's my point," Roach said. "It just don't seem likely to me that they would shit so close to their home nest."

"Did it ever occur to you, that is exactly what they want us to think? What do you think about it, First Sergeant?" Covington asked. He rubbed his hands together and blew against them, warming them with his breath.

"I figure it's more'n likely these here Injuns is the ones who done it," Dingo said. "But even if it ain't these, it don't matter, 'cause once this here war gets started, all Injuns is going to be the same."

"I think you are right, First Sergeant," Covington replied. "Captain Roach, how long will it take you to get your men to the other side?"

"Half an hour," Roach said.

"Then get your men into position, Captain. It looks like we have caught them completely by surprise, and I want to attack before it's light."

"Yes, sir. Uh, Colonel, what about the women and children in the camp? By attacking while it is still dark, I am afraid we will be putting them at great risk."

"Will we now?"

"Yes, sir."

"What about the women and children at Mr. Burke's ranch? Were they at risk?" Covington asked.

Roach was silent for a moment, then nodded. "Yes, sir. I guess I see what you mean."

"Once your men are in position, fire one shot,"

Covington ordered. "That will be our signal to attack from both sides."

"Yes, sir."

A small clinking sound of metal on metal came from somewhere among the soldiers. The sound was an unnatural intrusion into the soft whisper of wind in the trees. In her tepee in the village, Sasheena heard the sound while in the deepest recesses of her sleep, and her eyes came open as she wondered what it might have been. Automatically, she looked over toward her baby. He was sleeping nearby, dimly visible in the soft golden glow of the coals that still gleamed in the warming tepee fire. She felt the place beside her, empty now because Quinntanna and nearly every other young man in the village had gone hunting.

Sasheena smiled as she remembered the excitement her husband felt over the expedition.

"Why do you hunt for meat?" she had asked him. *"Our village has enough money from leasing grazing rights to the white man to buy all the pork, beef, lamb, and chicken that we need."*

"You are a woman, and I do not expect a woman to understand," Quinntanna had replied. *"But the traditional hunt is something a man must do. I only wish there were buffalo to hunt."*

The bed robes were warm, and Sasheena realized she must have dreamed the unusual sound. She closed her eyes, and quickly dropped off to sleep again.

* * *

Outside, the silent horses and the quiet men were now in position. They stayed motionless for several minutes. Then they heard what they were waiting for: the crack of a rifle shot echoing from the far side of the village.

"All right. Attack, men, attack!" Covington yelled. "Remember the Burke ranch!"

At Covington's orders, the militiamen galloped forward from both sides of the Indian camp, firing as rapidly as they could at the conical tepees that rose up in the darkness before them.

It had been so long since there was any battle between Indians and whites in this area that many of the Indian residents of the village hadn't even been born then. Because of that, the sleeping villagers had no instinctive responses to call upon. They poured out of the tepees, not to join in the fight, but to see what was going on.

"Keep calm, men," Covington shouted to his troops. "Keep calm and fire low."

Though the Indians were totally surprised by the unexpected attack on their village, they realized quickly that they were in mortal danger. Many of them tried to run, only to be cut down by the gunfire. One young Indian in his early teens suddenly burst out of one of the tepees and jumped on an unsaddled and unbridled pony. Covington started after him, not realizing that the boy was armed. The boy whirled around and fired, the bullet whizzing by Covington's ear. Then the boy, displaying unusual courage, rode directly toward Covington, firing twice more, but missing both times. Covington returned fire, killing the boy with one shot.

Sasheena had awakened as quickly as the others, and when she moved to the door flap of her tepee to look outside, she saw the swirling melee of soldiers and Indians. At first she was as confused as everyone else in the village. Then, looking around, she saw Stone Eagle going toward the soldiers, holding an American flag over his head. As a young girl she had heard stories around the council fires of the flag, for it had been given to Stone Eagle by the Great White Father in Washington, the man the whites called President Grant.

"Do not shoot!" Stone Eagle was shouting, waving the flag over his head and trying to be heard above the rattle of musketry. "We are friends to the white man! I am friend of Grant!"

Stone Eagle was shot down within twenty yards of his tepee. But it wasn't only Stone Eagle, for Sasheena could see old men, women, and children being shot as well, slaughtered by the indiscriminate firing of the soldiers. Suddenly, a fusillade of bullets punched through her tepee, and she knew she had to leave.

Grabbing a robe, Sasheena wrapped it around her naked body. Then she picked up her baby and left the tepee, running toward the edge of the trees. Two soldiers on horseback galloped after her. One of them reached down and grabbed the robe, then jerked it away.

Sasheena screamed, and tried, in vain, to cover her exposed body.

"I'll be damned! She's naked!"

"Hey, she ain't bad-lookin'! Get the kid away from her!" the other said. "Get the kid away from her, and we'll have us some fun."

"No!" Sasheena screamed, trying to keep the baby from being taken.

"Hell, don't fight her, Ed, just kill the damn kid."

Using the butt of his pistol, the first soldier hit the baby on the head, crushing its skull. Shocked almost senseless by the brutality, Sasheena felt the life leave her child. She screamed in anger and grief.

"Now, let's see what this little ole Injun gal can do for us," the other soldier said, dismounting and coming toward her, unbuttoning his pants as he did so.

Suddenly a shot rang out, and a bullet hit Sasheena right between the eyes.

"What the hell?" Ed said, looking around to see who'd shot her. He saw Dingo.

"We're here to kill Injuns," Dingo said. "Not make some half-breed brats that we'll have to deal with in the future. You want a woman, get yourself a whore like ever'one else."

"There ain't nothin' says we can't have a little fun now," one of the two men said.

"Yeah, there is somethin' says that," Dingo replied. He pointed to himself. "Me. I say it."

"The first sergeant is quite right," Covington said, arriving to see what the discussion was about. "We are here to conduct war against these people, not commit rape and other atrocities. You will conduct yourselves with dignity. Now, get on with it."

"Yes, sir," the two soldiers replied contritely.

"Good work, First Sergeant," Covington said. "It's a shame the young woman had to be killed, but it is serving a higher purpose." Covington turned his horse then, and rode back into the swirling melee of dust, running, screaming Indians, and mounted cavalrymen.

Very soon thereafter, most of the shooting had stopped, simply because there were no more targets of opportunity. Covington held up his hand, then described a circle, calling all his men together. The ground was strewn with Indians. Most were dead, though a few were still groaning.

"All right, men, I congratulate you on a fine victory

here today. Surely this will go down in history as one of the greatest Indian battles of all time. Now I want you to search all the tepees and remove anything of value, especially any weapons that you might find. And bear in mind that you are liberating contraband, not for yourself, but for the entire company. We will make a fair and balanced division of plunder once we return to Big Rock."

"Some of these people are still alive," Captain Roach said. "What do we do about them?"

"Shoot them, I guess," Covington said, almost in an offhand way. "That would be the humane thing to do. No sense in letting them lie here and suffer."

"What about the tepees?" Dingo asked.

"Burn them."

For the next several minutes the men of Covington's Militia moved through the encampment, removing blankets, cooking utensils, knives, furs, and anything else of value they could find, including, in several cases, money. There was an excited babble of voices as they displayed their treasure to one another, interrupted only by the occasional sound of a gunshot as the wounded Indians were killed.

"Colonel, I suggest that we not stay around much longer," Roach said.

"Why is that?"

"Have you noticed that there are no young men among the dead?"

"What are you suggesting, Captain?"

"I'm saying that, for some reason, all the young men are gone. If they come back from wherever they are, and see us here with all this"—he took in the camp with a sweep of his arm—"they aren't going to take it very well. And we would be very vulnerable right now."

Covington stroked his cheek, then nodded. "A

most astute observation, Captain Roach. Very well, give the order to withdraw back to Big Rock."

"Yes, sir," Roach said.

A few minutes later, with most of the tepees burning behind them, Covington led his militia back into the woods from which they had come. The bodies of 137 old men, women, and children lay on the ground, while the fires of scores of tepees sent a large column of smoke climbing into the air above them.

Sixteen

The travois of several horses were laden with the results of the hunt: deer, elk, wild turkey, and other game. It had been a good hunt, and as Quinntanna led the hunting party back to the village, he was thinking of the celebration they would have on their return. The meat would be put on spits and turned slowly over a fire, and the smell would cause everyone's appetite to grow. They would tell stories of the hunt, and some of the older men would speak of the early days when buffalo were plentiful.

Quinntanna could remember when, as a young boy, he had gone on a buffalo hunt. That had been one of the last hunts to actually take a buffalo, because the herds were all gone now. For hundreds of years the buffalo had served the Comanche. Then the white men had come and within one lifetime, the buffalo were gone.

None of the others were thinking about the vanished buffalo. They were thinking only about the last two days and the success of their hunt. They talked about it, reliving certain shots and honing the stories they would tell around the campfires. Everyone bragged of their exploits except Quinntanna.

"Quinntanna, have you no stories to tell?" Teykano

asked. "We are all waiting to hear how it is that you killed only one half of an elk."

"Yes," one of the others said. "Is the back half still running around somewhere in the woods, waiting to be taken at the next hunt?"

The others laughed.

"I will tell my story when there are better ears to hear it," Quinntanna teased. "Such a story to ears as yours would be a terrible waste."

"Quinntanna," Teykano said, pointing ahead. "Look ahead. There is smoke. Is it a forest fire?"

The hunting party stopped for a moment to study the smoke. Then Quinntanna shook his head. "I think it is not a forest fire," he said. "If many trees were burning there would be much more smoke."

"Grass, perhaps?"

"Perhaps it is grass, though it does not seem to me that the smoke is wide enough for a grass fire."

"Then what is the cause of this strange thing?"

"I don't know," Quinntanna admitted.

Quinntanna urged his horse ahead, and the hunting party followed him, riding quickly toward the smoke that rose before them. Though he didn't share it with the others, there was something about this that he found extremely troubling.

Then, when they reached the meadow where the village had been, Quinntanna realized what was bothering him. This was his dream, come to life, his worst fear realized. Ahead of him he saw several blackened circles. He also saw about fifty people moving through the pall of smoke. He wasn't close enough to see whether or not they were crying, but he knew without a doubt that they were.

Then he saw something that he had not seen in his dreams, even though he had always known they were there. He saw several bodies stretched out on the ground.

With a scream of rage, Quinntanna slapped his legs against the side of his horse. The steed bolted into a gallop, closing the remaining distance in but a few seconds. When he arrived, he leaped down from his horse and started searching for Sasheena.

"Sasheena!" he called. "Sasheena, where are you?"

"Quinntanna," an old man said. "Your woman and your child are here."

The old man who called him was Isataka, Sasheena's grandfather. Quinntanna looked down at the two bodies. The baby's head had been smashed like a gourd. Sasheena's face was deformed by the effect of the bullet that had ended her life. With grief and confusion in his eyes, Quinntanna looked up at Isataka who had summoned him.

"Who?" he asked. "Who did this?"

"It was white soldiers," Isataka replied.

"Soldiers?" Quinntanna was shocked by the answer. "Soldiers of the white man's army did this?"

"Yes. They came before light this morning, and began firing. Stone Eagle was going to reason with them, to ask them why they are doing this thing, but they shot him down before he could get to them. Then there was much confusion. Some of us got away during the confusion, and we hid in the forest and watched as they slaughtered those who did not get away."

Suddenly, Quinntanna recalled his conversation with Smoke Jensen. Jensen had told him that someone had attacked the family of a white rancher.

"I think I know why the white soldiers attacked," Quinntanna said.

"Why?" Isataka asked.

"The home of a white rancher was attacked, and

the rancher's wife and children were killed. According to the sign left, the attack was made by Comanche."

"That cannot be true," the old man said. "There are no Comanche on the warpath."

"We know that, but the whites do not. And I can think of no other reason why they would attack our village."

"I think they do not need a reason," Isataka said. "There is an evil in the white man that cannot be kept down. It has been many years since there was any trouble between our people. Perhaps the evil could wait no longer."

From all over what had been the village, Quinntanna heard the wails of grief and anger from the young men of the hunting party who were returning to find their own families slaughtered.

"Quinntanna, we must do battle with the white man," Teykano said angrily. Like Quinntanna, Teykano had lost his wife. He'd also lost two children.

"We can't fight the white man," Quinntanna said. "There are too many of them. There are as many white men as there are blades of grass. If we make war against them, we will all be killed.

"Better to be killed fighting than to die a coward. And that is what we will be if we do nothing," Teykano insisted.

"We will do something," Quinntanna promised.

"What? What will we do, Quinntanna?"

"I will talk with the spirits," Quinntanna said. "It is for the spirits to decide what we must do."

Quinntanna buried his wife and child, then went into the mountains to consult with the spirits. He took neither water nor food with him, for the nourishment he sought was for his soul, not his body. And to nourish his soul, he took a supply of peyote buttons.

He went high into the mountains, above the snow line, and there he sat, wrapped in a buffalo robe, looking out over the valley below. He didn't know how long he had been there when he saw a warrior mounted on a horse. The warrior was wearing a headdress of many feathers that stretched all the way to the ground. He also wore a shirt and trousers of beaded buckskin, and there was a glow around him that was so bright that it hurt Quinntanna's eyes to look at him.

"Shining Warrior!" Quinntanna said.

Shining Warrior looked at Quinntanna for a moment, but he didn't speak. Instead, he uttered a war cry, then urged his horse into a gallop. Shining Warrior rode for some distance away, then turned and rode back toward Quinntanna. As he galloped toward him, Shining Warrior held his war club over his head and leaned to one side as if he were going to strike Quinntanna. Quinntanna was frightened, but he knew, instinctively, that he must not flinch. Shining Warrior let forth a mighty yell, and swinging the club at Quinntanna's head, stopped it just inches away from smashing his skull.

Then Quinntanna noticed a very strange thing. Even though the horse had galloped back and forth across the snow-covered plain, it had left no tracks. Except for the footprints Quinntanna had left, the snow was completely pristine.

Shining Warrior leaned down then to put his hand on Quinntanna's forehead. Quinntanna shut his eyes, and when he did, he saw a vision of what was left of his people. In the vision, he saw that his people were being attacked yet again by soldiers.

"No!" Quinntanna shouted.

When Quinntanna opened his eyes, Shining Warrior was gone. There was no sign of his having been there at all, for the snow was still undisturbed. And now, amazingly, even his own footprints were gone. There had not been a fresh snowfall, yet the surface of the snow was brilliantly white, fresh, clean, and absolutely unblemished.

The Indians were still cleaning up the mess of what had been their village when Quinntanna returned from his sojourn into the mountains. He was met by Teykano and others.

"You have returned," Teykano said.

"Yes."

"And did you have a vision?"

"Yes. Teykano, Shining Warrior came to me," Quinntanna said.

"Shining Warrior?" Teykano repeated in awe. "Ayiee, your medicine is very strong. I have known many who wished to see him, but I have known none who have. What did he look like?"

"Like a warrior of old," Quinntanna said. "He looks like the warrior who visited Comanche in the story Stone Eagle told."

"What did he say to you?"

"He did not speak."

"He came to you, but he did not speak?" Teykano replied in a surprised voice.

"He did not speak to me with words, but he made me see here, and here," Quinntanna said, touching his forehead and his heart.

By now the other young men had gathered to hear what Quinntanna was saying.

"When we ride on the path of war . . ."

Hearing Quinntanna proclaim that they would be

riding on the path of war, the others suddenly shouted and howled in excitement, elated over the prospect of getting revenge for what was visited upon their village.

"When we ride on the path of war," Quinntanna said again, "our horses will leave no sign. Not even the most skilled of trackers will be able to find us."

"All creatures leave tracks," Teykano said. "Even an ant leaves a track."

"A bird leaves no track because it does not touch the ground," Quinntanna said. "We will be like the bird. The hooves of our horses will not touch the ground."

"How can this be? How can our horses travel without touching the ground?"

"I do not know," Quinntanna admitted. "But Shining Warrior showed me that it could be done." Quinntanna described the amazing sight of seeing Shining Warrior's horse galloping back and forth, yet leaving no mark upon the snow. Then he told how his own tracks had disappeared, even though there was no snowfall to cover them. "Perhaps it will appear to us as if our horses are touching the ground, but the sign will be invisible to everyone else."

"Yes," one of the other young men said. "If Shining Warrior has said it will be so, then I believe it will be so."

Quinntanna looked over to where the survivors were busy rebuilding as much of their village as they could.

"What are they doing?" Quinntanna asked.

Teykano took in the village with a motion of his hand. "Look. The village still lives. The lodges that weren't burned by fire have been put up again, and soon new lodges will take the place of those that were destroyed."

"No, our people must not rebuild here," Quinntanna said. "We must move the village."

"Why?"

"In my vision, I saw more soldiers come to this place. Many more of our people were killed."

"If you have seen it in your vision, then it is to be so and there is nothing we can do about it."

Quinntanna shook his head. "I do not believe this. I believe that I was shown the vision so that it could be changed. If the village is moved, then the soldiers cannot find it."

"Come," Teykano said to the others. "We will move our people."

"What about guns?" one of the others asked. "While we hunted with bows and arrows, our guns were left behind and the soldiers who killed our families stole our guns."

"Yes. Did Shining Warrior show you how we would get guns?" Teykano asked.

"No," Quinntanna said. "But I believe a way to get the guns will be shown to us."

Even as Quinntanna made that statement, they saw two riders approaching. Two of the hunters, still angry and grief-stricken, raised their bows and drew the string to shoot the visitors, but Quinntanna held out his hand to stop them.

"Wait. These are not soldiers. We will see what they want." As the two riders came closer, the villagers saw that they were Indian.

As they approached, the riders held up their right hands, palms out, in a sign of peace. Quinntanna returned the sign as a signal that they could enter without fear.

"I am Perry Blue Horses," one of the riders said. He pointed to the other. "This is Russell Swift Bear."

"You have white and Indian names," Quinntanna said.

"We have white and Indian blood," Blue Horses replied. He looked around at the destroyed village. "This was done by the white man?"

"Yes."

"I am shamed by my white blood," Blue Horses said.

"All the men were away," Quinntanna said. "When we returned, we learned that soldiers had attacked our village and killed our women and children and our old men."

"Are you at war with the whites?" Blue Horses asked.

Quinntanna nodded. "I think we are at war now," he replied. "For many years our people and the whites have been at peace. We lease our land to white ranchers so they may graze their cattle. We keep the money they pay us in the white man's bank. But some people attacked and killed a white rancher and his family. The whites think we did it."

"What?" Teykano replied. "A ranch was attacked? When did this happen? I know nothing of this."

"I think it happened a short time ago," Quinntanna said.

"Then we must go to the whites and tell them that we did not do such a thing. Perhaps then there will be no war," one of the older Indians said.

"I think they will not listen," Quinntanna said.

"Will you make war against the white men who did this?" Swift Bear asked.

"When we went away to hunt, we hunted in the old way, with the bow and arrow, as did our ancestors. Our rifles and bullets stayed behind. Now all our guns are gone, taken by the white soldiers when they attacked."

"We can get weapons for you," Blue Horses said, taking in Swift Bear with a wave of his hand.

"How?"

"Because of our blood, we can do business with the white man."

Quinntanna smiled broadly and looked at the others. "Did I not say that Shining Warrior would show the way?"

"Get guns for us," Teykano said. "Rifles and bullets. We will need these things."

"Fifty rifles with bullets will cost two thousand five hundred dollars in white man's money," Swift Bear said.

"How can we pay this? Our money is in the white man's bank."

"It is your money. Go to the bank and take it out," Swift Bear said.

"All right. I will get the money. When will we get the guns?"

"I will talk to the one who has them," Blue Horses said. "We will come with the guns when you have the money."

As Blue Horses and Swift Bear rode away, the others gathered around Quinntanna.

"Quinntanna, you will get the money?" one of them asked.

"Yes," Quinntanna said. "I will get the money."

"If you lead, we will follow," Teykano said.

Seventeen

The citizens of the small town of Stonewall weren't particularly surprised to see an Indian riding into town. The Indians frequently did business in the town, and though they had heard that renegades attacked a ranch over near Big Rock, they certainly didn't expect any trouble from *their* Indians. After all, the Indians did do a great deal of their business in Stonewall: everything from keeping their money on deposit in the Stonewall bank to buying goods from the local merchants. And because the Indians spent freely, the merchants often went out of their way to make certain that the Indians understood that their money was welcome in the town's stores.

The Indians had money because their great chief Quanah Parker had negotiated the grazing rights for all Comanches and Kiowa within a 240,000-square-mile area. With millions of acres to work with, Quanah Parker had arranged to lease pasturage to wealthy stockmen so they could run their cattle on Indian land. That brought in hundreds of thousands of dollars per year, and though the village of Quinntanna was much smaller, and had less land to lease, their percentage was enough to provide an income for every Comanche in the village.

Quinntanna was extremely cautious as he rode into

town. Although he had made a deal to buy rifles for 2,500 dollars, he had discussed the issue with Teykano, and they'd decided that he had better take five thousand dollars from the bank. They'd come to that decision because they didn't know when, or even if, they would get another chance to make a withdrawal. They had even discussed taking all their money from the bank, but decided that if they did that, there might be some sort of negative response to their action. And until all was ready, they wanted to minimize any chance of trouble with the whites.

If all whites believed that the Comanche were responsible for the attack on the ranch, then even the citizens of Stonewall, who were normally very receptive, might be antagonistic, and an attempt to close the account could set them off. Quinntanna also realized that the citizens of Stonewall might already consider themselves at war, so he was observant of everyone and everything. He kept his eyes on the roofs and second floors of the buildings, looking for any would-be shooters. To his surprise, no one seemed particularly interested in him.

He stopped in front of the bank, looped the reins around the hitching post, then went inside. There was still no reaction. But how could this be? Surely they have heard of the raid against his people by the soldiers. And yet, they gave no indication that anything was other than normal.

Quinntanna stepped up to the teller's window.

"Yes, sir, and what can the Bank of Stonewall do for our Indian customers today?" the teller asked, a wide, professional smile on his face.

"I want to sign paper to get five thousand dollars," Quinntanna said.

"Five thousand dollars? Oh, my, that is a great deal of money," the teller said. Checking a ledger, he looked up and smiled. "However, your village does have enough money in the account to cover it," he said. "In fact, you have much more than that. But in order to withdraw from the account, you will have to have the signature of either Mr. Running Deer or Mr. Stone Eagle. I'm afraid they are the only two names on the signature card."

"Dead," Quinntanna said.

"I beg your pardon?"

"Running Deer and Stone Eagle are dead."

"Both of them?"

"Yes."

"Oh, my," the teller said, clicking his tongue. "Oh, my. Well, this does complicate things."

"I am Quinntanna. I will sign paper for money."

The teller shook his head. "No, Mr. Quinntanna, I'm afraid that won't do. You can't get the money."

"It is money of the Indian people of my village, is it not?" Quinntanna asked.

"Yes, indeed it is," the teller said. "But surely you understand that, in order to keep just any Indian from coming in here and getting the money, only certain people are authorized to make a withdrawal. It is for your own protection. And the only ones who can take money from the account are Mr. Running Deer and Mr. Stone Eagle."

"Dead," Quinntanna said again.

"Yes, yes, so you told me. Wait here for a moment while I go to talk to Mr. Freeman. I'm sure he will know what to do."

The teller left the window and walked to the back of the bank to speak to an older man who was sitting behind a desk. As he spoke, he pointed back toward Quinntanna, and the man at the desk looked up toward Quinntanna.

Quinntanna saw the man, whom the teller had

identified as Mr. Freeman, shake his head, then go
back to work. The teller returned to the window.

"I'm sorry, Mr. Quinntanna, but Mr. Freeman says
we can't give the money to you. Now if you will have
Mr. Running Deer or Mr. Stone Eagle come into the
bank, we will be glad to give them as much money as
there is in the account."

"They are dead," Quinntanna said again, as if explaining something to a child.

"Yes, but they are the only ones who can withdraw
money, you see."

Quinntanna nodded, then, without further comment, turned and walked away.

"The nerve of that Indian," the teller said after
Quinntanna left the bank. "I suppose he thought he
could just come in here and take money out as if this
were his own private bank."

The others in the bank laughed.

Outside the bank, Quinntanna had started to
mount his horse when he saw the stock of a rifle protruding from the saddle holster of another horse that
was tied to the same hitching rail. Without a second
thought, Quinntanna pulled the rifle from its scabbard, jacked a round into the chamber, then went
back inside. As soon as he stepped through the door,
he fired at the table in the middle of the room, hitting
the ink bottle. The bottle shattered, sending a spray
of black ink spewing up into the air, then splashing
back down on everyone. Women screamed and men
shouted in alarm. Quinntanna jacked another shell
into the rifle, then stepped up to the same window
he had been at before.

"Give me money," he said, handing a buckskin
pouch to the teller.

"Y-yes sir," the teller replied. With shaking hands,

he began taking money from his cash drawer and stuffing it into the pouch.

Quinntanna stuck his hand out to stop the teller. "I don't want all money. I only want five thousand dollars of Indian money."

"Five thousand dollars. Yes, sir," the teller said.

"Write on paper that I, Quinntanna, took five thousand dollars of Indian money."

"Yes, sir." Quickly, and with nervous hands, the banker did as he was instructed.

Quinntanna signed the paper, then taking the money pouch, he backed out of the bank, pointing the rifle at everyone inside. Once outside, he jumped onto his horse, then with several whoops and shouts, rode out of town.

"The bank!" Freeman yelled, running out into the street a moment later. "The bank has been robbed!"

Freeman began firing his pistol down the street toward the fleeing Quinntanna. His bullets were going wild, ricocheting off the walls and whizzing by innocent citizens.

"Freeman, you dumb shit! Stop shooting!" a deputy shouted, running toward him. "You're going to kill someone."

"That Indian just robbed the bank!" Freeman shouted.

With Quinntanna in the lead, the village left the reservation. As they traveled, they took special pains to cover their tracks—sometimes moving across rock where no tracks could be left, other times using routes that were so well traveled that their tracks could not be discerned from those already on the ground.

A few of the young men wanted to let the villagers travel on their own. Now that they had money for guns, they wanted to meet with Blue Horses and Swift Bear, buy the guns, and go on the warpath; however, Quinntanna insisted that their first obligation was to the safety of the old people, women, and children who had managed to survive the attack.

Joe Mayberry, editor of the *Big Rock Sentinel*, removed the paper from the press, then took it over to the composition table to look at it. Big Rock was the fourth town in which Joe had started a newspaper. Joe had a history of coming into a town, starting a newspaper, then when the paper was going well, getting restless, selling it, and moving on. An indication of how solid a newspaperman Joe was was the fact that all of the previous newspapers were still going, being run by the people who had bought Joe out.

Joe wasn't afraid to take an unpopular stand, and often upset his readers with his pointed editorials. He had the notion that this editorial would be one of those.

WAS THE RAID ON THE INDIAN VILLAGE NECESSARY?

All of Big Rock, if not the entire state, knows about the tragic attack against the ranch of Tom Burke. And while most suspect that Indians were responsible for the attack, nearly everyone concedes that the attack had to be carried out, not by the law-abiding Indians we have come to know over the last several years, but by renegade Indians.

Last week Sam Covington, in his recently appointed guise as a colonel in the state militia, led a company of volunteer cavalry in a raid against Purgatory, the Comanche village that is

nearest Big Rock. The number of Indians killed
was quite substantial, whereas not one of Colonel Covington's men received so much as a
scratch. Colonel Covington is hailing it as a very
big victory.

But how big a victory is it? It is now known
that most, if not all, of the Indians killed were
women, children, and the elderly. There were
no young men present at the time of the attack;
therefore, the attack was virtually unopposed.
What that means is, the "Battle" of Purgatory
wasn't a battle at all. It was a slaughter, a slaughter of helpless and innocent Indians.

Yes, I said innocent, for even if those scoun-
drels who raided the Burke ranch were Indians,
they were acting on their own. And a peaceful
Indian village shouldn't be any more responsible for their outlaws than we are for ours. If jus-
tice is to be done here, let it be done against
those who are truly responsible for the evil deeds
done. For to do otherwise is to shift the evil from
the Indians to ourselves.

When Covington finished reading the article, he
let out a roar of displeasure and wadding the newspaper up, threw it into his trash can. The campaign
against the Indians had not generated the kind of
publicity Covington had hoped it would. It was barely
mentioned in the newspapers in the state, and when
it was mentioned, the articles were often as unflatter-
ing as this editorial was.

He wasn't sure that any out-of-state paper had carried any news about the campaign. Why this was, he
had no idea. It wasn't too long ago that every Indian
campaign, regardless of how small it might be, would
receive national coverage. In fact, people were still

talking about Custer's debacle, and that was over ten years ago. As a matter of fact, from the intensity of the interest in Custer still ongoing, Covington was willing to bet they would be talking about the Battle of Little Big Horn one hundred years from now.

So, why weren't they discussing the Battle of Purgatory? Unlike the Battle of Little Big Horn, where every soldier in Custer's command had been killed, in the Battle of Purgatory Covington had lost not one man. By all that was right, Covington should be regarded as a hero throughout the state.

Maybe he just wasn't well enough known yet. Yes, he thought, that had to be it. So, what could he do about it? Maybe he could arrange a speaking tour, telling of the dangers everyone in the state was facing today by being so complacent about the Indians. Yes, that would do it. He would write to Denver and secure the governor's sponsorship for a tour of the state. He knew that some photos had been taken out at Timber Notch Ranch. He could use those gruesome photos to arrange a magic lantern show to illustrate his talk.

He would call his talk "The Cost of Neglect," and he would use the graphic photographs to illustrate what could happen due to a lack of vigilance with regard to the Indians. At that moment, Covington's musing was interrupted by Dingo.

"Yes, First Sergeant," Covington said, "what can I do for you?"

"I was just wonderin' if you had heard about what happened over in Stonewall?"

"Something happened at Stonewall? No, what happened?"

"The Injuns come into a bank with guns blazing. Then they robbed it."

Covington looked up. "You don't say?" he asked,

his interest stirred by the news. "The Indians, you say. Are you sure?"

"Yes, sir, I'm sure."

"Where did you hear this?"

"Why, you can hear about it all over town," Dingo replied. "And they're especially talking about it over in Longmont's Saloon."

"Has Sheriff Carson gotten word of it?"

"I reckon he has," Dingo said. "I figure that's how ever'one else found out about it."

"He got word, and he didn't tell me," Covington replied, the tone of his voice showing his anger. "That's not right. The sheriff is obligated to tell me of any incident involving Indians. I think perhaps it is time I paid a little visit to our noble sheriff," Covington said, reaching for his hat.

"Yes, sir, I thought you might be interested in doing that."

Eighteen

"What do you mean, why weren't you informed?" Monte Carson replied, answering Covington's angry question. "It was a bank robbery. It has nothing to do with you."

"Oh, but I'm afraid it does, Sheriff," Covington replied. "You see, if the Indians robbed—"

"It wasn't Indians, it was one Indian. And the funny thing is, he didn't really rob the bank."

"What do you mean, he didn't rob the bank? You just told me that he did rob it."

"Technically, I suppose he did," Sheriff Carson admitted. "In that he took the money without proper authority. However, the money he took, five thousand dollars, was from the Indians' own account. He tried to write a draft for the money, but he couldn't because the only two men authorized to sign for the money, Stone Eagle and Running Deer, are both dead. You killed them, Covington."

"Are you telling me the Indians had five thousand dollars in their account?" Covington asked.

"Oh, yes. From what I understand, they have nearly fifteen thousand dollars in the account. Quinntanna merely tried to make a withdrawal, and when they wouldn't give the money to him, he took it at gunpoint." Monte chuckled. "And get this. He didn't rob them. He just forced them to accept his draft."

"Yes, well, it doesn't matter. If the person who took the money isn't on the signature card, then the draft is not valid. And if the draft isn't valid, then taking the money at gunpoint is bank robbery. He did take it by force, didn't he?" Covington said, rubbing his hands together excitedly.

"I'll be damned, Covington, if you don't look happy about it," Monte said.

"I'm happy only in that it will wake the people up. I think everyone needs to be aware of the dangers the Indians still present to the peaceful citizens of this great state."

"Bullshit," Monte said. "You're just wantin' an excuse to mount another campaign against them. Only, I don't think you will be able to steal anything from them this time."

"Steal from them?"

"That's what you did, isn't it?"

"It is not what I did. I made a legal confiscation of contraband," Covington said.

"Uh-huh. And if you had done that anywhere other than an Indian reservation, I'd have you in jail right now."

"Yes, well, that's the point, isn't it? I did do it on an Indian reservation."

"I don't know what you plan to take from them now. I'm sure that the Indians don't have anything left. I heard that, in addition to everything else, you also stole a thousand dollars in cash from them."

"As I informed you, Sheriff, the money wasn't stolen. It was part of the legal spoils of war," Covington said.

"Spoils of war," Monte said.

"You say it was Quinntanna who took the money from the bank?"

"Yes. But for the life of me, I can't see why you are so interested. Even if it was a bank robbery, and there is some question as to whether it was, it is a civil affair and has nothing to do with you."

"It does if Quinntanna's action is a direct result of the punitive raid we conducted against Purgatory. And such a reaction on the part of a principal member of the village means that the issue is still unsettled. I'm afraid this moves things to the next step."

"The next step? What do you mean, the next step?"

Covington pulled himself to attention. "Sheriff Carson, it is my unpleasant but necessary duty to inform you that, as of now, Big Rock and all of Las Animas and Costilla Counties are, and will continue to be until further notice, under martial law. From now on, you, your deputies, the mayor, and the city council will be responsible to me. No city or law enforcement business can, or will, be conducted without my express permission."

"What? Have you gone crazy? You can't declare martial law," Monte said in an exasperated and disbelieving tone of voice.

"Oh, but I can, and I have. My commission from the governor is very specific about that. If you have any questions, contact the governor."

"You are doing all this because of the act of one Indian?" Monte asked in disbelief.

"Indians are like cockroaches, Sheriff. Where there is one, there are many." Covington started to leave, but as he got to the door, he turned back to the sheriff. "Oh, please inform the mayor of my decision to declare martial law."

"I shall do so," Monte said. "I shall definitely do so."

Covington left a frustrated and disgusted sheriff behind as he walked quickly down the street to the telegraph office. When he pushed inside, the little bell that was attached to the top of the door rang merrily.

"Be right with you," Fred called from a room at the rear of the office. A moment later he came into the office, wiping his hands on a napkin. "I was just having my lunch," he said. "What can I do for you, Mr. Covington?"

"It is Colonel Covington for the duration," Covington replied.

"Duration? Duration of what?"

"The Indian uprising," Covington said. "But as for what you can do for me, I have a few regulations I am putting into effect."

"Go ahead," Fred invited.

"Effective immediately, you will send no telegram unless the sender has my express, written permission."

"What? I can't do that," Fred said.

"Also, no telegram will be delivered to anyone in town without my clearance. That means that all incoming telegrams must come to me first."

"Mr. Cov—"

"I told you, it is *Colonel,*" Covington said resolutely.

"*Colonel* Covington. I can't do what you ask. The rules and regulations of Western Union are quite specific. Our customers have the absolute right of privacy of communication. If we start running all incoming and outgoing messages through some official somewhere, people will no longer trust us."

"That's Western Union's problem, not mine," Covington said. "You will do what I say, or I will close your office."

"Yes, sir," Fred said contritely.

Leaving the Western Union office, Covington made

his next stop the *Big Rock Sentinel.* Joe Mayberry was sitting at the composing desk, setting type. Because his back was to the door, he didn't see who came in.

"If you have a news story, put it in the basket on the right. If it's an ad, put it in the basket on the left," Joe said without turning around.

"It is neither," Covington said.

Recognizing Covington's voice, Joe sighed and turned toward him. "What is it, Covington?" he asked.

"I did not appreciate the editorial you wrote about our operation," Covington said. "You impugned the action of many brave men."

"Brave?" Joe replied, scoffing. "What is so brave about going into a village in the middle of the night and killing sleeping women, children, and old men?"

"I wouldn't expect someone like you to understand. This was a military matter. What do you know of the military?"

"Sonny, where were you in the first week of July 1863?" Joe asked.

"July 1863? Why, I don't know," Covington replied. "Anyway, what is so significant about that date?"

"I was at Gettysburg, with the First Missouri Brigade," Joe said. "And unlike your midnight murder, Gettysburg was a real battle."

"All right, you were at Gettysburg. I admit that those who fought at Gettysburg may have faced more danger than we faced at the Battle of Purgatory. But unless you have had a command of your own, I still submit that you aren't qualified to discuss things of a military nature."

"Oh, I had a command," Joe said.

"You had a command? What was your command?"

"The First Missouri Brigade."

"Yes, yes, you told me that. What was your command within the brigade?"

A wry smile spread across Joe's face. "The brigade was my command," he said.

Covington gasped. "You?" he asked. "You are a brigadier general?"

"I *used* to be a brigadier general," Joe answered. "Now I'm a newspaperman. Now, are you here just to complain about my editorial? Or do you have something else in mind? What are you doing here?"

For a moment it looked as if Covington was still trying to absorb the fact that this man who published a weekly newspaper in a small Colorado town was once a brigadier general in the greatest war in America's history. "What?" Covington asked, almost distractedly.

"I asked what are you doing here," Joe repeated. "What do you want?"

"Oh, yes," Covington said, regaining his composure. "I want you to print an announcement for me. Effective immediately, all of Las Animas and Costilla Counties are under martial law."

"Martial law? Why?"

"I should think the reason would be obvious to you, Mr. Mayberry. We are in the midst of an Indian uprising. Martial law is necessary to protect the lives of our citizens."

"What exactly are the terms of this martial law?"

"Well, to begin with, I am establishing a ten P.M. curfew. No guns can be carried within the city limits. No guns can be sold without my permission. All legal matters, both criminal and civil, will come through my office. The text of all telegrams, sent and received, must be approved by me. Any gathering of ten or more people shall be construed as an unlawful assembly and those participating in such a gathering will be arrested."

"Are you going to arrest people for going to church?" Joe asked.

"Churches are exempt."

"That's big of you. Schools?"

"Yes, of course, schools are also exempt."

"What about Longmont's? On a good night, he'll have as many as forty patrons. Are you going to close Longmonts?"

"I will allow Longmont's to stay open in order to conduct its normal business. But the patrons of Longmonts will be put on notice that they will not be permitted to conduct a meeting of any sort. And the establishment will be closed by ten P.M."

"You don't really expect to make any of this stick, do you?" Joe asked.

"I do indeed. And finally, Mr. Mayberry, I want it understood by you that any article you print from now on is subject to military censorship."

"What?" Joe exploded in anger. "You can't do that! That is a direct violation of the First Amendment!"

"Disabuse yourself of any idea that you are covered by the Constitution or the Bill of Rights. Those are elements of civil law and authority. Big Rock is now under military law and authority and those personal rights normally guaranteed are withdrawn for the duration of the Indian emergency. I have the authority to prevent assemblies, suspend habeas corpus, close church and school, ban firearms, and censor the press, and I intend to do just that. Do I make myself clear, Mr. Mayberry?"

"Painfully clear," Joe replied.

"Good. See to it that this information is published at once. Don't wait for your next issue. Get an extra edition out."

* * *

Before nightfall that very day, an extra edition of the *Sentinel* was published and distributed. In addition, Covington had signs printed and posted all over town:

To all seeing these greetings
be it known that a state of
EMERGENCY EXISTS BETWEEN OUR
CITIZENS AND HOSTILE INDIANS
Resulting in the Declaration of
MARTIAL
LAW
To be administered by
SAMUEL COVINGTON
COLONEL, CMNDG

One such poster was placed on the batwing doors leading into Longmont's Saloon. Also prominently displayed was notice that a ten o'clock curfew was in effect, and would remain in effect for the duration of the emergency.

As a result of the implementation of martial law, the mood inside Longmont's was somber. Gone was the laughter that was normal when patrons gathered for drinks and friendly card games. Instead of conversation and congenial banter, there were mutterings and complaints about the new order.

"What gets me is why Monte Carson don't do nothin' about it," one of the patrons said.

"What can he do?" another replied. "Since martial law, he ain't actually the sheriff no more."

"Then why don't he send a telegram to the governor and get this changed?"

"Have you forgotten? Any telegram sent out of here has to be approved by Covington. It ain't likely Covington would let that kind of telegram go through."

"I hear tell the militia's getting ready to go after the Injuns again."

"They say they are."

"Well, I never thought I'd hear myself say it, but by God, when it comes to Covington and the Injuns, damned if I wouldn't be on the side of the Injuns."

The comment brought laughter, a rare commodity on this night.

Nineteen

Quinntanna and Teykano watched as Blue Horses and Swift Bear rode toward them, leading two packhorses. Word spread quickly that the weapons had arrived, and by the time the two gunrunners were on the scene, nearly all the young men of Quinntanna's group had gathered around, waiting anxiously for the opportunity to get their hands on a rifle again.

As soon as Blue Horses and Swift Bear arrived, the Indians rushed toward the packhorses and began opening the parcels, disclosing the rifles tied together in bundles of five.

"Ayieee!" one of the Indians shouted in excitement, grabbing a Winchester and holding it over his head in triumph. He pumped his arm and shouted again, his shout igniting excitement in the others.

"You have kept your promise," Quinntanna said.

"You have the money?" Blue Horses asked.

Quinntanna held out the sack of money he had taken from the bank. "Two thousand five hundred dollars. That is what you asked for."

Blue Horses took the money as the Indians began unpacking everything. The excitement waned somewhat when they saw the ammunition.

"Quinntanna, there are not many bullets," Teykano

said, looking at the pitifully few boxes. "There are not even enough bullets to fill all the guns."

"Why is this?" Quinntanna asked angrily. "We have given you much money, all that you asked for."

"This was all the bullets we could get this time," Blue Horses said. "But for one thousand dollars more, we can get many bullets."

"You did not speak of one thousand dollars more," Quinntanna said. "You spoke only of two thousand five-hundred dollars."

"Maybe we will kill you and take the money back," Teykano said, pointing his rifle at the two.

Blue Horses and Swift Bear reacted in fear, but Quinntanna held up his hand. "No," he said. "If we are to make war, we will need bullets and they are the only ones who can bring bullets to us." Then, to Blue Horses, he said, "Bring more bullets. But don't bring them here. We are going to leave this place."

"You will have one thousand dollars more?"

"Yes."

"Where do we bring them?"

"Do you know the place of Howling Winds?"

"Howling Winds is high in the mountains, near Raton Pass," Blue Horses said.

"Yes."

"It is not good to go high in the mountains now. There will be much snow there. Nobody goes high in the mountains when there is much snow."

"That is why we go. There, our people will be safe from the soldiers. If you want to sell more bullets, you must come there."

Blue Horses and Swift Bear looked at each other for a moment. Then Blue Horses nodded. He turned back to Quinntanna. "We will bring bullets to the place of Howling Winds."

* * *

As Cal approached the edge of town, two men came out into the road, holding up their hands to stop him. They were wearing military uniforms. Curious, Cal hauled back on the reins, stopping the team.

"What's going on?" he asked.

"We'll take your gun," one of the soldiers said.

"The hell you will," Cal answered. "Why should I give you my gun?"

"It's the law."

Cal shook his head. "I've lived here a long time," he said. "And I've never heard of such a law. In fact, I don't think Sheriff Carson would even let such a law get passed."

One of the men spat a wad of tobacco at the wheel of the buckboard, then wiped his lips with the cuff of his shirtsleeve.

"Carson ain't got nothin' to do with it," the tobacco-spitting soldier said. "This here town is under martial law."

"Martial law? What does that mean?"

"It means you do exactly what we tell you to do, or else."

"Or else what?"

"Or else you go to jail. Now, you goin' to give us the gun, or not?"

"Take it," Cal said menacingly.

One of the soldiers made a move toward Cal, but almost quicker than he could see it happen, a gun appeared in Cal's hand. The other soldier raised his rifle and started to jack a shell into the chamber, but even as he was operating the lever, Cal was firing. His bullet hit the rifle stock, right in front of the soldier's hand, causing him to drop the weapon.

Both soldiers were stunned into submission.

"You," Cal said, looking at the soldier who still had his rifle, though he wasn't holding it in a threatening way. "Jack out all the shells."

The soldier pumped the lever several times.

"Gun empty?" Cal asked.

"Yeah," the soldier replied.

"Good. Point it at your friend here, and pull the trigger."

"What?"

"You heard me."

The soldier pointed his rifle at his friend.

"Amon, no! What are you going to do?"

Amon hesitated for a second, then jacked the lever one more time. Another cartridge flipped out. He pulled the trigger, and there was a snapping sound as the hammer fell on an empty chamber.

"Now, empty the other rifle and do the same thing."

Again the lever was jacked up and down several times, until a metallic click of the hammer falling on an empty chamber proved that the rifles were empty.

"Pick up the shells and put them in the back of the buckboard," Cal ordered.

The soldiers responded and a moment later, there were fourteen shells lying in the back of the buckboard.

Cal's next move was to make them drop their rifles in a nearby watering trough. Then, and only then, did he feel safe enough to present his back to the two soldiers as he drove into town.

Cal left the buckboard in front of the general store, provided the store clerk with a grocery list, then walked across the street to Longmont's Saloon. He had just greeted Louis Longmont when four armed soldiers suddenly rushed into the room behind him. All had their guns drawn.

"Put you hands up, mister!" one of the soldiers said gruffly. "You are under arrest."

"For what?" Cal said, turning toward them.

The soldiers considered the abrupt turn threatening, and the one nearest Cal slammed the butt of his rifle into Cal's face. Cal went down and out.

Sally wasn't too worried when Cal didn't come back right away. He was young, and enjoyed getting into town, so she figured he had found something to occupy his time. When she happened to look outside late in the afternoon, she saw the buckboard coming up the lane. She smiled and stepped out onto the porch, intending to ask Cal if he'd had a good time. But the smile left her face when she saw that the team wasn't being driven. The horses had returned to the ranch on their own.

The team headed straight for the barn, then stopped. Sally hurried out to the buckboard and looked around. She saw no sign of foul play, but neither did she see any sign of Cal.

"Cal?" she said aloud. "Cal, are you hiding somewhere, playing a trick on me? Because if you are, it isn't funny."

One of the horses whickered, and stamped his foot. Sally went over to him, and patted him gently. "You've been in harness all day, haven't you, boy?" she said gently. "Let me get you out of there."

Sally unhitched the team and turned then into the corral. Then she went back inside and changed out of her dress and into a pair of denim trousers and a red wool shirt. She tied up her hair, then covered it with an old felt hat. After strapping on her Colt .44, she topped the ensemble off with a sheepskin coat. The coat not only provided warmth against the bracing chill, it also completed the picture so that, on casual glance, one would think they were seeing a young man. That was exactly the way Sally wanted it.

It was dark by the time she reached Big Rock. She was just riding past Josh Dobbins's livery when she was challenged.

"Halt!" a voice commanded.

"Halt? Did you say halt?" Sally replied, surprised by the call. She pitched her voice low.

Two men, dressed as soldiers, stepped out of the shadows of the livery. "You packin', mister?"

"What's going on here?"

"We're askin' the questions," the talkative soldier replied. "Are you carrying a gun?"

"Yes."

"Take it out real slow-like, and drop it in the dirt."

"Why should I?"

The talkative soldier jacked a shell into the chamber of his rifle. "Because, by God, I told you to," he said. "Now, do you have any more questions?"

"No," Sally replied quickly. "I'd say that pretty well does it for me." Sally slipped the pistol from its holster and let it fall. She had another one in the pocket of the jacket, but she made no move toward it, nor did she mention it.

"Case you're wonderin' about things, this here town is under martial law."

"Martial law?"

"Yeah. Case you ain't heard, we got us a Injun war goin' on."

"No," Sally said. "I haven't heard anything about it."

"Colonel Covington, he's done took over ever'thing—sheriff's office, telegraph office, the newspaper even. You goin' to spend any time in this town, you better watch your p's and q's."

"Yes," Sally said, still keeping her voice low. "Thanks." She started on into town.

"And whatever it is that you're a-doin', best you have it done before ten o'clock. That's curfew."

As Sally rode down the middle of the street, the sound of her horse's footsteps echoed back from the dark buildings. She had been in Big Rock after dark many times before, but the entire town seemed changed now. It took her a moment to figure it out; then she realized what it was. There was very little sound coming from any of the saloons, no boisterous conversation, and most noticeable of all . . . no laughter.

Sally dismounted in front of Longmont's. Ordinarily, she wouldn't go into a saloon alone, especially at night, even a place like Longmont's. But this wasn't an ordinary situation. Looping the reins around the hitching rail, she went inside.

Longmont's was doing a brisk business, but it didn't look as if anyone was enjoying himself. Rather, the customers were all sitting around with glum expressions on their faces, drinking almost mechanically. Even the bar girls, who normally flitted around like brightly colored butterflies, were sitting together at one table, engaged in quiet conversation. The only animation came from the half-dozen or so men who were in military uniforms.

As usual, Louis was sitting at his table in the back of the room. He was playing solitaire, and he dealt three cards, face-down, then studied the layout in front of him. Sally walked straight to his table.

"What can I do for you, mister?" Louis said, without looking up.

"Louis," Sally said. It was all she said.

Looking up, Louis recognized her, and his face became animated and he started to say something, but was cautioned against it by a small, almost impercep- tible nod from Sally.

"Uh, sit down, mister," Louis said.

Sally sat across the table from him. "Louis, have you seen Cal?" she asked.

Louis nodded. "They've got him in jail."

"Monte has Cal in jail?"

Louis shook his head. "Not Monte. The Army. We're under martial law now."

"Yes, that's what the men said at the edge of town when I rode in. They took my gun."

"One of the first things Covington did was declare that no guns could be carried by anyone but members of the militia."

"What about Monte? Where does he fit into all this?"

"He doesn't fit," Louie said. "In fact, he's not even in town now. He took the afternoon train to Denver to see the governor."

"Why didn't he just send a telegram?"

Louis shook his head. "No telegrams can come or go without Covington's permission."

"Why is Cal in jail? What did he do?"

"Far as I know, the only thing he did was not give up his gun when they asked for it."

"Smoke gave him that gun," Sally said. "He's not likely to give it up to anyone without a fight." She sighed. "I'm going to get him out. Do you know if bail has been set?"

"Bail? I doubt if Covington will allow bail."

"Well, bail or no bail, I'm going to get him out. I can't let him stay there."

"How do you plan to do that?"

"I don't know yet," Sally replied. "But if you've got any ideas, I'd be more than happy to listen to them."

"I've got one idea," Louis said, breaking into a broad smile.

Fifteen minutes later, Louis Longmont was standing in the dark just outside town, behind an old tannery building. The building was unoccupied now, and had been for a few years, ever since the tanning operation went out of business. Now there was nothing left of the once-thriving business, except four walls and a caved-in roof. Louis had bought the property and had plans to build a boot store there, as soon as he cleared the old building away. Tonight was the night he decided to clear the building away.

Louis was holding a bow and four arrows. Each arrow was wrapped in cloth, and each of the cloth wrappings had been soaked in kerosene. Louis lit one of the arrows, fitted it to his bow, pulled the string back, then let the arrow fly. The arrow described a long, high, beautiful, flaming arc through the sky. It landed on what was left of the shake roof of the old tannery building, and almost immediately, the building began burning.

Louis let out a long, bloodcurdling scream, yelling the way he perceived an Indian would yell. Another flaming arrow arced through the dark sky.

"Indians!" someone shouted. "Help, someone! We're being attacked by Indians."

Louis changed positions before he launched the third arrow.

"Where's our guns? Give us our guns so we can defend ourselves!"

A fourth flaming arrow arced through the night sky and though no one in town realized it, this would be the last arrow of the "Indian" attack.

Suddenly, those who did have guns, the militamen,

began shooting out into the dark, toward the direction from which the arrows had been launched. Louis was in no danger, however, because by the time the militia got organized enough to return fire, he was gone. He could hear the ripple of fire as he stepped up onto the porch of his saloon.

"I see 'em!" someone shouted. "There's hundreds of them!"

"Yeah, I see them too!" someone else shouted.

The gunfire increased as the soldiers fired into the woods just out of town. Now, every shadow was an Indian and every branch a warrior, waiting to take their scalp. As Louis stepped into his saloon, he saw Covington running up the middle of the street, heading toward his panicked men.

Louis laughed as he sat back down to the card game.

"All right, Sally, girl, the rest is up to you," he said quietly.

Sally waited in the dark behind the jail. When she heard the shooting, she moved through the shadows to the jail window.

"Cal?" she called. "Cal, you in there?"

"Sally!" Cal said. His head appeared in the window. "What's goin' on? What's all the shooting?"

"Don't worry about it," Sally said. "Anyone else in there?"

"No. The fellas who were here ran outside when the shooting started.

"Any other prisoners?"

"No."

"Good," Sally said. "Get away from the wall, far as you can. Take the mattress off your bed and get under it."

"What are you going to do?"

Sally held up a stick of dynamite. "I'm going to get you out of here," she said.

"I hope you know what you're doing."

"What is there to it besides lighting the fuse?" Sally replied. She struck a match, then held a flame to the fuse. When the fuse started sputtering, she looked up and saw that Cal was still at the window, watching with great interest. "If I were you, I'd get back," she said calmly.

"Oh, shit! I nearly forgot!" Cal said, scurrying to get to the far side of the room. Sally too hurried to get out of the way.

The fuse snapped and sputtered for a moment; then the stick of dynamite exploded with a flash of light and a loud boom. A substantial part of the back wall of the jail came tumbling down.

Sally ran to the wall, then started waving her hand against the smoke and the dust. "Cal!" she called. "Cal, you all right?"

Cal appeared then, coughing and wheezing. "Yeah," he said. "Yeah, I'm fine."

"Let's go."

Cal picked his way through the rubble.

"We're going to have to ride double," she said.

"Wait," Cal said.

"Wait? Wait for what? We've got to get out of here!"

"I ain't goin' anywhere without my pistol," Cal said. "Smoke give me that gun and I'm not leavin' it."

"Cal, don't be an idiot. We can get it later."

"I don't trust these sons of bitches," Cal said, moving along the side of the jailhouse, heading for the front. "I'm going to get it back."

"All right, get it," Sally said. "But hurry up!"

The shooting was still going on at the far end of town, augmented by the shouts of the soldiers and

even a few townspeople. The old tannery was burning
fiercely by now and half the street was lit by the wa-
vering orange glow. Cal sneaked around the corner
of the jailhouse, then slipped inside. He jerked open
the desk drawer, removed his pistol, and strapped it
on.

"What are you doing?" Someone said suddenly,
and Cal looked up to see that one of the men who
had been watching the jail was back. He was standing
in the door, pointing his gun at Cal. "Get back in
the . . ." When he saw the entire back wall gone from
the jail, he gasped. "What in the hell? How did
that . . . *uhng!*" He was interrupted in mid-sentence
by a blow to his head. He fell to the floor unconscious.
There, behind him, stood Sally, her pistol in her
hand.

"Come on, let's go," Sally said. "I don't know how
long he'll be out."

"You're really something, Sally," he said. "If you
weren't already married and if you weren't so old, I'd
marry you."

"Old?" Sally said sharply. "How'd you like to walk
home?"

Cal laughed out loud. "I was teasing, Sally. I was
just teasing," he said.

Hurrying out front, both of them mounted Sally's
horse. Then she urged it into a gallop. Even though
it was carrying double, the horse responded quickly,
and they were out of town before anyone knew they
were gone.

Twenty

Jack Tatum lay on a flat rock halfway up a hill that overlooked a stage depot known as Miller's Switch, named after Tony Miller, the man who ran it. He watched as the coach from Stonewall to San Luis pulled into the station. Even when the stage was several hundred feet away, he could see the horses' sides heaving and the clouds of steam from their nostrils, evidence of the effort they had put out pulling the stage up the long hill. The driver brought the team to a halt, then set the brake.

A middle-aged, heavyset man came out of the way station to meet them.

"Hi, Tony," the driver said to the man who had come to greet them.

"Hey, George," Tony replied. "You made good time this morning. You're about fifteen minutes early."

"It's a good, strong team," George replied.

"Keep this up, you'll be into San Luis before three. How many passengers you carrying?"

"Just four this trip."

"Hope they're all hungry. The missus cooked for eight passengers. You all go on inside, I'll take care of the team."

"Thanks," George replied. Then, yelling down to

the coach, he added, "Okay, folks, we'll change teams here. There's food inside for anyone that wants to eat, and the facilities are out back."

George climbed down from the box. The shotgun guard climbed down as well, leaving his gun under the seat. When the coach door opened, four passengers got out: three women and a man.

From his position on the rock, Tatum watched them cross the yard toward the main building, where they were met at the door by a woman wearing an apron.

"Welcome folks," Tatum heard the woman say. "Come on in. We've got baked chicken and dumplin's today."

Two liverymen who worked at the way station joined Tony then, and the three of them started unhooking the horses so they could change the team.

Tatum slid back down from his position on the rock.

"What's it look like down there?" Pigiron asked.

Tatum smiled. "Looks like we're going to have chicken and dumplin's for dinner," he said.

"That's good, because I'm getting plenty tired of beans, I don't mind telling you."

"Let's go," Tatum said as he mounted his horse.

Tatum and the others moved in single file down the narrow trail that led to the road and Miller's Switch below. They rode by the coach, which was now standing empty and devoid of its team, and headed straight toward the corral. Just inside the corral fence, Tony and his two workers had rounded up fresh horses and were just beginning to put them in harness.

Tony looked up as the riders approached. The expression on his face showed that in addition to his curiosity as to why they were there, he was also a little wary of them.

"Something I can do for you gents?" he asked.

"Yeah," Tatum answered. He pulled his pistol. "You can die." He pulled the trigger and Tony went down.

"What the hell?" one of the liverymen yelled, and both of them started running toward the main house. Tatum's men started shooting at them, and they were hit half-a-dozen times each. One fell facedown in a horse pile in the middle of the paddock; the other made it as far as the fence before he was hit. He fell onto the fence and hung there, half over.

Hearing the shooting outside, George and his shotgun guard came running out of the way station to see what was going on. Although both had drawn their pistols, neither got off a shot, as they were cut down by gunfire almost as soon as they set foot on the front porch.

"Let's go get us somethin' to eat," Tatum said, riding over toward the main house.

The men dismounted in front, tied their horses to the porch-roof support posts, then went inside. Four women and an old man were cowering against the wall on the opposite side of the room, having gotten up from the dining table. The table itself was filled with food-laden plates.

"Who . . . who are you?" the woman with the apron asked, her voice quivering with fear. "And what have you done with Tony?"

"Tony? Would that be the name of the man who runs this place?"

"Yes. Tony Miller. I am Mrs. Miller. This is Miller's Switch and we are host and hostess here. Where is Tony? I want to see him."

"Oh, we shot him," Tatum said matter-of-factly.

"No!" Mrs. Miller cried out. She started toward the door.

"Pigiron," Tatum said, and Pigiron grabbed Mrs. Miller, then pushed her back toward the wall by the others.

"Please, let me help my husband," Mrs. Miller pleaded.

"Lady, there ain't no helpin' him left," Tatum said. "I told you, we shot him. He's dead."

Mrs. Miller hung her head and began weeping quietly.

"See here," the male passenger said, speaking for the first time. "This is an outrage. An outrage. Do you know who I am?"

"No, old man. Who are you?"

"I am John Pierpoint Northington, a member of the State Legislature."

"Is that a fact?" Tatum asked.

"It certainly is a fact, sir."

"What is that supposed to me to me? You expect me to vote for you?" Tatum joked. The others laughed.

"It means that I intend to see to it that you are arrested, brought to trial, and sentenced," Northington said.

"You mean, you don't even intend to bargain for your life?"

"I do not," Northington said.

"Then there is no sense in going on with this conversation, is there?" Tatum pulled his pistol and shot Northington between the eyes. The women screamed as Northington's body was thrown back, then slid down to the floor, leaving a smear of blood on the wall behind him. The old legislator sat on the floor, almost as if it were by design, with his arms down to each side, his palms up, and his eyes open. It was only the ugly black hole in his forehead that belied the tranquil scene.

"My, oh, my, this looks good," Tatum said, putting his pistol away and taking a piece of chicken from one of the plates. He popped the chicken into his mouth. "Uhm, it is good," he said.

"You can't eat that," Mrs. Miller said quietly. "That food is for the coach passengers, the driver and shotgun guard, and those who work here."

"Is it? Well, doesn't look like any of the menfolk are around to enjoy it, does it?" Tatum asked.

"Please, if you'll just wait a short spell, I'll cook something for you and your men."

"Oh, you would do that for us, would you?" Tatum asked. "Well now, that's very . . . Christian . . . of you," he said, laughing at his choice of words. "Especially when we haven't been what you might call friendly since we arrived."

"I'd do it just to get rid of you," Mrs. Miller replied.

Tatum broke out in loud, raucous laughter. "Well, I'll give you this. You don't hold back your thoughts none. And it's a right generous thing you're doin, offerin' to feed us all, particular seein' as I got me a Mexican, two Injuns, and a colored fella ridin' with me," Tatum said. "Are you tellin' me you'd serve their kind in here?"

"Yes," Mrs. Miller said nervously. "If you'll just give me time to do it, I'll serve you and all your friends."

Tatum laughed. "Did you hear that, Jim?" he asked the black man, who was standing back by the wall with his arms folded across his chest. "She called you my friend."

Jim just stared impassively.

"Hell, lady, Jim's no more a friend of mine than you are. He's a colored man who just threw in with us, that's all."

"What are we goin' to do with 'em, Tatum?" Pigiron asked.

"Kill 'em," Tatum said.

The room echoed with the sound of gunfire as Tatum sat at the table and began eating from the plate in front of him.

At first it was just a thin wisp, like nothing more than a column of dust in the distance. But as Smoke, Pearlie, and Tom drew closer, the wisp of dust took on more substance until it became a column of smoke, growing thicker and heavier until finally it was a heavy, black cloud, filled with glowing embers and roiling into the sky.

The fire was still burning and snapping when the three reached Miller's Switch, but there was little left to burn. The main building, the barn, and the outhouses were nothing more than collapsed piles of blackened timbers, with just enough wood remaining to support the dying flames. Not even the stagecoach had escaped, for it sat in front of what remained of the depot, burned down to the wheels.

In addition to the fires, there had been a wanton slaughter of the replacement teams. A dozen horses lay dead in the corral, and there were even several pigs killed. Animals weren't the only victims. They found half-a-dozen bodies lying around as well, including two that were burned beyond recognition.

"Help! Help me, somebody." The voice that called was strained with pain.

"George!" Smoke said, running toward the stagecoach driver, finding him on the ground near the watering trough.

"When did this happen?"

" 'Bout noon," George said.

"Who did it? Was it Indians?"

George shook his head. "Don't know exactly who or what they were. They was whites, Injuns, Mexicans. They even had 'em a colored man with 'em."

"Comancheros," Smoke said. "I knew it. Same as hit your ranch, Tom."

"What happened?" Tom asked.

"I don't rightly know," George replied. "Me'n Pete was inside havin' lunch when we heard someone shootin'. We come out here to see what was goin' on, and the next thing you know, they shot us. I must'a passed out then, 'cause when I come to some later, everything was on fire."

"So you didn't see which way they went?" Smoke asked.

George shook his head. "I don't have the foggiest idea," he answered. "But I can tell you the name of the fella that was leadin' 'em. I was sort of in and out, but I heard 'em talkin'. They called him Tatum."

"Jack Tatum," Tom said. "Yes, it figures now."

Smoke looked George over. He had at least three bullet holes in him, two in the thigh and one in the arm. They were painful, and he had lost a lot of blood, but he would probably live.

"Pearlie, get him patched up as well as you can," Smoke said. "I'm going to look around for sign. This is the closest we've been to those bastards, and I don't plan to let them get away."

"What'll we do with him after I get him patched up?" Pearlie asked.

"George, what time is the next stage due through here?" Smoke asked.

"If nothin' has happened to it, it ought to be here before supper time," George replied.

"We'll wait here with him until then," Smoke said.

"Then we'll put him on the stage and send him back to Stonewall."

While Pearlie attended to his patient, Smoke began looking around. After a few minutes, Tom came over to stand beside him.

"Find something?"

"They came down this way," Smoke said, pointing to the place where a small trail joined the road. "And they left that way," he added, pointing toward another climbing trail.

"Into the Sangre de Cristo range?" Tom asked. "They're going higher into the mountains? That's sort of dumb, isn't it? Nobody goes up there this time of year."

"That's what they are counting on," Smoke said. "They plan to get over on the other side before the pass is closed. If they can do that, they'll get away."

"Lord, I'd hate to think of those murderin' bastards getting away."

"Then don't think about it," Smoke said with a wry smile. "Because they aren't going to get away. We're going to find them, and they are going to pay."

"Now you're talkin'."

Twenty-one

Quinntanna sat astride his horse and watched as the little band in his charge moved slowly by. Some rode horses, some walked, while others—the very old, and those who had been wounded but survived the attack—rode on travois that were pulled behind the horses. All were bundled against the cold. As the people passed by, they looked neither right nor left, but stared straight ahead as they moved laboriously toward the mountains rising in the distance.

Quinntanna had arranged to meet Blue Horses and Swift Bear at the place of the Howling Winds because it was on the trail and it fit in conveniently with his plans. He intended to move the entire village, or at least what was left of it, to the other side of Culebra Peak in the Sangre de Cristo mountain range. If he could get them over the top before the heaviest of the winter storms came, all the passes would then be closed by snow and his people would be safe. But getting them there was easier said than done.

The little party of travelers made a pitiful sight, for there was scarcely one among them who had not lost one or more members of his or her family. There were dozens of children without mothers, mothers without their children, as well as old men and women who had survived the attack but now had no one left to care for them. Quinntanna saw Teykano coming toward him.

"The trail is clear," Teykano said.

"Will we get through before nightfall?" Quinntanna asked.

Teykano shook his head. "I think not. The top is too far away and our people are not moving quickly enough."

"They can't go any faster. They are old, weak, and tired. Some are sick and injured."

"I know," Teykano said. "Some of the others, the young men, want to leave now. They want to find the white men who did this and fight them."

"They would abandon our people?" Quinntanna asked.

"They say we can leave two or three to help our people get across the mountains. The rest can fight. We have guns now."

"What do you think?" Quinntanna asked.

"I think if we did this, who would we leave behind? All want to go, but some must stay because our people cannot get over the mountain alone."

"We will all stay until the people are safe. Then we will all go," Quinntanna said.

Teykano smiled. "I told the young men that you would say this."

"And do they understand?"

"Yes. They did not like it, but they understand."

"Good."

"We will get revenge against the evil ones who did this, won't we?" Teykano asked.

Quinntanna sighed. "How will we get revenge?"

"How? We have guns and some bullets. We are not helpless the way the people of our village were. We will fight the whites."

"Someone attacked the ranch of a white man and

killed many of their people. The whites thought Indians did it, so they attacked our village and killed our people. They didn't know who did it, but their blood was hot so they killed. Would you have us kill innocent whites?"

"Yes!" Teykano replied without hesitation.

"What is to be gained by that? If we kill the innocent, and the guilty go unpunished, how is our revenge satisfied?"

"We must do something, Quinntanna," Teykano insisted. "Our young men have blood that is hot. We cannot tell them that they cannot seek revenge."

"I will find a way to kill the ones who are responsible," Quinntanna promised.

"How will you do this?"

"I don't know," Quinntanna replied. "But if you will tell our young warriors to trust me, I will find a way."

"You are my friend, Quinntanna, and I will trust you," Teykano said. "I will counsel the others to trust you as well. But look into your heart and into your mind and find a way to do this thing you say."

"I will find a way," Quinntanna said again, though even as he was saying the words, he was searching for some way to carry out his promise.

Quinntanna knew about the place where the white man's people-wagons stopped on their journeys between Stonewall and San Luis. It was called Miller's Switch, and it was located just as the trail started climbing into the mountains. He was certain that by now the people at Miller's Switch would have gotten word that a white ranch was attacked and burned. If so, like everyone else, they would believe the Indians were responsible.

If he could have done so, he would have gone around the way station, but because they were following the only passable trail up into the mountain range, that wasn't possible. Therefore, the only thing he could do would be to scout the way station, then pass by as quietly as possible and hope they weren't seen. Informing the villagers to stay where they were for a while, he and Teykano went ahead to check out the depot. When they moved to the edge of the woods, they were surprised to see nothing but burned-out buildings and a burned-out stage.

"Ayiee, what happened here?" Teykano asked.

"I believe the ones who attacked and burned the white ranch did this," Quinntanna said.

"It does not matter who did it. The whites will think we did."

"Yes," Quinntanna. "That is why we must . . ." Quinntanna stopped in mid-sentence. "Teykano, here is where we will get our revenge," he said.

"Here?"

"Yes. It is as you said. It does not matter who attacked here. The whites will think we did it. I believe they will send their soldiers here. I believe they will send the same soldiers here who attacked our village and murdered our people."

Teykano smiled. "And when the soldiers come, we will be here, waiting for them."

"Yes. In the meadow beyond the first rise."

"That is a good plan, my friend," Teykano said. "That is a plan worthy of the warriors of old. But what will we do with our people?"

"We will find somewhere for them to stay. Then we will come back to the meadow and wait for the soldiers."

* * *

As soon as the coach rolled into Big Rock, the driver hurried down to the sheriff's office.

"Monte," he called, stepping inside. "Monte, where are you?" When he saw the big hole in the back wall, he let out a low whistle. Covington was standing inside the open cell, supervising the repair work on the wall. "Oh, my, what happened here?" the driver said.

"We had a prisoner escape."

"I'll say you did."

"What can I do for you?" Covington asked.

"I'm looking for the sheriff."

"He's in Denver. I'm in charge here now."

"You're in charge? Who are you?" the driver asked.

"Colonel Sam Covington, temporarily the military administrator for Las Animas and Costilla Counties."

"Military administrator? I've never heard of such a thing."

"I've placed both counties under martial law," Covington said. "Now, I'll ask you again. What did you want with the sheriff?"

"Well, since you're in charge, I suppose I can tell you," the driver said. "Miller's Switch has been hit."

"Hit?"

"Attacked and burned. Miller, his wife, the men who worked for them, all the coach passengers were killed. Jeb, the shotgun guard was also killed, but looks like the driver might pull through. I dropped him off at the doc's office back in Stonewall."

"We've got 'em!" Covington said, hitting his fist in his hand and grinning broadly. "First Sergeant Dingo, assemble the troop! We're going to Miller's Switch."

"What about these two?" Dingo asked, indicating the two men who were laying brick to patch the hole in the back wall.

"Them too," Covington said. "We'll let Sheriff Carson worry about his wall. I don't intend to let these Indian bastards get away from us."

"Yes, sir," Dingo said. "Come on, men, help me round everyone up."

"Excuse me," the driver said after the others left. "Did you say you didn't intend to let the Indians get away with this?"

"That's right."

The driver shook his head. "It wasn't Injuns."

"What wasn't Indians?"

"Them people that hit Miller's Switch. They wasn't Injuns."

"What makes you say that?"

"George told me. He was there, he seen it all. He said they was just a bunch of outlaws."

"Are you trying to tell me that it wasn't Indians who did this?" Covington asked.

"George said they might have been one or two Injuns with 'em, but it was white folks, Mexicans, they even had 'em a colored man with 'em."

"And Indians," Covington insisted.

"Well, yeah, that's what I said. But accordin' to George, there was only one or two of 'em was Injuns."

"That's good enough for me," Covington said. "One Indian, one hundred Indians, far as I'm concerned, they're the ones behind it."

"Yeah, well, whatever you say. I've got to get back over to the depot. The stage is goin' on through to Trinidad."

The driver started toward the door, but Covington called to him. "What's your name, driver?"

"Simpson. Arnold Simpson."

"Simpson, you keep quiet about what you have told me here. I don't want you shooting your mouth off to anyone."

"You mean about it not being Injuns?" Simpson replied.

"I mean I want you keep your mouth shut, period. This is a military matter now, and if I find that you have been shooting off your mouth, you could wind up on the gallows."

"On the gallows?" Simpson replied. "What the hell have I done that you can threaten to hang me?"

"If you start spouting off military information, some of it might get back to the Indians we are going after," Covington said. "If that happens, and if even one of my men are killed because they have advance information, then you'll be tried for murder, you will be found guilty, and you will hang."

"You've got no right to talk to me like that," Simpson said.

"On the contrary, Mr. Simpson. I have every right. That is the nature of martial law. The administrator, that's me, has absolute authority. The citizens, that's you, have no rights except the rights I let you have."

Sheriff Monte Carson sat in the outer chamber of the Governor's office at the capital building in Denver. He had been waiting for some time, and as he held his hat in his hand, he fiddled with the hatband. Finally, the governor's personal secretary came over to him.

"Sheriff, Governor Cooper will see you now."

"Thanks," Monte said, rising from his chair.

Governor Cooper was a large man with puffy cheeks and a well-groomed handlebar mustache. A lawyer, he had moved to Colorado from Illinois several years ago and had become wealthy, not only in the law business, but also in insurance, mining, and

WARPATH OF THE MOUNTAIN MAN   201

cattle. With a politician's smile and an extended
hand, he came halfway to the door to greet Monte.

"Sheriff Carson, it's good to see you again," the
governor said. "How are things down in Las Animas
County?"

"Not good, Governor," Monte answered.

"Oh? I heard about the Indian uprising, but it was
my belief that Colonel Covington had things well under control."

"Perhaps too much control," Monte suggested.

"What do you mean?"

"Governor, Sam Covington has established martial
law. And under the auspices of that declaration, he
has suspended all civil rights. No telegrams can be
sent or received, the newspaper is under his direct
censorship, I have been relieved of my duties, the
mayor and city council have been relieved of their
duties, he has established a ten o'clock curfew, and
abolished the right of peaceful assembly. And he has
done all of that under your authority."

"What?" Governor Cooper replied, barking the
word out. "Has the man lost his mind? I granted him
no such sweeping power as you describe!"

Monte smiled. "I'm glad to hear you say that, sir.
In fact, I was sure you would say that. That's why I
came up here to see you."

The governor returned to his desk, then took out
a piece of paper and began writing. "I am hereby
revoking this martial law. In fact, I am revoking his
commission. Sheriff, I am charging you with the re-
sponsibility to reestablish civil law. Do you want a
document to that effect?"

"Thank you, Governor, but with Covington out of
the way, I don't need any further documents. As the
duly elected sheriff, I already have the mandate to

reestablish and uphold civil law. And that I intend to do."

"I'm glad you came to see me," the governor said. "And please keep me informed of what happens down there."

"I will, sir," Monte said.

Twenty-two

Covington's Cavalry had been on the trail for half the morning the next day, when Dingo came across Indian sign indicating scores of horses, plus the tracks of a dozen or more travois. He pointed it out to Covington, who immediately halted the march, then ordered his officers and noncommissioned officers to a conference.

As the officers and NCOs arrived, Covington was sitting casually in his saddle with one leg hooked across the pommel. He was distractedly tapping that leg with his riding quirt and he smiled broadly at his officers.

"Well, gentlemen, it would appear this is our day," he said. "Do you see this?" He pointed to the ground behind him where the Indian trail could be easily seen, from the hoofprints and travois tracks to the horse droppings. "The hostiles have made it easy for us. They have practically sent us an open invitation."

"Colonel, doesn't that worry you a little?" Captain Roach asked.

"Worry me? No. Why in heavens name should it worry me?"

"I mean, think about it for a moment," Roach said. "These are people who can make their trail disappear. Now, all of a sudden, it's almost as if they are putting up signposts saying, 'This way.' And that's not bothering you?"

"What are you suggesting, Captain Roach?"

"I'm just saying that we aren't exactly sneaking up on them. From the looks of things, they're moving their entire camp, including women, children, and dogs. It just doesn't seem right they would make it so easy for us to track them."

"Well, Captain, have you considered the fact that they may have no choice?" Covington asked.

"I'm not following you, sir."

"I mean, even Indian horses have to eat," Covington said, as if explaining something to a child. "And what goes in at the front of the horse, inevitably comes out at the rear." Covington pointed again to the trail. "Unless they have their squaws following behind picking up horse turds, they are going to be easy to follow."

Several of the others laughed at the mental image of a group of Indian women walking along behind the horses, picking up the horses' droppings. Captain Roach, without laughing, took his hat off and examined it for a moment.

"That's what I'm talking about, Colonel. You see, I've seen squaws do just that."

"You've fought Indians before, have you, Roach?"

"I have."

"Why is it you haven't mentioned it before now?"

"I was with the Seventh during the little fracas we had up in Montana a few years ago. Custer rode into a trap, and you see what happened to him."

"You were with Custer?"

"That's right. In Reno's Battalion. The reason I haven't mentioned it before is because it isn't something I'm very proud of. Fact is, I joined with you to sort of even up the score."

"And now you're getting nervous that something like that might happen to us?"

"I'm saying that we could be riding into a trap, yes, sir."

"Nonsense. What happened to Custer was the result of pure numbers. There were a lot more Indians than there were soldiers. Well, plainly, we don't have that situation here. We outnumber the Indians. And as far as riding into a trap?" Covington laughed, a scoffing laugh. "Believe me, I know Indians, and I know that they aren't smart enough to conceive such a thing."

"I hope you are right."

"I am right," Covington insisted. "Now, here is my plan. I'm going to form four squadrons. Captain Roach, you will take one squadron, go south for one mile, then ride west, parallel with our line of march. Lieutenant Conklin, you will take one squadron to the north of our line of march, then proceed west in parallel with our course. That will leave two squadrons, which I will lead, right up the middle of the trail until we encounter the savages. And then, gentlemen, we will attack, leaving the squadrons on each wing in position to cut off any possible retreat."

"Colonel, you are going to divide the command?" Roach asked.

"Do you have a problem with that?"

"If we divide our command, no single element will outnumber the Indians. And I would remind you, Colonel, that Custer divided his command."

"Stop comparing me with that fool Custer," Covington said.

"Very well, sir. Shall we agree upon some signal for assistance?" Roach asked.

Covington chuckled. "I scarcely think that will be the problem," he said. "No, sir, the problem will be in keeping them from running away. All right, gentlemen, let us proceed."

Roach and Conklin pulled their squadrons away in accordance with Covington's instructions, while Covington continued right up the path of broken and chewed grass and brown and green horse apples.

"Well, First Sergeant Dingo, it's clear to see that Roach doesn't agree with me. What do you think of my plan of battle?" Covington asked.

"You're the commander, Colonel, and it's your plan. It don't matter what Roach thinks."

"My sentiments exactly," Covington said. It didn't dawn on him that Dingo's reply was rather nonspecific without offering an endorsement.

Covington stopped the advance while he stared through a pair of field glasses. "Damn," he said aloud. "How the hell did they get over there?"

"Beg your pardon?" Dingo asked.

Covington pointed toward a cloud of dust in the distance, south of the direction they were traveling.

"It would seem that the Indians have left us a broad highway to travel while they positioned themselves for an attack at my flank. Captain Roach is about to be engaged. Dingo, I want you to overtake Captain Roach. Tell him that I will send Conklin around to cut off any possible retreat, and instruct him to strike at the enemy at once. Do you have that? He is to attack at once."

"Yes, sir," Dingo said.

The ground over which Dingo rode ascended in a long, gradual slope that made riding relatively easy, and a short time later he pulled up at the head of Roach's column.

"Has Covington seen them?" Roach asked, indicating the Indians in front of him. Here, the trail had opened into a high meadow.

"Yes, sir. He says you should strike against them from the front as soon as you can engage them."

"A frontal assault?" Roach asked.

"That's what he said. He's moving Conklin's squadron in position to block the Indians' retreat, while he comes to your support."

"He is coming to support?"

"That's what he said, Captain."

Roach sat his saddle for a moment, then sighed. "All right," he said. "Will you be joining me, Sergeant Dingo?"

"Yes, sir."

"I'm glad. It'll be good to have another man with experience. You take the left side, I'll take the right." Roach stood in his stirrups and addressed his command.

"Men, I think you should understand that this won't be like the attack on the village. There, we killed women, children, and old men. They were unarmed and they were asleep." He pointed toward the Indians. "These are warriors, armed, deadly, and ready for us."

What had started out as a lark suddenly changed, and the men experienced fear for the first time. The horses as well seemed to sense the impending danger, perhaps from the men atop them, and they grew a bit skittish. A couple of the horses began nervously prancing around, moving in and out of the line. A couple of the riders had to turn their mounts in a full circle to get them back into position.

"Forward at a trot!" Roach shouted, and the squadron started out across the meadow.

"They are coming," Teykano said.

Although the total number of soldiers was greater

than the total number of Comanche, Quinntanna had outmaneuvered Covington. In addition, Covington had split his forces so that, as the two bodies of men came together, the Comanche would be the superior force on the field.

"Good. We are ready for them," Quinntanna replied.

The soldiers' advance surged forward at top speed, and soon the sound of galloping horses' hooves was like rolling thunder. Above all the noise, though, the soldiers could clearly hear the Indians as they whooped and shouted in anticipation of battle. They hurtled toward one another. There were two armies: one uniformed, the other in buckskin—both determined.

As the two groups closed on each other, both sides opened fire. In the opening fusillade, both Indians and soldiers went down with bleeding bullet wounds. Then the enemies came together in closer, more brutal combat, saber against war club. In that battle the Indians had the clear advantage, for they had used war clubs their entire lives for everything from games to hunting, whereas the soldiers were, for the most part, unfamiliar with and untrained in the use of the saber.

Dingo was one of the first to go down, his head bashed in by a blow from a war club. Seeing Dingo killed, many of the men panicked and started running. Roach tried to rally them, but he was killed as well. When the others realized that they no longer had anyone in command, they quit fighting and turned to gallop away, leaving three fourths of their original number dead on the field behind them. Some of the Indians started after the few remaining survivors, but Quinntanna called them back.

"Let them go!" he shouted. "More soldiers are coming. We must be ready for them!"

When Lieutenant Conklin brought his squadron up, he thought he would be providing support for Roach. Instead, he arrived at the spot where the battle had taken place, marked by the bodies lying on the field. And among the dead, there were many, many more wearing uniforms than there were wearing buckskins.

"Lieutenant! There's Captain Roach!" one of the men said, pointing to Roach's bloodied body.

"And Dingo!" another said.

Suddenly, and from all around them, Indians sprang up, screaming hideous war yells. It was as if they had just materialized, so good had been their concealment. The Indians opened fire, shooting as fast as they could cock and fire their rifles. Bullets whistled through Conklin's command, slamming into men and horses. There were shouts of panic and screams of pain as the Indians pressed their attack, firing almost methodically into the demoralized soldiers. Very few soldiers even had the presence of mind to return fire.

"Retreat! Retreat!" Conklin shouted. He would have given the order a third time, but he was hit in the temple with a bullet. As if shooting cows in a pen, the Indians continued to work the levers on their rifles, firing at the soldiers until every last one was dead. Then, and only then, did the shooting stop.

"Aiyee!" one of the Indians yelled, realizing that their victory was complete. The others began yelling and shouting as well.

"Collect the guns and bullets!" Quinntanna said.

"Hurry! We must go now! We must return to our people and get them through the pass to safety."

Colonel Covington, who had started toward Roach to support him, was surprised to see just over half-a-dozen men in uniform galloping toward him. They were shouting long before they were close enough to be heard or understood. Finally, the gallopers reached Covington's two squadrons.

"Hold it!" Covington shouted. "Hold up here! What's going on?"

"Dead!" one of the men said. "They're all dead!"

"Who is all dead?"

"All of them! All the rest of Roach's squadron. And Conklin's squadron as well."

Covington shook his head. "No, that's impossible," he said. "They can't all be dead."

"Colonel, you want to go look for yourself?" one of the six soldiers said. All had panic-stricken faces, and all were breathing hard from the exertion of their wild flight.

"Give me those glasses," Covington said, reaching his hand out toward a nearby sergeant. The sergeant handed the binoculars to Covington, who raised them to his eyes to study the meadow. He swept his vision back and forth across the field in front of him.

"I don't see anyth . . . holy shit!" Covington said in mid-sentence. He trained the glasses on one spot.

"What do you see, Colonel?" asked the sergeant.

"Bodies," Covington replied. "Lots of bodies." Sweeping the field beyond the bodies, Covington saw several Indians leaving the field.

"Do you see any Indians?" someone asked fearfully. Covington continued to study the retreating Indians. By rights, he should be going after them. Sighing, he lowered the glasses.

"What are they doing?" his sergeant asked.

"What is who doing?" Covington replied.

"The Indians. What are they doing?"

Covington sighed. "There are no Indians," he said. "They seem to have left the field. Come on, lets take care of our dead, then go back home. We are going to have to reorganize before we can continue this campaign. By God, maybe people will listen to me now. We have a full-blown Indian war on our hands, as big and dangerous as any uprising in the past."

"For many years, our people will sing around the campfire of our great victory on this day," Teykano said excitedly as they rode back to the place where they had left their people.

"I think not," Quinntanna answered.

"What? How can you think that? In all the stories of our people, there has never been a war chief like you. And there has never been a victory like the one we had today."

"Perhaps this is so," Quinntanna agreed. "But I think our village will be no more. Too many were killed. There are no young women for our young men. There are no children to grow up to be warriors and wives, no squaws to have new children. I think soon our young men must go to other villages and other places to find women, and when they do, they will not come back."

"You are right," Teykano said. "The village of Stone Eagle is no more." He was silent for a moment, then he smiled. "But those who came in the night to murder our people are no more as well."

"Yes," Quinntanna agreed, joining Teykano's smile

with his own. "At least those who came to murder our people are now dead."

"What about the place of Howling Winds?" Teykano asked. "Shall we go there now to buy bullets?"

"There is no need to buy bullets now. The white man's army has provided us with many bullets, and we did not have to spend one thousand more dollars."

Twenty-three

Much higher in the mountains, almost all the way to the top of the pass, Tatum relieved himself, then turned back toward Blue Horses and Swift Bear. "You are certain they said they would meet us in the place of the Howling Winds?"

"Yes," Swift Bear replied.

"And you are sure this is the place of the Howling Winds?" Pigiron asked.

"I think it must be," Sanchez said. "Can you not hear the winds howling like the cry of El Diablo?"

"This is the place," Tatum said. "I've been here before."

"Maybe the Injuns ain't goin' to show up," Pigiron suggested.

"They'll show up. They want the bullets," Tatum insisted.

"How long are we going to wait for them?"

"As long as it takes."

"For a lousy thousand bucks, we are going to stay here for as long as it takes?"

"More than a thousand bucks," Tatum said.

"What do you mean, more than a thousand bucks?" Pigiron asked. "Ain't that what we said we'd sell the rest of the ammunition for?"

"Well, for one thing, there ain't no more bullets to

sell. We didn't get any more. So what difference does it make how much we told Quinntanna we would sell the bullets to him for? And for another thing, if Quinntanna has a thousand dollars, then you can believe he has much more than that on him. So I figure that when we meet up with him, we'll just take all of it."

"Yeah, well, I don't like being this far up in the mountains at this time of the year," Pigiron said. "What if the snow comes in and traps us? What then?"

"You afraid of a little snow?" Tatum asked.

"Damn right I'm afraid. Ain't you ever heard of the Donner Party?"

"Donner Party?" Tatum replied. He shook his head. "No, I ain't never heard of nothin' called a Donner Party."

"They was a group of people tryin' to go West by wagon train," Pigiron explained. "Only, they got started too late, and they wind up getting theirselves caught up in the mountains at a place called Donner Pass. Thing is, Donner Pass was filled up with snow, and they couldn't go through it, and they couldn't go back, so they had to just stay there. But pretty soon, just staying there where they was, they run out of food."

"You tellin' me a whole wagon train of people starved to death?" Tatum asked.

"Not all of 'em starved. Some of 'em made it through by eatin' the dead."

"They done what?" Tatum gasped.

"They got so hungry they et the ones that had already died."

"They did no such thing!" Tatum said.

"Yes, they did. I can't believe you ain't never heard that story. It was in all the newspapers and everything."

"Yeah, well, it ain't goin' to happen to us," Tatum said. "Now, ever'body pick 'em out a position and stay there 'till the Injuns come. Once they're here, open up on 'em. We'll kill 'em all, ever last one of 'em. Then we'll take whatever money we can find on 'em." Suddenly, and inexplicably, Tatum smiled broadly. "Not only will we get the money, we'll get the credit for killin' off the Injuns that's been raisin' hell around here. Why, we'll be heroes."

It was very cold, and as Quinntanna moved his village higher into the mountains, vapor clouds formed around the noses and mouths of the horses and people. The tops of the mountains were shrouded by a low-lying bank of clouds, and here and there Quinntanna could see patches of snow, lying brilliantly white in the sunshine and dark azure in the shadows. To spare the horses for the climb, Quinntanna made all but the very lame dismount, or leave the travois, and walk, so as not to overtax the animals. Teykanno came up to walk beside him.

"I do not know if our people will get through," he said.

"We must," Quinntanna replied. "For only after we are on the other side will we be safe."

Teykano pointed to the cloud-covered spine at the mountain's top. "It is as if the Great Spirit himself is guarding the pass."

For the next hour they continued up the trail, step by laborious step. What little sun there had been earlier was gone now, and it turned into a dark, dreary day—so heavily overcast that the exact position of the sun couldn't be made out, even by the faintest glow. Individual clouds couldn't be seen either, for a thick blanket shrouded the towering mountains so effectively that the peaks disappeared into the slate gray sky itself. Finally, as they reached a high plateau, Teykano came to Quinntanna and asked him to call a halt.

"We can't stop now," Quinntanna said. "We are not even halfway up the mountain."

"Night is coming," Teykano said. "If we continue, some of our people might get lost in the darkness. Is it not better to keep everyone together?"

With every fiber of his being, Quinntanna felt that it was best to keep going, but as he looked into the faces of the people he was trying to lead to safety, he gave in. "Very well," he said with a surrendering sigh. "We will stay here tonight."

They camped where they stopped. Later, when they threw their blankets and skins out on top of the snow, Teykano came over to Quinntanna.

"Quinntanna, I am sorry if you think I betrayed you."

Quinntanna looked at Teykano in surprise. "Betrayed me? How do you think you have betrayed me?"

"I know you wanted to go on."

"Yes, but I think you are right. I do not believe our people could have gone any farther."

A flash of golden light suddenly illuminated the area. Along with the light came a wave of heat. Quinntanna looked toward the source of heat and illumination, and saw that someone had set fire to some mossy scrub brush.

"Uhm, that is good," Quinntanna said. He and Teykano moved their blankets and skins closer to the burning bush, joining with the others who were also finding positions around the fire. They sat there for a long moment, as if mesmerized by the flames. The burning shrub popped and snapped as it was consumed. And because they were exhausted by their labors, they fell asleep easily, warmed by the fire.

They were oblivious to the cold, oblivious to the precariousness of their position, and oblivious to the large flakes of snow that, just after midnight, began tumbling down through the blackness.

The snow fell silently, moving in unnoticed by the sleeping Indians.

When Smoke Jensen woke up in the morning, he was immediately aware of the change that had taken place since the night before. Last night, he had gone to sleep on top of the snow. This morning, he awoke under it. A pristine blanket of snow covered everything in sight. The trail that he had been following was no longer visible. Neither was the trail behind them. There were no footprints, no signs of the encampment that he, Pearlie, and Tom had made. Everything was completely covered in a mantel of white. It was as if man had never been here before, and yet he knew that the ones who had attacked Miller's Switch, the people he suspected had attacked Tom Burke's ranch, were ahead of them.

The scenery was spectacular this morning, not only because of the new-fallen snow, but also because the air had been washed clean. Whereas low-hanging clouds had shrouded the mountains yesterday, today the clouds were all gone, and even the most distant mountains were clearly visible.

"Pearlie, Tom, wake up," he said.

Tom and Pearlie woke up, then tossed their snow-covered blankets aside to look around

"Holy shit, look at this," Tom said.

"So, what do we do now?" Pearlie asked. "Do we backtrack, or do we go ahead?"

"If Tatum and his bunch got over the pass, it won't do us any good to go ahead," Tom said. "There's no way anyone can get through that pass now."

"On the other hand, if they didn't get through the pass before this snow, there is no way they can get through either. That means that we may have them trapped, and they can't get away without coming back through us," Smoke said. "I think we should press on."

"Damn! If this ain't the shits!" Pigiron said, looking up toward the pass. He turned toward Tatum. "I told you last night, we didn't have no business staying here. Now what?"

"We go back down, that's what," Tatum said.

"Even goin' back down ain't goin' to be all that easy," Pigiron insisted. "I mean, look at those folks in the Donner Party."

"Will you shut up about the Donner Party?" Tatum said. "I don't believe there was such a thing anyway. Everyone up. Get saddled, but we'd better lead the horses down."

There was a good deal of grumbling as the men started breaking camp.

"You know what I think?" Wheeler said. "I think we ought to divide up the money and go out on our own."

"That's what you think, is it?"

"Yeah. I mean, we've got enough money to have near three hundred dollars apiece if we was to divide it now. That's pretty good money."

"You'd have it spent on liquor, women, and cards in one night," Tatum said.

"Yeah, but at least I'd have me a good time that one night," Wheeler said.

"How would you know?" Pigiron asked. "You'd get drunk first thing; then you wouldn't remember any of it."

The others laughed.

Swift Bear had been leading the way back down the trail. Now he came back up the trail quickly.

"Men come," he said.

"Men? What men? Injuns?" Tatum asked.

"White men."

"Who the hell could that be?" Pigiron asked.

"I don't know," Tatum said. "But whoever they are, it ain't good."

"What are we going to do?"

"We're goin' to kill 'em," Tatum said. "Everyone, get in position. Soon as you figure you got yourself a pretty good shot, take it."

"What about the horses?" Pigiron asked.

"Leave 'em, they ain't goin' nowhwere," Tatum said. "They can't move any better'n we can."

Tatum, Pigiron, Wheeler, Sanchez, Arino, Swift Bear, Blue Horses, and Jim moved on down the trail for a short distance, then found places of cover and concealment while they waited for whoever was coming up the trail. Jim, because he had the buffalo gun, and also because he tended to keep himself separated from the others anyway, moved a little farther down the trail.

Smoke, Pearlie, and Tom trudged through the deep snow as they climbed the trail. They had left their horses behind them for the simple reason that they couldn't ride them anyway, and there was no need to wear them out. The man in the lead had the most difficult task of the three, since he had to break through the snow, whereas the two following could move through the trail he cut. Because of that, they traded off the lead position about every fifteen minutes. They had just traded positions, and now Tom Burke was in the lead.

"You think we'll find them on this side of the pass?" Pearlie asked.

"I hope we find them," Tom said. "I hope we find them half froze to death."

Pearlie laughed. "Just half froze to death?"

"Damn right. I want the pleasure of finishin' them off my—"

Tom's sentence was interrupted by the angry buzz of a bullet. It creased his cheek, bringing blood, then ricocheted off a snow-covered rock. The sound of the rifle shot rolled down the mountainside.

"Down!" Smoke shouted, diving for cover behind a nearby rock. The other two did the same.

"What the hell was that?" Pearlie asked.

"From the sound of it, I would say that was a .52-caliber buffalo gun," Smoke said. "Isn't that what you would say, Tom?"

"Sounded like it to me," Tom replied.

"You all right?"

"Yeah, just a nick in the cheek. You see anything?" Tom asked.

Even as Tom was asking the question, Smoke was looking up the trail. He saw a flash of light and a puff of smoke, followed by the angry whine of a bullet. An instant later, he heard the sound of the gunshot.

"Tom, do you see that cone-shaped rock off to your left about five hundred yards up the trail?"

"No," Tom said.

"See the three rocks together there?"

"Yes."

"Look just to the left of them. What do you see?"

"Nothing," Tom said.

"Damn, you aren't in position."

Another bullet whined by.

"Toss your buffalo gun to me," Smoke said.

Tom raised up to his knees, then tossed the rifle to Smoke. Smoke caught it, then got back down in position. He rested the rifle on the log in front of him while he drew a bead on the cone-shaped rock about five hundred yards up the trail. He waited until he saw a shoulder, then half a head, then an entire head move into position. It was Jim, getting ready to take another shot.

"Damn," he said. "It's a black man."

"The driver said there was a black man with the ones who hit Miller's Switch," Tom said.

Smoke put the front bead right on the black shooter's forehead, then squeezed the trigger. The rifle boomed, and rocked back against his shoulder. A second later, his target fell out from behind the rock, face-down, arms spread in the snow. His rifle slid down several feet in front of him.

"You got 'im!" Pearlie said.

"Tatum, they got Jim!" Pigiron called.

"I saw it. You think I'm blind?" Tatum replied.

"Who is it? Who's down there?" Pigiron said.

Suddenly Tatum got a glimpse of two of the men. One was Jensen, the other was Tom Burke.

"Son of a bitch. It's Jensen!" Tatum said.

Twenty-four

"Tom!" Smoke called. "See if you can work your way over here to where I am!"

Tom nodded, then drawing a deep breath, made a run from his position behind a tree over to the log where Smoke had taken cover. As he dashed across the open area, Tatum and all of his men shot at him, and their bullets whined passed him, but he wasn't hit. When he closed to within five yards of the log, he dived headfirst, and slid through the snow for the last couple of feet. He lay behind the log for a moment, panting for breath.

"You all right?" Smoke asked.

Still drawing air in in deep, cold gasps, Tom nodded his head in the affirmative.

"Good," Smoke said. He handed Tom's rifle back to him. "Here's you rifle."

Tom's eyes grew wide. "You called me over here to give me my rifle?"

"Hell, yes," Smoke said, laughing. "You didn't think I was going to run across that open area to give it to you, did you?"

Tom blinked, not certain if Smoke was teasing or not.

"I called you over here because you've got a better view from here," Smoke said. "I want you to use that long gun to cover us while Pearlie and I move up the hill toward them."

"Whoa!" Pearlie said from his position about ten feet away. "You and me are going to charge up that hill after them? We didn't vote on that, did we? Because I don't remember casting my vote."

"I voted for you," Smoke said.

"Oh, well, that's different then," Pearlie replied. "I mean, as long as I got a chance to vote."

Tom took a handful of shells from his pocket, then wiped the snow away to have a place to put them. He opened the breech, flipped out the empty shell casing from the shot Smoke had taken, then slid a new shell in. Closing the breech, he laid the weapon across the log and pointed it in the general direction of Tatum's men.

"All right," he said. "I'm ready. If I see anyone drawing a bead on either of you, I'll pick him off."

"Good man. Pearlie, you ready?"

"I guess I have to be, seein' as I've already voted on it," Pearlie replied.

Smoke pointed to the left. "Looks like there are several rocks, trees, and logs over there," he said. "You work your way up on that side. I'll go up the right."

"Give me the word," Pearlie said. Gone was the joking. He was all business now.

Smoke and Pearlie started up the trail toward Tatum. They were violating every dictum in the book of military strategy, a book that says that those on the attack need many more men than those in defense in order to balance the scales. And if the attack is made against higher ground, then the number needs to be even greater.

Smoke and Pearlie were only two men, and they were attacking seven men, seven men who had good positions of cover on higher ground. As Smoke and

Pearlie worked their way up the hill, they heard Tom's rifle bark from behind them, and at almost the same time, they saw one of Tatum's men pitch forward in the snow.

Now there were only six.

"Sanchez!" Tatum shouted. "Damn you, Jensen, you just killed Sanchez. He was my friend!"

"Who are you trying to fool, Tatum?" Smoke replied. "People like you don't have friends."

"I'm going to kill you, you son of a bitch!" Tatum shouted.

Smoke saw one of Tatum's men rise up slightly to have a look around. That little bit of exposure was all Smoke needed and he fired, then saw his target fall back.

"Tatum, he got Paco," someone yelled.

"Shut up, Pigiron! No need lettin' him know about it!" Tatum replied.

Now there were five.

Another of Tatum's men tried to get into position to take a shot, and when he did so, he exposed himself to Tom's buffalo rifle. A loud boom, and he went down. Almost immediately after that, Pearlie got one. In less than a minute, Tatum's numerical advantage had disappeared. There were now only three of the outlaws left.

"I'm getting' the hell out of here!" Pigiron shouted.

"Me too!" Wheeler said.

"Don't you leave me here, you cowardly bastards!" Tatum shouted.

The two men stood then, and firing wildly back down the hill, tried to run. Pearlie and Smoke took them out with one shot each.

* * *

"White men!" Teykano said, hurrying back down the trail to join Quinntanna.

"Soldiers?"

"No."

"Then who?" one of the other Indians asked.

"I think I know who," Quinntanna said.

"Who?" Teykano asked.

"Those who burned the stagecoach house. I believe also they are the ones who attack the white man's ranch."

"Then they are the ones who brought trouble to us," Teykano said.

"Yes. They are the reason our families are no more," another said.

"Let us make war on them, Quinntanna," Teykano said. "Let us make war on them. Then our revenge will be complete."

Quinntanna looked at the little band of people he was leading. He did not want to leave them unprotected. But neither did he want the opportunity for revenge against those who brought so much sorrow to his village to pass him by. He looked into the eager faces of the warriors around him.

"Very well," he said. "We will make war."

Quickly, Quinntanna moved his people into shelter. The shelter played the dual role of keeping them out of the elements as well as safe from discovery. Once they were safely in place, Quinntanna moved up the trail a few yards, then examined the area thoroughly. Not until he was satisfied that the encampment was totally secure did he give orders to the others.

"We go now," he said.

One of the Indians let out a war whoop, but he was quickly shushed by the others, who realized the importance of silence for this particular war party.

* * *

One mile up the trail from where the Comanche were making their encampment, Smoke, Pearlie, and Tom were waiting. It had been several minutes since Pigiron and Wheeler were killed, and Smoke was certain that only one man remained. That one man was Jack Tatum, but so far, Tatum had stayed under cover.

"Smoke," Pearlie called. "Smoke, you think he's still there?"

"He's there."

"How come he don't say nothin'?"

"Tatum!" Smoke called. "Tatum, you're all alone now."

There was no answer, but Smoke didn't really expect one.

"Tatum?"

Still now answer.

"Hey, Smoke, maybe we got 'em all," Pearlie suggested.

"I don't think so. At least, he's not one of the bodies I can see."

"He could've been hit and just died up there where he was," Pearlie said.

"No, I think it's more likely that he's just hiding up there," Smoke said. "Tom!" he called.

"Yeah?"

"Come on up here, then you and Pearlie keep your eyes open. I'm going the rest of the way up to see if I can root him out."

"All right," Tom called back.

Smoke waited until Tom worked his way up the trail to a place that was even with Smoke and Pearlie. Then, getting in position to provide cover, Tom nodded at Smoke.

"Anytime you're ready," Tom said.

Smoke nodded back, then started toward the area where Tatum had set up his defense. He passed by Jim's body first. The black shooter was already stiffening in the cold, his rifle lying on the snow beside him.

Damn nice rifle, Smoke thought.

A few more feet farther up, he saw the two Mexicans, then the two Indians. Finally, he passed by the bodies of Pigiron and Wheeler.

But he still saw no sign of Tatum.

Suddenly, he heard a sound behind him and turning, saw Tatum leaping at him, knife in hand. Tatum made a slash with his knife, and the blade sliced into Smoke's gun hand, causing him to drop his pistol into the snow. Smoke made a quick grab for the pistol, but another slicing motion of Tatum's knife forced Smoke away. Smoke started backing away from Tatum.

"Where you goin', you son of a bitch?" Tatum asked. He shook his head. "Ain't nowhere you can go now that'll get you away from old Jack Tatum."

Tatum continued to advance toward him, an evil smile on his face. He was holding his knife in front of him, the point facing Smoke, weaving back and forth slightly, like the head of a coiled snake.

"I'm goin' to cut you good," Tatum said with a snarl. "I'm goin' to open up your belly and let your guts spill out onto the snow."

All the time Smoke was backing away from Tatum, he was reaching for his own knife. Because he was wearing a heavy coat, his knife wasn't that easy to get to, but finally he found it. His fingers wrapped around the knife handle. Then he pulled it from its scabbard and brought it around to the front.

When Tatum saw that Smoke also had a knife, the smile, as well as some of the smug confidence, left his face. He stared at the knife clutched in Smoke's bloody hand.

"You didn't expect this, did you?" Smoke said.

Trying to regenerate his own sense of self-confidence, Tatum turned his left hand, palm up, and began making a curling motion with his fingers, as if beckoning Smoke to him.

"Come on," Tatum said. "Come on and get some of this."

"Now then, you were saying something about opening up my stomach, I believe?" Smoke challenged.

Tatum's attempt at bravado fell short, and he began licking his lips nervously. For a moment it looked as if he might take flight. Then, from somewhere deep inside, he summoned up one last bit of courage. With a defiant yell he leaped forward, making a wide, slashing motion with his knife.

Had Smoke not been wearing his sheepskin jacket, had this been a fight in the summertime, Tatum's attack would have been devastatingly effective. As it was, Tatum succeeded only in cutting a long, deep slash in Smoke's jacket. Uninjured, Smoke then made a counterthrust under Tatum's extended arm. Smoke drove his knife, point-first, into Tatum's abdomen. Smoke's knife was turned flat, allowing it to penetrate between the third and fourth ribs. The point of the knife punched into Tatum's heart, and dark, red blood spilled out around the wound.

Smoke withdrew his blade, then stepped back. Tatum put both hands over the wound, then looked down, as if surprised to see the blood spilling through his fingers. He staggered a few steps away from Smoke, then fell on his back in the snow. His arms flopped out to either side of him as his eyes, still open, stared into the sky. The white snow around his body turned crimson from his flowing blood.

By then both Pearlie and Tom had joined Smoke, and the three men stood there, looking down at

Tatum's body. At Tatum's throat, something flashed in the sunlight. It was a shining gold chain from which was suspended a brilliant diamond pendant.

"Isn't that what you gave Jo Ellen for her anniversary?" Pearlie asked.

"Yes," Tom replied in a choked voice. Then, he shouted at Tatum's body. "You son of a bitch!" Tom raised his boot and kicked Tatum so hard in the head that some of his teeth popped out. "Bastard! I wish you were still alive so you could feel this!" Tom kicked him several more times, until Tatum's face was all but unrecognizable. Then he dropped to his knees and removed the chain. When he stood up again, there were tears in his eyes.

Smoke put his hand on Tom's shoulder. "I'm sorry, Tom," he said. "I'm very sorry."

"Yeah," Tom replied. He sighed, then wiped his eyes. "Well, at least I have the satisfaction of knowing for sure that we got the right ones. Now, I won't have to go through the rest of my life wondering who did it."

"Let's go home," Smoke said.

"What about them?" Pearlie asked, pointing to the bodies that were lying around.

"What about them?" Tom replied.

"Shouldn't we bury them or something?"

"To hell with them," Tom said.

"To tell the truth, I don't think the bastards deserve to be buried either," Smoke said. "But if we just leave them here, it's going to be awfully ripe-smelling around these parts come next spring's thaw."

"All right, but one hole for all of them," Tom said.

Smoke chuckled. "Oh, I agree. I didn't say I was in favor of giving them a funeral."

The first thing they did was to go through everyone's pockets. They were surprised to find twenty-five hundred dollars in cash on Tatum. Then they looked around for a place to bury the outlaws, and finding a narrow ravine, pushed them into it. After that, they collapsed the ravine's sides down onto the bodies, then piled several rocks on top. The result was a grave that would be secure against predators, as well as keep the bodies from deteriorating on the open trail.

"Good enough," Smoke said. He handed the packet of money to Tom. "By rights, this should be yours."

"Mine? Why?"

"He took more from you than he did anyone else," Smoke said. "I know this can't compensate you for your family, but it might help build your barn and granary back."

"Thanks," Tom said, taking the money.

"And if nobody has any objections, I'm going to take this rifle," Smoke said, picking up the rifle Jim had used against them. "It looks to me like it's a pretty good weapon."

"It is a good rifle," Tom agreed, looking at it.

"What are you going to use it for?" Pearlie asked, laughing. "There's no buffalo to hunt anymore."

"Well, you never know when a good rifle like this might come in handy," Smoke replied.

At that very moment a bullet whizzed by so close they could all hear its angry buzz. Then, looking ahead, they saw several Indians coming up the hill toward them.

"Like now, for instance!" Smoke shouted. "Get down!"

And once more, the three men found themselves scrambling to get behind cover as they were being attacked, this time by a band of wild, screaming Indians.

Twenty-five

Smoke got behind a rock, then raised up to look at the Indians who were working their way up the snowy trail. He shoved a heavy round into the buffalo gun he had picked up from beside Jim's body, took aim, and fired. As it so happened, Tom had picked out his own target and fired at the same time.

Two of the attacking Indians went down, one with a bullet in the heart, the other with a bullet in the head. The Indians had thought themselves well out of range at this distance, and when they saw two of their number go down, they stopped their advance and looked around in surprise. They stopped, but they failed to seek cover. As a result, two more shots dropped two more of the Indians.

"They are devils with guns!" one of the Indians said. He and the remaining Indians scattered, running to both sides of the trail to find places of cover and concealment.

Quinntanna looked back toward the four Indians who were lying in the snow. Three were dead, the fourth was wounded. The wounded Indian was Teykano.

"Teykano!" Quinntanna called. "Teykano, are you still alive?"

"Yes," Teykano answered, his voice strained with pain.

"I will come get you," Quinntanna said.

"No. If you come, the devils with guns will shoot you too."

"I will come get you," Quinntanna said again. Laying aside his rifle, Quinntanna got down on his stomach and started moving through the snow, slithering on his belly.

Smoke saw the Indian slithering across the snow. To his left, he saw Tom raising the rifle to his shoulder.

"No!" Smoke called to Tom. "Don't kill him."

Nodding, Tom lowered his rifle. Smoke raised his rifle, and fired, not aiming directly at the crawling Indian, but aiming at the snow in front of him. His bullet hit just in front of the Indian, sent up a spray of snow, then whined on down the mountainside.

The Indian quit crawling, but only for a moment. Then he started crawling again.

"That fella's not going to give up," Smoke said, shooting a second time, again just in front of the Indian.

The Indian stopped a second time, waited a moment, then resumed his crawling. This time, just before he resumed crawling, however, he glanced up the hill toward Smoke's position . . . almost as if challenging him to shoot again. That was when Smoke got a good look at him.

"Damn!" Smoke said. "That's Quinntanna!"

"Quinntanna? I thought you and Quinntanna was old friends," Tom replied. "Sharing that elk and all, like you done."

Smoke cupped his hands around his mouth.

"Quinntanna!" he called.

Surprised to hear himself addressed by name, Quinntanna looked up the hill again.

"Quinntanna, it's me, Smoke Jensen? Let's parley!" Smoke tied a white handkerchief to the end of his rifle, then held it above the rock and waved it back and forth. Quinntanna raised to his knees, then turned toward Smoke. In so doing he was making himself an obvious target, a way of showing his own trust.

"What now?" Pearlie asked.

"I'm going to go talk to him," Smoke said. "I want to know why he started shooting at us."

Smoke stepped out from behind the rock, held the rifle up, then tossed it to one side. It was a symbolic disarmament only, for he still had his pistol strapped around his waist, though it was covered by the heavy coat he was wearing. Holding his arms out to his side in a non-threatening manner, he started down the sloping path toward Quinntanna.

For his part, Quinntanna stood up and started up the path toward Smoke. The two men walked toward each other for a moment, meeting approximately halfway between their respective starting points. At this position, both Quinntanna and Smoke made easy targets for those who had stayed back.

"Smoke Jensen," Quinntanna said. "It is good to see you."

Smoke chuckled. "Good to see me? You tried to kill us."

"I didn't know who you were," Quinntanna said. "I thought you were here to kill us."

"Why would we want to kill you?"

"Because the whites think Comanche people burned the white man's ranch, and burned the buildings where people-wagon stops."

"People-wagon? You mean the stagecoach? Are you talking about Miller's Switch?"

"Yes," Quinntanna said. "We saw that place. It was burned, and there was much death there."

Smoke shook his head. "We know you didn't do that," he said.

"How do you know that?"

"The driver wasn't killed. He told us who did it. It was Comancheros."

"It does not matter. They think we burned the ranch and. . . ."

Smoke held out his hand to stop Quinntanna in mid-sentence. "No," he said. "We know you didn't do that either. The Comancheros who burned the stage depot also burned Tom Burke's ranch, killed his wife, children, and all his hands."

"If this is known, why have the soldiers attacked us?"

"Nobody knew until now," Smoke said. "But when we get back, we will tell what we have learned."

"And the soldiers will go after the Comancheros?"

Smoke shook his head. "It's too late for that," he said. "My friends and I have already killed them all."

Quinntanna was quiet for a moment. Then he sighed and nodded his head. "Then there can be peace between us," he said. "I will let you go. But I think there can be no peace between the Comanche and the whites. We have killed too many of their soldiers."

"If the Indians will make no more war, I will see to it that the whites will make peace," Smoke promised.

Quinntanna looked back down the hill and saw that Teykano was now sitting up, holding his hand to his shoulder. His fingers were red from the blood that had flowed from his wound.

"You are a mighty warrior, Smoke Jensen. I believe

you when you say there will be peace. From this day, I will fight no more war forever."

Smoke and Quinntanna put their hands on each other's shoulders as a sign of friendship. Then each turned and started back toward their own. After a few steps, Smoke turned back toward Quinntanna. "One of the men with me, Tom Burke, is pretty good at doctoring people," he said. "If you would like, he can take a look at your friend."

"Yes," Quinntanna said. "White man shoot, white man make well. That would be good."

Tom Burke didn't go all the way back to Big Rock with Smoke and Pearlie, but left them when they reached the road that turned off to his ranch. Pearlie headed on to Sugarloaf to tell Sally that they were back and in one piece.

In town, Smoke went straight to the sheriff's office.

"Well, look what the winter winds have blown in," Monte said, getting up from his desk and crossing over to extend his hand in greeting.

"That coffee sure smells good," Smoke said, nodding toward the pot that simmered on top of the stove.

"Have a cup, sit down, tell me what's been going on," Monte invited.

Smoke poured his own coffee, then sat in a chair across the desk from Monte. He took a swallow of his coffee, slurping it between extended lips to cool it. Then he looked up at Monte and smiled.

"We got them, Monte," he said.

"Got them? Got who?"

"We got the people who raided Tom's ranch."

"Indians?"

Smoke shook his head. "Comancheros. Mixed pack

of outlaws—whites, Indians, Mexicans, and a black man. Tatum was the leader."

"I'll be damned," Smoke said. "You're sure they are the ones who did it?"

"There's no doubt. You remember that diamond on a chain that Tom bought for Jo Ellen? Well, he pulled it off Tatum's neck after we killed him."

"So the son of a bitch is dead then?"

"Yes. All of them are."

"Probably just as good. Save us a trial."

"Colonel Covington won't like it. Won't get a chance to show off in the courtroom anymore."

"Oh, he isn't a colonel anymore," Monte said.

"He's not? What happened?"

Monte told about going to see the governor to get martial law lifted, and Covington's commission revoked.

"Bet he didn't take that too well."

"No, he's been pouting around here for a few days now. Ever since he got back from his last expedition against the Indians. He got about forty of his men killed in that little fracas."

"If you ask me, just getting his commission taken away isn't enough," Smoke said. "I'd put the son of a bitch in jail, if not for murder for killing a lot of innocent Indians, then for manslaughter for getting his own people killed."

"Funny you should say that," Monte said. He picked up a yellow envelope that was lying on his desk. "This telegram just came from the governor. It's a warrant to be served against Covington. The governor wants him arrested for exceeding the scope of his authority. But now that you mention it, I may just add manslaughter to the charge."

"When you going to serve it?"

"I was getting ready to just before you came in," Monte said. "Would you like to come with me?"

"No, I'll let you worry about that," Smoke said. "If it's all the same to you, I'll just finish my coffee, then get on out to the ranch. It's been a while since I was home, and I'm anxious to get back to Sally."

Although Smoke didn't realize it, Sally had been coming in town to do some shopping anyway, and when she met Pearlie on the road and learned that Smoke was back, she slapped the reins against the animals' backs, hurrying them into a trot. She was every bit as anxious to see Smoke as he was to see her.

At the opposite end of the street from the sheriff's office, Fred Dunn, the telegrapher, was standing in Covington's office. Earlier, Fred had been incensed by Covington's insistence that he share every telegram with him, in violation of Western Union rules. What he was doing now was a violation of those same rules, but he had no compunctions about sharing this one. In fact, he was going to take particular pleasure in looking into Covington's face as he read the telegram.

"What is this?" Covington asked as Fred handed a copy of the telegram to him.

"Why don't you just read it and find out, Mr. High and Mighty, Call Me Colonel Covington," Fred said with a sneer. "I guess you won't be coming in my office anymore, demanding to see all the telegrams. According to this, you're all through."

"I don't know what you're talking about," Covington said.

"I'm talking about that telegram. I gave a copy to the sheriff. It's from the governor, telling Sheriff Carson to arrest you. And as far as I'm concerned, it's good riddance."

Covington read the telegram with increased irritation, reacting exactly as Fred had wanted him to react.

"This will never stick," Covington said in a blustering voice. "I was well within the scope of my authority with everything I did."

"Yeah? Well, there are a few widows and family folk around town who don't think so. They think you got their men killed."

"Preposterous," Covington said. "We'll just see about this."

Brushing by Fred, Covington went outside. Just as he stepped into the street, he saw the sheriff striding purposefully up the street toward him. All of a sudden he lost his resolve to have it out with him. At the same time, he saw Sally Jensen climbing down from a buckboard, not ten feet away from him.

"Covington! Hold it right where you are!" Monte shouted. "You're under arrest!"

Sally was at a disadvantage. She was halfway down from the buckboard, and her pistol was still on the seat, under the buffalo robe she had wrapped around her to keep warm for the drive into town. Had she not been at that disadvantage, Covington would never have been able to do what he did next.

Stepping over to her quickly, he put his left arm around her neck. With his right hand, he pointed his pistol at Sally's head.

"Stay back, Sheriff!" he shouted. "Stay back, or I'll kill her!"

Monte stopped. "Don't be a fool, Covington," he said. "Let her go."

Covington started dragging Sally across the street, in the direction of the livery.

"I'll be waiting in the livery," he shouted to the sheriff. "You go down to the bank and clear out my account. Bring it and a saddled horse to me."

"Covington, you know I can't do that," Monte replied.

"Oh, you can do it, all right. You can and you will, because if you don't, I'll kill this woman."

Hearing the shouting from the street, Smoke stepped out of the sheriff's office to see what was going on. When he saw that Covington had Sally, and was holding a pistol to her head, he started running up the street toward them.

"Covington!" he shouted. "Let her go, you son of a bitch!"

Covington fired at Smoke. The bullet hit the dirt just in front of Smoke, then ricocheted up between his legs, and he got an uneasy, tingling sensation in his groin when he realized how close the bullet had come to it.

Smoke pulled his pistol to shoot back, but realized that he couldn't do it without fear of hitting Sally. Laughing out loud, Covington pulled Sally into the shadows of the livery.

"Covington!" Smoke called again, cautiously moving closer to the livery.

"That's far enough, Jensen," Covington called from inside. "If you come any closer, I'm going to kill your woman."

"You don't want to do that, Covington. There's no charge of murder against you. Why don't you give yourself up?"

"There's no charge of murder against me," Covington replied, "but I'm sure there are charges of manslaughter forthcoming. I could get ten years in prison for manslaughter. I don't intend to serve one day in prison."

"Sally. Sally, are you all right?" Smoke called.

"Yes, I'm fine," Sally said. "Smoke, if you get the chance, kill him."

"Shut up, bitch!" Covington snarled. Even from outside, Smoke could hear the sound of him hitting her. Sally cried out in pain.

"If you hit her again, you'd better turn that gun on yourself," Smoke shouted angrily. "Because I'll be coming after you."

"You're going to war with me, are you, Jensen?" Covington asked in a taunting voice.

"I'll give you a war you won't believe," Smoke said menacingly.

Covington took another shot at Smoke, who heard the pop loudly as it snapped by just inches away from his ear.

Covington laughed. "My advice to you, Mr. Jensen, is to go find out what's keeping the sheriff. I'm getting a little antsy in here. If I don't see the sheriff with my money and a saddled horse here in two more minutes, I'm going to start shooting."

Smoke realized that he was an easy target in the street, so he moved over to stand behind the barber-shop pole. There, he was out of Covington's immediate line of fire, and he also had a view of the front of the livery.

"Covington, give it up," Smoke shouted. "You know you aren't going to get away with this."

By now several people had been drawn to the area. They stood as close to the action as they could, without exposing themselves to Covington's fire.

One of the people who had gathered in the street was Abner Norton, the prosecuting attorney.

"Sam," Norton called. "Sam, this is Abner Norton.

I urge you to give yourself up. I promise you a fair trial."

"A fair trial?" Covington replied. "Who would I get to defend me, sir? I am the best defense attorney in the state of Colorado, of that there is no doubt. But I'm quite sure you are aware of the old chestnut, 'The lawyer who defends himself has a fool for a client.' "

"Don't throw away everything you've worked for all these years," Norton said.

"Don't you understand? I've already thrown it away," Covington replied. Another shot rang out, and those people who had gathered dangerously close to the livery stable hurried to get out of the line of fire.

"If the sheriff doesn't get here soon, I'll kill this girl. Someone had better find him and explain that to him."

While Covington was engaged with Norton and the other people out front, Smoke managed to slip around the corner of the barbershop, then run to the drainage ditch that ran along the back. He ducked down into the ditch, then ran to the back of the livery barn. Once behind the barn, he ran from the ditch to the barn, then climbed up into the hayloft. Moving quickly but silently from the back of the hayloft to the front, he found himself in position to look down on Covington. He was in a good position to take a shot, but it would have to be a perfect shot, because Smoke was holding Sally close to him. Smoke raised up to take aim.

Two pigeons had taken roost in the hayloft very near where Smoke was standing, and when he stood up, they were frightened into flight. The rapid beating of their wings caused Covington to look up, and when he did, he saw Smoke. He pulled the hammer back on the pistol he was holding against Sally's head.

"Drop your gun, Jensen!" Covington called. "I mean it! Drop your gun, or I will kill her!"

For an instant, Smoke started to shoot him anyway. He had an opening, though it was very tiny. Then, almost as if sensing that the opening was there, Covington shifted his position slightly so that it was too risky for Smoke to take a chance. Slowly, Smoke lowered his gun hand.

"I said drop it!" Covington called up to him.

Smoke dropped his pistol, but he dropped it only to the floor of the hayloft, not to the ground below.

"Very smart," Covington said sarcastically. "Now, kick it off onto the ground."

Smoke moved the gun with his foot, advancing with it slowly, until he was standing at the very edge of the hayloft.

"Kick it off," Covington said, and as he spoke, he took his gun away from Sally's head and used it to point.

Sally had been waiting for that very moment. Suddenly she rammed her elbow into Covington's gut, then spinning out of his grasp, turned and kicked him in the groin.

Smoke didn't hesitate for a second. He leaped from the hayloft the instant he saw Sally make her move. Right on the heels of Sally's kick to the groin, Smoke's leap terminated on top of Covington, sending Covington to the ground. Covington managed to squeeze off one shot. Although Smoke was singed by the flash, the bullet thudded harmlessly into the roof of the barn.

Smoke was on top of Covington now, and with his left hand he jerked the gun out of Covington's grasp. He tossed it a full thirty feet away. With his right hand, Smoke backhanded Covington, driving the man's head down against the dirt. Then, still with his right hand, he caught Covington with a wicked cross, driving his head into the dirt again. He repeated the maneuver time and time again, until Covington was just lying there, inert against his blows.

"Smoke! Smoke!" Norton shouted. "You're going to kill him!"

Smoke put his left hand to Covington's collar and twisting it, raised Covington's chin for another punch. He drew back his right hand and held it for a moment. Then, with a sigh, he let his hand drop. He got up and stared down at Covington's unconscious form.

"I wanted to kill the son of a bitch," Smoke admitted.

"Killing him is too good for him," Norton said. "Let him spend ten or twenty years in prison. Believe me, he would welcome death over that."

"All right, I guess we'd better get him down to the jail," Smoke said.

"I'll get a couple of men to carry him."

"No need for that," Smoke said. Looking over toward one of the livery stalls, he saw that a horse was already saddled. Taking a rope from the saddle, he looped one end of the rope around Covington's feet, then tied the other end to the saddle pommel. He clicked at the horse, then led the horse down the street toward the jail. He guided the horse so that it dragged Covington through every pile of manure along the way.

Covington sputtered awake after a few feet.

"Hey! Hey, what are you doing?" he shouted.

"I'm taking you to jail," Smoke said.

"You're dragging me through shit!" Covington shouted. "I'm all covered with shit!"

Smoke stopped and looked back at him.

"Now how the hell can you tell?" he asked. The

question was met with uproarious laughter from those who had gathered to see the show.

It was two weeks later when Tom Burke showed up unexpectedly at Sugarloaf Ranch.

"Tom," Smoke said. "Good to see you. Come on in. Sally will have lunch on the table soon. Eat with us."

Tom smiled. "I promise you, I didn't time my visit just to get an invite," he said. "On the other hand, I'd be a fool to turn it down. Especially since I've been having to eat my own cooking lately."

"You're more than welcome here anytime," Sally said.

"Thank you, Sally. I appreciate that." Then to Smoke: "Did you see the paper? Covington got ten years."

"I saw it," Smoke said. "When you consider all the Indians he murdered, it should've been twenty years."

The two men engaged in small talk for a few minutes more, until Sally had the meal on the table and called them to dinner. After they sat down, Tom asked if he could say grace, and Smoke and Sally agreed.

It was a quick grace. Then when the others looked up, they saw that Tom was holding something in his hand. "Sally," he said. "It would pleasure me more than I can say if you would accept this."

"What is it?"

"It belonged to Jo Ellen."

Covington opened his fingers and there, in his hand, was the gold chain and diamond pendant he had given Jo Ellen less than two months earlier.

"Oh, Tom! I can't take that!" Sally said. "That was Jo Ellen's!"

"Please take it," Tom said. He looked at Smoke. "That is, if you take no offense, Smoke."

"No, I take no offense," Smoke said.

"I know it was Jo Ellen's, and she was proud of it. But I know in my heart she would dearly love to look down from heaven and see that pretty thing hanging around the neck of her best friend. Would you do that for me, Sally?"

Sally took the chain and pendant in her hand and stared at it for a moment.

"If you put it that way, of course I'll wear it. I'd be happy to. No, I would be proud to," she said. "Would you put it around my neck?"

"Smoke?" Tom asked, looking at him for permission to personally hang the necklace around Sally's neck.

"Yes, of course you can," Smoke said.

Sally tilted her head forward slightly as Tom slipped the chain and pendant around her neck.

"Beautiful," he said.

"It's the most beautiful thing I've ever seen," Smoke agreed.

Sally looked up at them. The diamond at her throat was glistening brightly, but no brighter than the tears that were glistening in her eyes.

Look for
William W. Johnstone's
next novel

THE LAST GUNFIGHTER: IMPOSTER

Coming in October 2002
from Pinnacle Books

Here's a sneak preview. . . .

Frank Morgan reined up and called out to the lone figure sitting by the tiny campfire. "I'm friendly! You want some company?"

"Shore. Come on in and pull up a piece of ground and take a load off."

Frank walked Stormy, his big Appaloosa, into the clearing and swung down from the saddle. "That coffee sure smells good."

"Come on over and have a taste," the man said. "I got plenty."

Frank dug his cup from the packsaddle of his pack horse and poured a cup of the hot brew, squatting down by the fire. "Fire feels good too," he said. "It's turned chilly."

"For a fact," the man replied, his eyes narrowing suspiciously as he looked at Frank.

Frank wondered about that, but said nothing.

The man, a miner from the look of his clothing and lace-up boots, inched a bit closer to his shotgun.

"Finding any color around here?" Frank asked.

"Enough to get by." The man looked hard at Frank for a few seconds. "Why, you figurin' on robbin' me?"

Frank returned the hard look. "Don't be stupid!" he snapped back at the man. "I'm no thief."

"Since when?" the miner came back at him.

Frank set his cup on the ground. "What the hell are you talking about?"

The miner moved a hand toward his shotgun. Frank leaned over the hat-sized fire and grabbed the scattergun.

"I knowed it!" the miner said. "You're gonna kill me, ain't you, Val?"

"Who the hell is Val?" Frank asked, breaking open the double-barrel gun and tossing the shells to one side.

The miner blinked a couple of times. "You is."

Frank sighed and picked up his cup, taking a swig of the strong brew. Tasted good. "My name is Frank, not Val."

"Says you! I know who you is. You're Val Dooley."

Frank laid the scattergun to one side. "Friend . . . I never heard of anyone called Val Dooley. And personally, I don't give a tinker's damn if you believe that or not."

"Then he's your twin brother!"

"Nope. I don't have a twin brother." Frank took another gulp of coffee and held out the cup. "Fill it up, friend. That's good coffee."

The miner carefully picked up the battered old pot and filled Frank's cup, then his own. "Might as well have me one too. Be my last cup on earth. I ain't scared to die, Val."

"Damnit, man, I am not this Val person!"

The miner stared at Frank. "Shore look like him."

"Oh, hell, forget it," Frank said, disgust evident in his voice. "How far to the nearest town? I need supplies."

" 'Bout twenty miles southwest. But you'll get a rope if you go there, Mr. Whoever in the Hell You Is."

"A rope?"

"Val Dooley is wanted dead or alive, and you is the spittin' image of Val."

"If this Dooley person is so famous, how come I never heard of him?"

"He ain't been outlawin' long. But in the few months he's been rampagin', he's been a-rapin' and a-killin' and a-stealin' to beat the band. And that ain't all he's been doin'."

Frank waited, then asked, "Well . . . what else has he been doing?"

"Liftin' the dress tails of a lot of good women. You're . . . I mean, *he's* a mighty handsome man, you is, ah, he is. Women get all flighty and stupid around you . . . *him*. You right shore you ain't Val Dooley?"

"I'm sure."

"I guess you ain't. But if you want some good advice, you'll get back on your horse and head east. Get the hell out of this part of California. 'Cause if you stay around here, you gonna be a shore 'nuff dead man."

"Mister, look hard at me. Think of a a gunfighter. A very well-known gunfighter. Now, who am I?"

"Val Dooley. I done told you that 'bout a dozen damn times."

Frank shook his head. "I've got to get to the bottom of this." He drank the rest of his coffee and stood up. "I think I'll head for this town. What's the name of it?"

"Deweyville. The sheriff there is damn mean too. Name's Carl Davis. But you're a damn fool if you don't hightail it out of this state, Mr. Whoever You Are."

"I've been called a lot worse than a damn fool. Thanks for the coffee. Hey, how far's the road that'll take me to Deweyville?"

"Couple of miles." The miner jerked a thumb. "That way."

"Old coot," Frank muttered as he rode away from the miner. "Surely he's not right in the head."

He made camp with about an hour of daylight still left. He hobbled the horses so they could graze, and then fixed food for himself and Dog. While his bacon was sizzling in the pan and his bread baking in the small Dutch oven, he looked over at Dog and said, "If I tell you to get, boy, you get, you hear me?"

Dog looked at him and cocked his head to one side.

"That old rummy back there might have been about half right, and I don't want you to get shot. So if I tell you to get, you run."

Dog growled.

"I'll take that as a yes. You just do as I tell you."

Dog walked closer and licked Frank's hand.

"All right. Good boy."

After his meal, Frank sat by the fire, smoking and drinking coffee and thinking. "Maybe I'll get lucky this time, Dog. Maybe I can find me a little place where folks don't know me and I can buy me a little spread and we can stop this eternal wandering. Would you like that?"

Dog looked at him, unblinking.

Frank laughed. "It doesn't make a damn to you, does it, boy?"

Dog again cocked his head to one side.

Frank patted the animal's big head. "Well, I like to dream about having a place where I can settle down and live in peace. But I know it's just a dream."

Frank Morgan was a gunfighter, but it was a profession he did not choose. When he was in his mid-teens, working on a ranch in Texas, a bully pushed him into a gunfight. It was a fight the boy did not want. But

the bully died from the bullet Frank fired into his
chest. Frank drifted for a few months, then joined
the Confederate Army, and at war's end he was a captain of Rebel Cavalry. He headed back West, looking
for work; that's when the brothers of the bully who
had forced him into a fight caught up with Frank.
One by one, they stalked Frank, forcing him into gun-
fights. Frank killed them all. His reputation spread.

Frank Morgan was just a shade over six feet tall. He
was broad-shouldered and lean-hipped. His hair was
dark brown, lightly peppered with gray. His eyes were
a pale gray. Women considered him a very handsome
man.

Frank wore a .45 Colt Peacemaker on his right side,
low and tied down.

Frank had married once, right after the end of the
War of Northern Aggression. That marriage pro-
duced a son; a son that Frank knew nothing about
for many years. The woman's father had forced Frank
to leave, and had had the marriage annulled, not
knowing his daughter was with child. The woman,
Vivian, had gone back East, married well, and built a
new life for herself, becoming very wealthy. Vivian
and Frank reunited briefly, Frank learning then he
had a son. After Vivian's tragic and untimely death,
Frank learned she had willed him a portion of her
estate, making Frank a moderately wealthy man. But
the son never really warmed to his father and the two
went their separate ways, seeing each other only oc-
casionally.

Frank drifted aimlessly, looking for a quiet place
where he could build a home and hang up his guns
forever. But that was something he knew in his heart
he would probably never find.

Frank had earned the nickname The Drifter. He
was both feared and hated by many, idolized by some.

There had been many newspaper articles written about him—most of them untrue—and a number of books, penny dreadfuls, published, supposedly chronicling his life. There was a stage play touring the country, a play about his exploits—most of those exploits pure fiction. Frank had had people tell him the production was awful.

Frank drifted, trying unsuccessfully to escape his reputation. And now he was in northern California and had been told he looked just like a local desperado named Val Dooley.

"I'll get this straightened out and be on my way," Frank muttered. "The last thing I want is a bunch of locals taking pot shots at me."

At mid-morning, Frank rode slowly into the town of Deweyville. People began coming out of stores to line the boardwalks on both sides of the street, to stand silently and stare at him. Frank cut his eyes to Dog, padding along beside his horse. The big cur seemed tense, his ears laid back.

"Steady now, Dog," Frank whispered.

"You got your nerve, Val!" a woman called from the boardwalk.

"Somebody shoot that murderer!" a man yelled.

"Get him!" a man hollered. "Don't let him get away!"

Crowds from both sides of the street rushed toward Frank, yelling and calling him all sorts of names.

"Go, Dog!" Frank yelled. "Go!"

Dog took off running just as Frank put the spurs to Stormy. The big App leaped forward, the pack-horse trailing at a run.

A local grabbed Frank's leg and tried to pull him from the saddle. Frank kicked the man off. Another tried to grab him from the other side and missed, falling beneath Stormy's hooves. The citizen yelled in pain and rolled away.

"What the hell's the matter with you people?" Frank yelled as dozens of hands attempted to drag him from the saddle.

There was no answer from the wild-eyed crowd as several men tore the reins from Frank's hand and brought Stormy to a halt. Dog was nowhere to be seen. He had ducked into an alley and disappeared.

Frank was dragged from the saddle and thrown to the ground.

"Somebody get a rope!" a man yelled.

"Yeah!" another hollered. "Hang the murdering scum!"

A pistol boomed, and the crowd suddenly fell silent. "That's it!" a man yelled. "I won't tolerate any lynch mob. Back off, all of you. Now, damnit. Get your hands off that man and stand away. Move!"

"But it's Val Dooley, Sheriff Davis!" a woman protested.

"I don't care if it's Satan himself!" the sheriff said, pushing his way through the crowd. "He gets a trial." He looked down at Frank. "Get up slow, Dooley. And keep your hand away from your gun."

"I'm not Val Dooley!" Frank said, getting to his feet. "My name is Frank Morgan."

"Bull!" Sheriff Davis said.

"Frank Morgan?" a woman yelled. "The famous gunfighter? In a pig's eye you are. You're Val Dooley and now we've got you!"

"And now we get to see you hang, you murdering scum!" another woman yelled.

"You're goin' to have to do better than that, Val," Sheriff Davis said. Then he chuckled. "Frank Morgan? That's a good one, Val. You must not have heard the news."

"What news?" Frank asked.

"Frank Morgan's dead," the sheriff said. "He was killed last week in a gunfight over in Montana."

"Yeah," a deputy said. "It come over the telegraph wires just hours after it happened. It's true. Move, Val. You got a date with the hangman."